The Suggested Assassin

David West

GW00392074

The Suggested Assassin

Anchor Locker

Wardrobe Cupboard

First lieutenants Cabin

Guest cabin 2

Guest Heads

Guest cabin 1

Mast

Under-floor cool lockers

Hammocks

Saloon Table

Gun locker

Chart Table

Stove

Cupboards

Steps

Heads

Stores

Captain's Cabin

Wardrobe Cupboard

Gimballed Cots

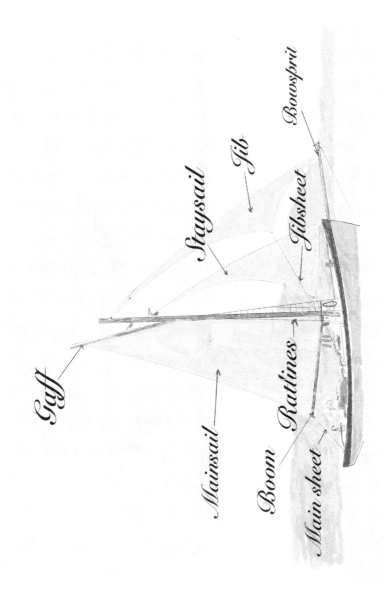

Gaff

Staysail

Jib

Bowsprit

Jibsheet

Mainsail

Boom

Rattlines

Main sheet

ACKNOWLEDGMENTS

I would like to thank my wife Claire and my editor, Debz Hobbs-Wyatt for their valuable input to this book. Any remaining errors are entirely my own. I would also like to thank Jacqueline Abromeit for another brilliant cover design.

CHAPTER ONE

Roberto Cavalli grinned as he watched Maria at the helm, her hands gripping the handles of the spoked wheel. A week ago, she had told him that her only experience of sailing had been a ferry across the lagoon to Venice and back. Now she was easing the spoked wheel as the pressure of the wind dropped, then pulling when the wind freshened. The boat surged forward, leaving a clean stern wave, spreading out, chasing the bow wave, but never quite catching it.

'So how do you like her, Signorina Standen?' he asked, knowing what the answer would be.

'She is beautiful, so fast. We seem to have caught and overtaken every other vessel on the water.'

'You can thank your father for that,' he said, slapping Sir Anthony on the back. 'This is the first boat I have built around a gaff sail, rather than a square rig. Where did you say they started using this form of rig, Sir Anthony?'

'I understand that they adopted it in Sweden, around fifty years ago. The fishing boats I sailed on in the North Sea were gaff-rigged. I thought nothing of it because it was my first real sailing experience. But we ran rings around any square-rigger we met.'

'Clearly those Swedes know a thing or two about sailing, that I hadn't given them credit for. I hope I'll get a lot more orders from the owners of the boats we are overtaking.'

'I trust I'll get a commission?' Anthony laughed, exchanging a smile with his twenty-year-old daughter, her black hair streaming in the wind, her lithe figure flexing and blending with the movements of the wheel and the deck. 'You have done a good job, Roberto. She is everything I asked for and more. I think the test sail is complete. Shall we head back to harbour now?'

'Of course, I shall be happy to relieve you of the weight of the last payment, Sir Anthony.'

'Ready about!' Anthony called out, as he took the mainsheet in his hands, and Maria steered the bow through the wind.

'Lee ho!' she called, stepping around the wheel as the bow passed through the wind and the mainsail came across. Anthony released the sheets of the jib and staysail on the starboard side and crossed down the sloping deck to the port side, hauling in on the block and tackles of the two foresails, pulling them across to the new tack. He then tensioned the mainsheet of the big, four-cornered sail as it began filling with wind again. He tensioned the running stays to support the mast on the new tack, before easing the sails out as Maria adjusted the boat's course towards the harbour of Ostia, at the mouth of the River Tiber.

'Have you decided what to call her, Sir Anthony? The signwriter is eager to do his work.'

'What do you think, Maria?' Anthony called across the wind.

'How about Maia?' She replied. 'The eldest of the Pleiades, daughter of Atlas, and mother of Hermes.'

'It's a nice name why not.'

'Nice and short, that won't cost too much in paint,' Roberto added.

Half an hour later, with the wind dropping, they were

gliding towards the harbour entrance. Anthony untied the long sculling oar from its brackets fixed into the starboard bulwarks. He took it and lashed it in place between the thole pins on the stern, then lowered the blade into the water. He began levering the blade through the water in a figure of eight movement, adjusting the angle of the blade on each stroke.

'The gondoliers make it look so easy,' Anthony muttered under his breath.

'You'll soon get the hang of it,' Roberto smiled. 'There, you've got her moving now, slow and steady. Use your weight, not your muscles. That's better, Sir Anthony.' The wind had died, but as Anthony got the hang of stern sculling, they made steady progress towards the quayside. 'I suggest, Maria, that you lash the wheel amidships, then Sir Anthony can use the oar to turn Maia beam onto the quay as we come alongside. That leaves you free to jump ashore with the mooring lines.'

'What will you do, Roberto?' Maria asked as she lashed the wheel.

'Watch with interest. She's your boat now. I won't be with you after today, so you'd better get used to it.'

Maria opened a locker and took out two coiled ropes. She dropped one on the deck at the stern and took the other to the bow, where she uncoiled it. Then she leant over the side and passed an end through the fairlead and secured it on the deck-cleat. She took the other end and walked with it, placing it on the deck amidships. Then she did the same with the other rope from the stern before taking the remaining coils of both mooring ropes into her hands, standing ready to jump with them onto the quayside.

'Keep going, Sir Anthony. That gap between the galleon and the carrack is your berth in the boatyard, when you're not using her.' Roberto called out. Anthony kept sculling until he judged they had just enough carry to make the gap. As Maia's stern cleared the bow of the schooner, he swung the oar over and they turned into the gap. 'Stern rope first,

Signorina.' Maria stepped off onto the quay and wrapped the stern line around a bollard. The rope tightened and groaned as it absorbed Maia's remaining momentum. She tied a bowline in the end and dropped it over the bollard. Walking forwards, she took the bow line from where she had left it, draped over the gunwale amidships. She secured that to another bollard on the quay, near Maia's bow. 'Well done, Signora! Good sculling, Sir Anthony! If you could accompany me to my office with your purse, Sir Anthony, we shall complete the paperwork, and then she's all yours. I'll send the signwriter over too.'

'I shan't be long, Maria. Could you get the sail down and tidied away while I'm in the office? Then perhaps you could get the log burner going. I'll check on the horses in the stable when I've finished with Roberto. There are a few more cases I want to bring over from the wagon, then we'll start on dinner.'

'Yes, Papa.'

It took Anthony several trips to carry the remaining stores from his wagon over to Maia.

'Maria, give me a hand with these, would you?'

Maria's head popped up through the companionway hatch. 'What have you got there?'

'I'll show you once we've got them all aboard.'

Maria climbed on deck and hurried to the side, taking the long wooden case that Anthony handed to her. She put it on deck before taking a sack of onions and a leg of salt beef. Anthony then passed her a barrel of brandy and another small barrel before climbing aboard. Maria took the onions and beef and descended the companionway. Anthony followed her with the long wooden case. There was a warm glow coming from the iron galley stove. Maria stowed the provisions in the galley lockers, while Anthony carried the long case through into the saloon, and placed it on the table.

'Father, I can't work it out. What's the cast-iron box

around the stove chimney, there, screwed into the deck above?'

'Ah, that was Roberto's idea. Because I wanted a tight fit between the deck and the stove pipe, to avoid water dripping on us when we're eating, he was concerned that if the stove pipe got too hot, it would char the deck. He suggested fitting that integral water tank. We can fill it through a brass deck-fitting that unscrews. The water absorbs most of the heat from the stove pipe, so we can take hot water from this tap,' he said, pointing at a tap on the side of the tank. 'I'm rather pleased with the stove. There's a sliding ventilator control on the fire box, at the bottom, so you can open it to increase the rate of burn, or you can close it to let the embers glow all night. Above that is the oven, with a hot plate on top. The hot plate has a fiddle around the edge, to stop pans falling off when there's a sea running. Anyway, let's get things stowed away.' He went forward into the saloon and lifted the hinged locker lids set into the floor to reveal the lead-lined, cool storage compartments in the bilge. Being beneath the waterline, the sea kept the lockers at an even, cool temperature, and the lead lining kept them dry. Beneath the lockers, lead ballast ran the full length of the keel. He had specified lead rather than iron despite the cost. Its higher density enabled full sail to be carried longer in a freshening wind than iron would and was a major factor in the boat's impressive speed.

Anthony stowed the barrel of brandy along with the barrels of beer and flagons of milk in the cool lockers. He noticed Maria had finished in the galley, so he lowered the locker lids one by one. Maria then joined him in the saloon and sat on the bench running along the port side. Maria gasped as he opened the long case and handed her one of six flintlock rifles. 'You want to see the world, and the world's a dangerous place, particularly the Mediterranean. Cannon would be a bit out of place on a sixty-foot yacht, so I had these rifles made by a gunsmith in Austria. A rifle is so much more accurate than a musket or cannon. Our main defence against the Barbary pirates will be our speed, but these may come in handy too.'

'Oh they're beautiful.' She ran her fingers along the barrel and the wooden stock. 'What's that?' She pointed at a small wooden case set in the long case.

'It's a mould for making lead projectiles. The gunsmith said that he's been experimenting with pointed-oblong projectiles, rather than the traditional musket balls. He says that with a rifled-barrel they improve the accuracy considerably. I have several boxes, ready made, in the case, and a block of lead for making more. The other barrel is gunpowder. We should stow that in the lead-lined locker under the galley floor. There are some spare flints in the case, too.'

'Right, shall we put these away and get on with dinner?' Maria suggested, 'It's getting dark. I'll make a stew. Can you light the oil lamp?'

◇ ◇ ◇

After dinner, Anthony got on with the washing up. He took the galley bucket from its recess in the worktop and attached a length of light rope to the rope handle. He went up on deck, lowered the bucket over the side and scooped up seawater. He carried it below, removed the light line and set the bucket into the worktop. He took a bar of soap and a brush from one of the galley drawers and started scrubbing the tin plates, spoons and iron pot clean, placing them on the elevated draining board, which was angled to drain down a channel back into the bucket. When he finished, he pushed the draining board aside, took the bucket back up on deck, and threw the dirty water overboard. Maria was just coming out of the heads as he replaced the galley bucket.

'Good night, Papa,' she said, kissing his cheek.

'Sleep well, love,' he replied.

Maria made her way forward through the saloon, and down a narrow corridor past the fixings on the starboard side, to take the hammocks for her younger siblings, and the two cabins on the port side to accommodate either her twin brother Antonio or guests. She opened the door to the V-shaped fore-cabin, undressed and hung up her canvas breeches and smock in the hanging locker before climbing into the swinging cot, pivoted fore and aft. She pulled the blanket over her. She heard her father enter the heads. There was a brief pause, followed by a soft moan, and the sound of him relieving himself into the lead-lined wooden bucket. She heard the click of the locker being opened, and pictured her father taking out his tooth rag, applying the rock alum, and rubbing it around his teeth. He could be quite vain, but it seemed to work. Few men of his age had so many teeth left. The teeth that he had lost had been knocked out, rather than succumbing to decay. He'd be using the quill now, to pick out the meat stuck between them. She heard a trickle of water again, then the sloshing noise before he spat into the sink bucket. God knows why he so gently lifted the sink bucket out of its cradle, before tipping it into the latrine bucket. Doesn't he know you can hear every single sound? There he goes, tiptoeing up the companionway and emptying the bucket overboard. She smiled at the joy of having a father, only wishing that he had entered her life three years earlier.

Anthony awoke at first light, got up and dressed. He left his cabin and opened the stove ventilator slats. He opened the burner door and knelt down to blow on the embers. There was soon a flame, so he chucked in another couple of logs, before closing the burner door again. He put a frying pan on top of the stove to heat before climbing the companionway up onto the deck. It was a fine morning, and he took a few deep lungfuls of air. He then set off towards the baker's shop in the town. As he returned, he could smell bacon frying.

'Good morning, Papa,' Maria called out, the boat rocking as Anthony climbed aboard.

'Did you sleep well, Maria?'

'Yes, Papa. Do we have to go home next week? It would be such fun to explore further afield. We could circumnavigate Sicily, perhaps.'

'Your mother is expecting us, and there will be lots of time for sailing. Perhaps we could sail down to the bay of Naples and explore Capri and the other islands there. Sicily is too far for now,' Anthony said, as he put the loaves on the saloon table. Maria cracked four eggs and added them to the pan. 'How many slices of bread do you want?' Anthony squeezed past Maria to fetch the bread-knife from the galley drawer.

'Two please, Papa,' Maria replied, taking two plates from the locker over the work surface. She slid eggs and bacon onto each plate and put them on the table. Then she put the pan into the sink bucket, that she had already filled with seawater. 'Thank you,' she said, sliding onto the port-side bench opposite him, as he passed her two slices of buttered bread.

They ate in silence, and were both soaking up the last of the egg yolk and juices, with the last scraps of bread, when they heard raised voices on the quayside. They listened for a while, but couldn't hear clearly. Anthony got up and climbed the companionway onto the deck. Maria followed him. They could see a smartly dressed man in a red silk jacket, blue breeches, and a tall black hat arguing with a seaman. The smart man had a neatly trimmed beard and long black hair. He could be anything between thirty and mid-forties in age, Anthony thought. He was talking excellent Italian, but with a French accent. Beside him was an even more smartly dressed woman, who seemed to be about Maria's age. She was radiantly beautiful, with fair, smooth skin, and fine features. She wore her fine clothes well, with a nicely proportioned figure, but the contrast of beauty with his daughter was stark. The woman on the quayside reminded him of a feline: a domestic, pampered, but not overfed cat. Maria was a leopardess, stalking her next kill. The man caught Anthony's gaze and turned back to the seaman.

'Look over there, my man. There is a woman on that boat. What do you say to that, eh? It's still afloat, isn't it?'

'I don't care if it's afloat or not afloat. I'm not having a woman on my boat, sir. It's bad luck,' the seaman waved his hands above his head. The smartly dressed man turned and walked over to Maia.

'Excuse me, sir, could you explain to this fellow that it's not bad luck to take a woman on a boat, please?' he called up to Anthony.

'its pure superstition, of course, sir, but seamen are superstitious people. Now that I come to think about it, I've never been on a boat with a woman, other than a gondola, or a short ferry ride, until buying my boat with my daughter.'

'Well, I have to get to Tunis, and I'm not going without my wife. We were only married the week before last. Would you take us? You have your daughter anyway. I'm sure my wife won't bring any additional bad luck.'

'I'm sorry, sir, we have to get home. We've been away a week already.'

'I can pay well, sir.'

'How much will you pay, sir?' Maria called out.

'I would have paid this fellow forty ducats.'

'We could do it for fifty ducats, sir,' Maria replied.

'What are you saying? Your mother is expecting us. Ignore her, sir, we are not for hire.'

'A hundred ducats then, sir.'

'I'll help you with your bags, sir,' Maria said, jumping down onto the quayside. 'Mother won't be too worried, Papa. She's grown accustomed to your long absences.'

CHAPTER TWO

Anthony helped carry their passengers' trunks aboard and took them through to the guest cabin.

'I am Sir Anthony Standen, sir, and this disobedient wench is my eldest daughter, Maria. Who do we have the honour of conveying to Tunis, may I enquire?'

'I am most grateful, Sir Anthony. I am François Savary de Brèves and this is my wife, Anne. She is the niece of the eminent historian Jacques Auguste de Thou. Perhaps you have read his works?'

'I fear I have not, sir. May I enquire what business you have in Tunis?'

'I am to be Good King Henry's ambassador to Uthman Dey, the Ottoman ruler of Tunisia.'

'Mon Dieu!' Anthony exclaimed, flitting to French. 'I have met Good King Henry the fourth of France, and I knew his wife — Marie, when she was but a small child. I have much to thank her for. If I had not taken her on a walk to feed the ducks when she was grieving, I would not have met my wife.'

'You have confused me, sir. You are clearly a Frenchman, yet I had assumed, from your name, that you were English. What are you?'

'I am English, but I grew up playing with the children of foreign diplomats, and developed an interest and ability in languages. We may use French aboard. Maria is almost fluent, and the practice will do her good.'

'My wife will appreciate it. Her Italian has come on leaps and bounds in the last year, but she has found it a strain. Will we be departing soon?'

'In a couple of hours, François. Sorry, may I call you that?'

'Of course.'

'You must call me Anthony. I will need a little time to prepare. We only have charts for this coast of Italy. I shall need to buy charts for the whole of the Tyrrhenian Sea, and the approaches to Tunis, in particular. I shall also need to buy some more provisions, as I have enough for two people for a week, not four people for a week, or perhaps more. The charts must come first so I can check how long the voyage will take. Maria will take care of you in the meantime. Maria, would you show our guests around Maia, so that they feel at home, and know where everything is. Then if you could start preparing to sail, I will be back as quickly as I can.'

'Yes, Papa, of course.'

Roberto Cavalli had all the charts that Anthony required. He borrowed a pair of his dividers and laid out the chart of the Tyrrhenian Sea on Roberto's desk. He set the dividers to measure fifty nautical miles on the longitude axis and walked the dividers across the chart from Ostia to Tunis.

'Three hundred miles. That's around two full days with a good wind. I'd better make provision for two weeks, there and back, just in case.'

'You can borrow my trolly, Sir Anthony, to ferry the stores to your boat.'

'That's kind of you, Roberto. Do stop calling me Sir Anthony. We have achieved a lot together. It has been a pleasure working with you on Maia. You have brought many of my flights of fancy down to earth, with sound, practical alternatives.'

'And you have given me many ideas for new and faster boats, Anthony.'

Anthony smiled, paid for the charts, and shook Roberto's hand. He walked down the steep steps from Roberto's office, rolled charts under his left arm, and kept his right hand on the banister, to the boat-building shed below. The noise of sawing and hammering was deafening, and the sawdust in the air made him cough. He made his way between the unfinished hulls to the door and put his charts in the trolly outside. Then he wheeled it around the small town of Ostia, buying dried pasta, a staple of Italian mariners since roman times, a dozen loaves of bread, six barrels of beer, a dozen flagons of wine, some salt pork and beef, sacks of onions, carrots and turnips, three bars of soap and some more paper for the heads. The apothecary had run out of rock-alum, but he did buy some pepper, cloves, ginger and herbs. Then he returned to Maia. Maria helped him to load everything aboard and stow it. After returning the trolly to the boatyard, he and Maria made final preparations to sail.

'The wind has died away, and we don't have room to manoeuvre with stern sculling. I think we should lower the rowing boat and I'll climb in. You fix a line to the bow cleat and throw the rest down to me. Then let go the shore lines and I'll row out to pull the bow off. Once she's clear, you can scull from the stern to help me. By the time we get her into clear water, the sea breeze should kick in.'

'What if she's too heavy for you to pull her off, Papa?'

'I'll take the kedge anchor with me. If I can't pull her off by rowing, I'll tie the bow line to the anchor and drop it. Then I'll row back and we can use the anchor windlass to pull us off.'

'Good idea, Papa,' Maria unlashed the rowing boat from its storage frame on the foredeck, and attached the gaff halyard. Anthony rummaged around in the lazarette locker and pulled out the rope ladder, which he attached, ready to run over the side. He helped Maria haul on the halyard's block and tackle, and when they were sure the rowing boat would clear the ship's side, they swung the gaff across and then lowered the rowing boat into the water. Anthony climbed down the rope ladder and got in as Maria passed the oars down to him.

'Is there anything I can do to help?' François asked.

'No, Papa knows what he's doing. He spent time as a fisherman, and in the navy,' Maria replied, as she secured the bow line and tossed the coiled rope down to Anthony, followed, more cautiously, by the kedge anchor. Anthony rowed the small boat into position while Maria jumped down to the quay and removed the mooring lines, coiling them as she climbed back onboard. The line joining the boats came taught, and slowly, but surely, the bow came off the quay. As the stern also came clear, Maria fixed the sculling oar in place, over the stern, and began sculling. 'Actually, François, you could call ahead to Papa. He can return on board now. I have her.'

'Aye aye, skipper. Is that what you say?' François replied, smiling, as he walked to the bow and called out to Anthony. Ten minutes later, Anthony was back aboard. The rowing boat was lashed down on deck again, and the equipment was all stowed away.

'Right, let's get the sail up ready for the sea breeze.' Anthony unfastened the sail ties and reattached the gaff halyard; hauling the mainsail up. 'Now we wait.' Twenty minutes later, the sculling oar was lashed to its stowage brackets, and Maia was leaning into the freshening breeze, charging south.

They had a good wind as they sailed south by south-west from Ostia. Maria was at the helm, the wind flicking her hair, as she adjusted the helm and the mainsheet when gusts came and went. Anthony studied the Italian coastline on their port side, from time to time, going below deck to consult the chart. On one visit to the chart table, François was exiting the heads. He came over to see what Anthony was doing.

'How do you know where we are, Sir Anthony?'

'We are crossing the Tyrrhenian Sea, between the Italian peninsula and the island of Sardinia, and we are about here.' He placed his index finger on the chart. When I see prominent, identifiable features on land, such as a castle, a church, or a headland, then I stand by the compass in front of the helm and check the bearing of the feature. Using this protractor,' he said, holding up a brass semi-circle with the degrees marked off around the edge, 'I can estimate our position. I then put away the chart in the chart locker and get out the log book, quills and ink. I make a note of the approximate time and our position. That is just to aid my memory, when the next feature comes into view.'

'Why do you put the chart away, Sir Anthony?'

'You're paying us for this voyage, you can just call me Anthony. Ink and expensive charts don't mix on a rocking boat. One day, someone, Galileo perhaps, will invent a magic quill that writes without ink, and which you can erase with a magic cloth. When that day comes, I will cover my charts with position lines drawn from bearings and horizontal quadrant angles, as they are on big ships with dozens of copies of the same chart. Until then, we will keep sailing south-south-west, trying to miss Italy on our left, and Sardinia on our right.' Anthony climbed half-way up the companionway and popped his head out of the hatch. 'Is all well, Maria?'

'Yes, Papa.'

'I'll prepare tonight's stew and get it in the oven. Shout out if you have any concerns!' Anthony climbed back down. 'There is no need to look so concerned, François. There will be a full moon tonight and we will see either coastline long before we need to change course. Tomorrow, I will take sun sights with my octant, as we approach noon.

The highest of my altitude readings will give us our latitude. The navigation of this voyage is not difficult.' He opened one of the cool lockers, and fished out some of the beef, a few onions, carrots and turnips. He took them to the galley and began preparing them in the sink. 'I have made up some small-beer, in that barrel, François,' Anthony indicated with a glance. 'Would you mind pouring us each a tankard? I'm getting thirsty. The tankards are in there,' he also indicted the locker with his eyes. Do you mind telling me the reason King Henry sends you to Tunis?'

'I am afraid I cannot.' François replied, passing Anthony a tankard filled with small-beer. He took another tankard and poured some small-beer for himself. 'Although I cannot discuss the king's motives, the local history may be of interest. The Ottomans took Tunisia from Spain in 1574. Since then, it has been ruled by a military regime headed by the beylerbey, that is the provincial governor. The governors are appointed on terms of one year. The local diwân of Tunis then nominates the next governor for approval by the sultan. In 1591 the janissaries, the Ottoman troops rebelled because of mistreatment by their officers. Since then, there appears to have been a shift of power from the sultan towards the local families.'

'I see,' Anthony said, putting the prepared vegetables with the meat and some herbs and spices in a ceramic pot. He decided to add water ,while it was still fresh, before putting on a glove, and putting the stew in the oven. 'After dinner, I suggest you and Anne retire to your cabin. It is difficult to sleep well on a sea voyage, particularly on the first night at sea. Maria and I will alternate watches, two hours on, two hours off.'

Anthony filled bowls for his passengers, seated at the saloon table. He then filled a bowl for himself and took it up on deck. Steam rose from the bowl, and he breathed deeply through his nose, savouring the salty, spicy aroma.

'As soon as I've finished this, I'll take over,' he said to

Maria.

'No need to rush, Papa. It's a beautiful evening.'

'You won't think it quite so beautiful when I wake you, two hours after you've gone to bed, and half an hour after you've fallen asleep, if you're lucky. And make sure that you lash the wheel, and wake me as soon as you feel yourself getting drowsy.'

'Yes, Papa.'

'I'm serious. I can't have you falling asleep before you've woken me.'

'So am I, Papa. I'll wake you. I heard you talking to François,' she whispered. 'What do you think King Henry's interest is in Tunis?'

'I don't know, but the Ottomans and France have a common enemy in Spain, and the Ottomans have been threatening the Holy Roman Empire to the east. Beyond that, I can only guess. Right, I've finished. I'll take over now. Your stew is in the oven.'

'Here you are then, Papa. Course, south by south-west. We passed a merchantman to port half an hour ago. Estimated speed, seven knots. You have the ship.' Maria grinned as she stood aside, and Anthony took the helm. She kissed him on the cheek, then went below for her stew.

On the morning of their second day at sea, the wind blew steadily, and they made good progress. Anthony made his noon day observations of the sun with his octant and calculated that they were at a latitude of thirty-nine degrees north. He went below, checked the chart, put away his octant, and came back up on deck.

'I'm just going up the mast,' he called out to Maria, before climbing the ratlines. From the top of the ratlines, about two thirds of the way up the mast, he had a good view all around. After a few minutes, he came back down again. 'We are doing very well. I can see the peaks of the southern tip of Sardinia, on our starboard side, and Sicily to port. We have around a hundred and twenty nautical miles left until Tunis. If this wind keeps up, we will be there by early morning tomorrow. However, the wind is unlikely to blow this steadily. Nevertheless, I hope we shall be there before tomorrow nightfall.'

They saw a few sails on the horizon in the afternoon, and a pod of dolphins accompanied them for half an hour, leaping through their bow wave. As the dolphins headed off, they took the wind with them. The bow wave the dolphins had enjoyed ebbed away, and they continued at a third of their previous speed.

'I spoke too soon about our good progress,' Anthony mused.

'Don't worry, Anthony. A day or two is neither here nor there,' François said. 'I didn't think we were going to get to Tunis at all yesterday morning. Do you mind if I have a go on the helm, while it is calm?'

'Not at all, please do. Maria will stand by you, just in case,' Anthony replied, as Maria stepped to one side, and François gingerly took hold of the wheel.

'Well, I never thought I would steer a ship. Is it still south by south-west that we need?' he asked, peering at the compass in front of the wheel.

'No, we've been steering more or less due south since noon,' Anthony replied. 'Try not to over-correct as much,' he said, as François turned the wheel first to port, then to starboard. 'Just look at the compass, and pick a cloud on the horizon that is to the south, then steer towards that. Then look at the compass again in a few minutes and choose a new cloud if necessary. There, that's much better.' François continued to steer for a few minutes.

'I think the wind is picking up a little. Perhaps it's time to hand back to the professionals,' François said.

'If you want, but you're doing fine now.'

'No, I'm getting tired. Would you mind?' he said, turning to Maria.

'Would I be able to have a go?' Anne called from the

companionway, from where she had been watching her husband.

'I don't think you should, my dear. The wind is freshening, it's practically a gale now,' François called back, as Anthony and Maria raised their eyebrows in unison.

'Surely if Maria stood next to me, we should be in safe hands,' Anne said, climbing onto deck and lifting her skirts an inch, as she walked over to the helm.

'Will it be all right?' François asked, turning to Maria.

'Certainly it will,' Maria said, taking the wheel from him as he changed places with Anne. 'There, that's it. Just pick a spot on the horizon or a cloud dead ahead and steer towards that. Perfect! Ah, there is a bit more breeze coming. I can see ripples on the water ahead.'

'Should you take over?' Anne asked.

'No, you're doing fine. I will if I think I should,' Maia leaned a little as the wind arrived, and accelerated. 'I think you're a natural,' Maria smiled as Anne made slight adjustments to the wheel. 'Look behind us. See how straight our wake is? You're steering a very steady course. Well done!'

Maria made a beef pasta dish for dinner that evening. She took a bowl up to Anthony before re-joining their guests for dinner. Anthony smiled as he heard the conversation drift up from the saloon. Anne seemed to have enjoyed her period at the helm, much more than her husband had. As the upper limb of the sun dipped below the horizon, he heard the washing up being done. A little later, Maria came up on deck with the latrine bucket, and tipped its contents over the side. She lowered it down on the line to swoosh it clean.

'Our guests have retired to their cabin. Would you like anything to drink, Papa, or would you like me to take over?' she asked, picking up his bowl and spoon.

'A goblet of wine will wash that splendid dinner down. But I'll be fine for another couple of hours. You get your head down as soon as you've brought my wine.' A few minutes later, Maria came up with his wine.

'Well, good night, Papa.'

'Good night, Maria,' Anthony said, as she kissed him on the cheek, and went back below. Anthony watched the stars as they appeared. He found Orion, the hunter, with his distinctive belt, and tracked right and a little higher to find Taurus, the bull, and there between Perseus and Aries shone the Pleiades, the seven sisters. 'I don't know which of you is Maia, but thank you for your namesake. She's a good little ship,' he murmured, taking a swig of his wine. The wind was light, but steady. Anthony estimated they were making between four and five knots. The wind was on the beam, and Maia was perfectly balanced. Anthony tied a light line to the wheel and lay down on the deck, staring up at the stars. He wasn't sure how long he had been asleep, but the moon was now high in the sky, so he must have been asleep for several hours. He looked behind him and could make out, in the moonlight, the silhouettes of Sardinia and Sicily. He checked the compass, and they were still running due south. Well, that was a bonus. Feeling alert and refreshed, he thought he might as well carry on and let Maria get a great sleep.

◇ ◇ ◇

The third morning at sea dawned bright and clear. A few sails were visible on the horizon, and Maia ploughed on. Anthony took the log line and the half-minute sand-glass from the starboard cockpit locker. He turned the glass timer and threw the log over the side. He counted the knots in the line as they ran through his fingers until he saw the last grain of sand drain down through the neck of the timer. 'Seven knots and a bit,' he said to himself.

'Why didn't you wake me?' Maria asked, as she popped her head out of the companionway.

'I fell asleep for a few hours under the stars. When I woke, everything was fine, so I carried on,' he whispered, not wanting to alarm their guests. 'Could you rustle up some bacon and eggs? We're making about seven and a half knots. We'll be there by noon, if we keep this up.'

'Excellent. I'll get started on breakfast,' Maria replied, her head disappearing from view. Anthony put the log line and timer away, Maia sailing on with the helm lashed. Maria brought him his bacon and eggs, with some bread, and a tankard of small-beer. She scanned the horizon before going back below to do the washing up. François climbed up on deck, followed by Anne.

'What a fine morning, Anthony,' he remarked. 'We slept much better last night, didn't we, Anne?'

'Yes, dear. It is such a beautiful day, and the clouds are clearing. How long before we will reach Tunis, do you think, Anthony?'

'Well, I thought by noon, an hour ago. But the clearing sky may portend less wind. We shall have to see.'

Indeed, over the next hour, the wind dropped, as did their speed. By the time they were making only two knots through the water, Anthony retrieved a fishing line from the locker, baited it with a piece of bread, and threw it over the stern to see if they could catch anything. About ten minutes later, he saw the line twitch and hauled it in. 'I've caught something!'

'It's a sardine,' Anne said, as he lifted it out of the water and dropped it on deck. He extracted the hook from its lip and took a marlin spike from a rack beside the compass binnacle. Anthony killed the sardine with a blow to its head, then put another piece of bread on the hook and tried his luck again. He had landed four sardines by the time anyone noticed that the wind had died completely.

'I doubt that we'll catch anymore fish just lying here,' Anthony said. 'Still, that's a fresh supper for this evening.'

'Papa, I think I can see a boat, over there,' Maria said, pointing.

'So you can. I'm going up the mast to take a look,' Anthony said, making his way to the starboard ratlines. He climbed up and peered eastwards. Then he climbed down.

'There are two of them. The furthest one is the largest, and they're galleys. The nearest one has six oars on each side. Galleys are used virtually exclusively by the Barbary pirates.'

'Pirates!' Anne screamed.

'Have no fear, my sweet,' François said, putting his arm around her shoulders. 'I have diplomatic immunity. If they try to board us, I shall show them the king's warrant. We will not be harmed, neither will Anthony nor Maria.'

'I fear pirates have no respect for diplomacy, or warrants, François. If the wind picks up, we will outrun them. But if it stays like this, we will have to fight.'

'But what chance do we have?' Anne asked. 'If there are twelve oarsman, and heavens knows how many others, probably all men, we are outnumbered by the first boat, let alone the larger one.'

'The oarsmen will all be galley-slaves, chained to their benches. It's not them we have to worry about. Can you fire a rifle or musket, François?' Anthony asked.

'I'm a scholar, not a soldier, Anthony. I haven't even touched one.'

'How are you with a sword?'

'I've never held one.'

'Maria, start sculling,' Anthony ordered. 'We won't outrun them, but we can buy a little time. François come below. I can teach you to load a rifle, at least.'

'I will come with you,' Anne said. 'I may not be able to load a rifle, but I shall watch, and will put François right if he gets it wrong. I'm good at that.'

CHAPTER THREE

'All right, watch carefully,' Anthony said, picking up one of the rifles, 'this is the striking mechanism, the hammer. We can adjust these jaws to open or close, and they grip this piece of flint. The gun is not loaded, but if it were, I would pull back the hammer, like this, until it clicks. There, did you hear that click?' They both nodded. 'As you can see, the hammer is now held in position. If I squeeze the trigger, like this, there, as you saw, the trigger releases the hammer, which is spring loaded. The flint struck the steel and created sparks. The steel it struck is the priming pan lid, which is pushed forwards, allowing the sparks to enter the priming pan. If there had been gunpowder in the pan, it would have ignited, and a flash of flame would have passed through this small hole, into the barrel of the rifle, igniting the cartridge of gunpowder, and launching the ball, or projectile, out of the rifle towards the target. Now to load the gun, I take one of these paper cartridges of gunpowder, and bite off the end. I open the lid of the priming pan, and sprinkle a little of the powder in the pan. There, that's enough,' he said, showing them both the pan, and then closing the cover. 'Next, I push the cartridge into the muzzle of the rifle, like this, and I take out the ramrod, that's this rod in the tube under the barrel, and I use it to push the cartridge all the way down. Then I take one of these lead projectiles, and put it in the barrel, blunt end first. Then I push it all the way down with the ramrod. Finally, I take a piece of wadding, like this, and push that all the way down the barrel to hold the projectile in place. And that's it. The gun is loaded and ready to fire. You should reload the coolest rifle first. If the barrel is too hot to touch comfortably, then use this cleaning rod,' he said, taking a rod with some cloth attached to its end from the rifle case. 'Wet the cloth and run it up and down the barrel a few times, before inserting the cartridge. Any questions?'

'What if we run out of cartridges?' Anne asked.

'I doubt we will, but there is a barrel of gunpowder in the locker under your feet, together with paper for making more cartridges. Just put the gunpowder in the paper, roughly the same amount as in the already prepared ones. Roll it up and twist both ends.'

'And if we run out of projectiles?' François added.

'Even less likely, but I have some moulds here. Hack off a piece of lead, put it in a large metal spoon and put it in the stove. When it's molten, take it out with your hand wrapped in cloth, and pour the lead into these moulds. When they have cooled, there's a latch here which opens the back of the mould and allows the projectiles to drop out.'

'That sounds rather complex,' Anne said.

'If it came to that, we'd either have escaped, be dead, or be slaves. Now you both have a go at loading a rifle each, while I watch.' They each took a rifle and did as Anthony had shown them. 'Yes, that's right, you're both doing really well. Anne, don't cock the hammer. That was only demonstrating how to fire one. You'll need to be faster, but I've found that tends to happen naturally when the fighting starts. Maria and I will keep them at bay. The rifle is much more accurate than the muskets they will have. You stay down here. I'll take the loaded rifles up on deck. As we discharge each weapon, we'll throw them down the hatch. You pass them back up loaded as quickly as you can. Good luck!'

Anthony carried two rifles up on deck and laid them down. François passed him the other four, one by one. He studied the pursuing galley, which was steadily catching up with them. A Moor standing in the bows, aiming a musket. Anthony heard the crack as it was fired, but not the whistle of the musket ball.

'They're shooting at us!' François screamed. Anthony picked up a rifle and took aim, steadying the barrel on the gunwale. He held his breath and squeezed the trigger.

'Got him,' he smiled, as he passed the empty rifle into the waiting hands of François. Another two Moors took their fallen comrade's place, and Anthony heard two more musket cracks. 'Maria, stop sculling and shoot with me. Aim at the standing ones. The oarsmen are chained slaves, poor buggers, it's the others we need to take out. I'll take the one on the left.' Maria picked up a rifle and crouched beside him, taking aim. 'On the count of three. One, two, three.' Their rifles cracked as one, and both Moors dropped. 'Right, help me get the sails down,' he said, passing his rifle down the hatch. 'When the wind comes back, I don't want our sails full of holes.' There were four more musket cracks from the galley as they took down their limp sails. Anthony heard the whistle of one of them. 'Right, back to the shooting gallery.' The galley was getting much closer, and Anthony could count another ten Moors on board. Two of them were whipping the oarsmen, there was one on the helm, three were taking aim with muskets, and three were crouching, holding scimitars. The other seemed to be directing operations. 'The three with muskets, I'll take the one on the left again. You take the one on the right.' The three muskets cracked, and Anthony and Maria fired at the

24

same time. The two outer Moors dropped, just as their musket balls thudded into the cockpit coaming beside Anthony. He passed both their rifles down for reloading. 'In the locker opposite your cabin door, there are two swords. Pass them up, would you?' he asked, taking two fresh rifles from François.

'I got another one,' Maria said, taking a loaded rifle from Anthony. 'That leaves only seven.'

'And those in the galley behind them. That'll be here in another ten minutes,' he said, crouching down and taking aim. They dispatched three more pirates in the fifteen strokes of the oars that it took the galley to pull alongside. Anthony felt something hit his back, and he turned to see his swords that François had slid across the deck. He reached for them, passed one to Maria, and unsheathed the other. Anthony stood up, just in time to parry the scimitar slash of a Moor, as he leapt onto Maia's deck. He parried two more blows before lunging and feeling the tip of his sword parting ribs. He pulled his sword from the crumpling assailant and thrust it into the side of the nearest of two Moors, who were pushing Maria back as she frantically parried their blows. He tried to pull his sword free, but the Moor was falling at an awkward angle, and dragged Anthony down with him. As he tugged at his sword, he saw a shadow on the deck. He turned to see the pirate captain raise his scimitar. Anthony's hand was trapped under the dead weight of his last kill, and he was powerless to protect himself. He closed his eyes as he saw the blade slashing down at him. Instead of darkness, there was a rifle crack and silence. His attacker crumpled, an expression of surprise on his face. Maria had just lanced her adversary and stared at the companionway. Anthony turned and saw Anne, still pointing a rifle, smoke trailing from its muzzle.

The second galley continued its steady approach from the east. Anthony surveyed the carnage on his deck. He picked up the discharged rifles, and crossed to the companion way.

'I've just killed a man,' Anne wailed.

'Yes, and you saved my life, my daughter's life, your husband from slavery and yourself from the Harem. Thank you, you did really well, but it isn't over yet. Can you and François take these rifles, and the one you're holding below, and commence loading again? It might also be time to throw a few more logs in the stove and use the moulds to make some more projectiles. Maria and I will clear up here.' Anne went below, and Anthony turned to Maria.

'Let's get these bodies overboard,' he said, dragging the nearest Moor to the side, lifting him by the armpits, and tipping him over the side. Maria did the same with the lightest of the other three. Anthony then disposed of another, as Maria turned to the largest one, the leader.

'This one's got a ring of keys attached to his belt,' she said.

'Take off his belt and leave the keys on deck. I'll help you get him over the side. I don't think we'll ever get the stains out of the deck.' As the body splashed into the sea, Anthony picked up the keys, opened the rope locker, and took out a mooring warp. Then he jumped across into the pirate galley. He heard a babble of languages around him, French, Italian, Arabic, and others he didn't recognise. He gave the keys to an Italian man nearest to him. 'Free yourself and pass the keys on. I'm going to attach this line to the stern of the galley, and take it back and attach the other end to the bow of our boat. Your freedom depends on you all rowing westwards, away from the other pirate galley, as fast as you can, towing us. You saw how we dealt with your captors. We will keep up steady rifle fire at our pursuers. We have a joint interest in this.' As he attached the line to the galley's stern, he gave the same speech in French and then Arabic. He then jumped back aboard Maia and attached the warp to Maia's bow. 'That way!' he shouted in the three languages, pointing towards the clouds gathering in the west.

He peered down the companionway, and Anne passed up the loaded rifles. He saw François had hacked off some lumps of lead and was holding a spoon in the flames of the open stove door. 'Well done, François, well done Anne. We're going to be towed by the first galley now, and keep up a steady volley of fire at our pursuers. That's in both our interests.' Anthony took the rifles to the stern, where Maria was crouching. The pursuing galley started firing their muskets, but were too far off to have any effect. He turned and looked towards the bow, as the tow line came taut and the first galley was being rowed westwards. He looked back over the stern and noted the stern wave growing as they accelerated. Anthony and Maria picked off four pirates between them before they heard the whistle of musket balls getting closer. Antony beckoned François to crawl over to them with the fresh rifles, and he did. Anthony took aim again at the Moor with a musket on the starboard side of the galley, slowly but steadily catching them. He fired, and the Moor crumpled. Anthony watched the gun smoke lying motionless on the water, corralled between the waves spreading out from their stern. The musket fire was becoming increasingly accurate as the pirates gained on them. The pirate galley seemed to speed up. Anthony stared in disbelief, then noticed their wake fading to nothing. He turned around and peered forward.

'The bastards have let go of the tow line. We're drifting,' he shouted above the gun fire.

'What are we going to do, Papa? They'll be on top of us in a couple of minutes.'

'Well, I didn't want to, but I think our only chance now is to shoot some of the front rank of oarsmen. A couple of them slumped over an oar will cause their oar to clash with the one behind, and so on, slowing them down.'

'I agree, Papa. We have no choice. I'll go for the innermost oarsman, in the front rank, on their port side.'

'And I'll go for the outermost one,' he said as they both

took aim. 'Wait! Hold your fire.'

'Why, Papa?'

'The smoke is clearing, it's being blown away. The wind is back. Keep firing at the pirates while I hoist the sails. Be ready with the mainsheet.' Maria nodded as Anthony crawled to the foot of the mast. He uncoiled the main halyard and lay on his back as he hauled on the rope, for all he was worth. The sail rattled up the mast, and when the luff was taut, he hauled at the peak halyard until the mainsail set. A musket ball thumped into the mast, just above his head, and he turned to check on Maria. She was taking aim at the Moor who had just fired. Anthony saw François was crawling towards her with reloaded rifles. Anthony hauled on the jib halyard, and when the jib luff was tight, he cleated off the halyard and rolled across the deck to the port side. He grabbed the jib sheet and pulled. The wind filled the jib, and, bit by bit, pulled the bowsprit through the eye of the wind. The mainsail began to flap. 'Mainsheet, now!' he shouted back to Maria. He saw her heave it in. The mainsail filled, and he breathed a sigh of relief as Maia leant to the wind and sped away to the south. He gathered his strength for a few moments, then hauled up the staysail. He went forward and pulled in their towline that was now streaming out behind them, coiled it up and went back to join the others. Both Anne and François had now joined Maria on deck.

'Jesus, that was close, Papa.'

'Indeed it was. You did well, Maria. So did you, François, and Anne. You know, I think with all the blood already on deck, I may as well gut and fillet those sardines up here now, before washing the deck down.'

'Good heavens, Anthony. I don't know how you can think of your stomach now,' François exclaimed.

'Well, they'll take a while to prepare and cook, you know. Look, the large galley is chasing after the smaller one now, poor bastards.'

CHAPTER FOUR

The wind blew steadily from the west, and Maia made a good eight knots, due south. With Sardinia astern, and Sicily on their port side, they could see the Atlas Mountains ahead of them, and stretching away to the west, as far as they could see. They entered the Bay of Tunis as the sun fell, and the wind dropped, so rather than scull their way into the harbour, they dropped anchor in the bay, in six fathoms of water.

The following morning, Anthony used the ratchet windlass to winch the anchor up, hoisted the sails, and in a light breeze, they ghosted along towards the harbour. They passed a tower built on the end of a breakwater and turned to port. There were dhows of various sizes being loaded and offloaded along the quay. The quayside was bustling with heavily laden camels, horses, and donkeys. Anthony picked a gap between two dhows and aimed for it. Maria dropped the jib and staysail, and Anthony alternately let out the mainsheet to slow down, and hauled it in to prevent them from stalling. As they came alongside, he let the mainsheet out completely, and he and Maria stepped ashore with the mooring warps. They looped them around and tied them off to bollards fore and aft. Then they set two more warps as springs to stop them moving fore and aft. Even while they were tying Maia up, they were besieged by boys and men of all ages waving jewellery, foodstuffs, ceramics and a host of other items in their faces. They retreated aboard, and the vendors didn't follow them.

It was a matter of perhaps half an hour before a party of men, armed with scimitars, and dressed in white flowing robes, arrived. Their leader wore a red cylindrical hat and had an embroidered red tunic under his robe. He addressed them. Anthony recognised the language as Turkish, but he had devoted the time he had spent in Constantinople, or Istanbul as they had called it, to learning Arabic well, rather that several languages poorly. François stepped forward and conversed fluently with the leader of the troop.

'He insists on coming aboard, Anthony.'

'Well, we can hardly prevent him,' Anthony replied. François invited them aboard. The leader barked orders to his men, and two of them went down the companionway. François remonstrated with the leader and showed him his diplomatic papers. The leader took them and read them. Then he shouted further orders, and his men scurried back up on deck. There was a further conversation between François and the leader.

'We are all to go with them to the palace. This fellow is the captain of the Dey's guard. He will leave two men on the quay to guard your ship and prevent any pilfering. We will be presented to Uthman Dey, who is the ruler of Tunisia,' François said.

'I trust he won't mind me locking the ship, just to be sure?' Anthony asked. François talked some more with the captain, before François nodded. Anthony went below. He closed and bolted all the hatches from the inside. He returned on deck with padlocks and a key in his hands. He first locked the companionway hatch, then all the cockpit lockers. When that was done, they all climbed down onto the quay and followed the captain, escorted by the other troops. He led them through the crowds, who parted to make way for the captain. They passed several elderly, bearded men sitting cross-legged playing wooden flutes, as hooded snakes rose from the wicker baskets in front of them, and swayed from side to side. Maria paused to watch, but the guard behind pushed her, and they kept walking.

They left the harbour area and proceeded through narrow streets with shops on either side. The scent of spices was all around. Stalls were set out in front of the shops, with cloth, leather-ware, pots and pans, vegetables, fruit, fish, and meat. Shop keepers who weren't bartering with customers called out to them and held out their wares for inspection, but were brushed aside by the guards. They passed a rectangular tower, that Anthony estimated might be a hundred-and-fifty-feet high. François conversed with the captain before turning to Anthony.

'That is the Al-Zaytuna Mosque, which means the Mosque of Olive. It's the oldest mosque in Tunis and covers more than an acre. It has architectural features brought from the nearby ancient city of Carthage.' A little further on, they reached the Dar Othman palace. They approached it through a garden of sweet-smelling flowers. They reminded Anthony of the Topkapi Palace, where he had stayed during the year he had spent in Constantinople; although this was nothing like as grand. The entrance was an ornately carved wooden door under a striped, horseshoe-shaped stone arch. It was shaded by a wooden portico set on wooden columns, also with striped horseshoe arches connecting them. The paving in front of the door was laid out in a pattern of diamond shapes. Guards opened the door as the captain approached. They went through into a square vestibule, with stone benches along two sides. The captain spoke with François. 'Anne, I'm afraid you and Maria must wait here while Anthony and I are taken to meet Uthman Dey.' Anne sat down without argument. Maria also sat, but scowled.

'I'm afraid it's their way, Maria. I'm sure I won't be long. He's a busy man,' Anthony said.

François and Anthony were ushered into a large room decorated in the Arabic style, with geometric patterns and calligraphy. There were four men, seated on cushions, by a window with a view across to the Al-Zaytuna Mosque. The men stood up, and three of them bowed and left. The fourth man, tall and ornately dressed in silk robes, walked over to them. He spoke with François in Turkish, and then they switched to Arabic. François presented him with his letters from King Henry, which he read.

'Please, come, be seated. Would you like some mint tea after your long journey?' They both replied that they would. He clapped his hands, and a servant appeared. There was a brief exchange in another dialect, and the servant bowed and left the room. They both sat down, cross-legged, on cushions opposite Uthman Dey.

'Welcome to Tunis, Monsieur Savary de Brèves. Of course, we shall be happy to receive you as King Henry's ambassador. We shall make a house available nearby for you and your wife; and provide servants, as long as your stay here shall last. Who is your associate?'

'This is Sir Anthony Standen, Your Highness. I could not find a ship willing to convey my wife and I here, and Sir Anthony gallantly came to our rescue, with his own ship.'

'I am pleased to meet you, Sir Anthony. The captain of my guard informed me of bloodstains on your deck.'

'A small encounter with some pirates, Your Highness. It was nothing serious,' Anthony replied.

'These Barbary pirates are a curse on trade. However I have purchased some western women from them, for my harem. They provide an amusing diversity and please me. Will you be staying with us for long?'

'No, Your Highness, I am eager to return to my wife and

family,' Anthony replied.

'The woman with you is not your wife, then?' Uthman Dey replied, surprised.

'No, Your Highness, that is my eldest daughter, Maria.'

'Then when you are ready, my guard will escort you back to your ship and ensure you have an unobstructed departure. Ah, the tea arrives. Please drink.' The servant set down a tray with three glasses of green tea, a spoon, and a bowl of sugar on a small table beside them. They each took a glass. Uthman Dey took three spoonfuls of sugar, François took one, and Anthony declined the sugar. Anthony sipped his tea, as Uthman Dey explained how he had taken control of the country, following the mutiny of the janissaries. He had broken up the previous system of councils, and ruled in his own right, with the Ottoman Pasha confined to a ceremonial role. He had subdued the hinterland, as well as the city of Tunis, and had amassed an army of two thousand Zuwâwa troops, from the local tribes, and payed them the same as the Ottoman janissaries. When they had finished their tea, he clapped his hands again, and the servant came and removed the glasses. 'I have much business to deal with today and tomorrow. That will give you time to settle in to your new residence, Ambassador Savary de Brèves. Come and see me the day after tomorrow, after morning prayers. My captain of the guard will escort you and your wife to your residence, and Sir Anthony and his daughter, back to their ship.' He rose, and Anthony and François stood up as well. Uthman Dey left the room, and as the door was closed behind him, the door through which they had entered opened. The captain beckoned them over, and they re-joined Anne and Maria.

'We are to be taken to our new residence, Anne, then the guard will escort Anthony and Maria back to their ship.'

'Oh, but we left our trunks onboard, and I still have some packing to do. We must collect them first, darling,' Anne said.

'Of course,' François said and turned to the captain,

who seemed to only speak Turkish. He spoke with him for a while, then translated for the others. 'The guard will take us to Maia so that we can collect our things, and say our farewells to Anthony and Maria. Shall we go?' They were escorted back to the quayside. Anthony climbed aboard and unlocked the companionway. François and Anne climbed aboard and went below to their cabin. Maria remained on the quayside, watching a snake charmer. When François and Anne reappeared on deck, Maria climbed back aboard to help Anthony lift the chests up on deck. 'Well, I suppose this is goodbye,' François said, taking his purse from his belt and counting out a hundred ducats. 'It hardly seems enough for what you have seen us through. But I have to provide accounts to the king. I cannot thank you enough, Anthony and Maria. We are forever in your debt.'

'No!' Anne shrieked, 'this is not how the story ends. It can't be. Here's your money. Thank you very much. Have a safe voyage. I don't know how it ends, but this isn't it.'

'Are you all right, my darling? Is it the heat?'

'No, it isn't the damned heat. Yesterday, I killed a man. I did it to save Anthony, and myself, and you. They saved us from slavery, or death, or worse. You crawled through gunfire to pass them loaded rifles. Oh, I don't know what comes next, but it's not just goodbye.' Anthony watched a tremor begin around Anne's midriff, shaking like a ship's timbers crashing through one great wave after another, spreading with a relentless rush until her whole body was convulsing, tears cascading down her face. François pulled her to him and wrapped his arms around her.

'If I may speak,' Anthony said, 'it's shock. Battle is a brutal and bloody business. There is never an end to the story, but in my experience, the end of the chapter usually involves the surviving comrades-in-arms drinking an enormous amount of wine together and talking nonsense. We have lots of our own wine and brandy aboard. You are welcome to stay and drink with us. You don't have to meet the Dey again until the day after tomorrow.'

'I think it will be good for us, darling,' Anne whispered, wiping the tears from her cheeks.

'Yes, of course, my dear,' François said. He went to Maia's side and called down to the captain. After a brief conversation, he turned back to Anthony. 'That is fine. The captain will return tomorrow to escort us, and he will leave a guard on the quayside to ensure that we are not disturbed.'

They sat around the saloon table, a flagon of Anthony's Sangiovese in the centre. They had all downed their first wine without a word. Anthony refilled all their goblets.

'Well, someone's got to say something. Where did you learn Turkish, François?' Anthony asked.

'Mainly from my cousin Jacques. He's a brilliant linguist, and fluent in Arabic, Turkish and Persian. I say he is a brilliant linguist, he may be dead, for all I know.'

'Go on,' Anthony said, taking a swig from his goblet.

'He's a bit of a hothead. He can't toe the line. The former King Henry appointed him ambassador to Constantinople in 1585, and he took me with him. All went well to start with, and my fluency in the eastern tongues advanced tremendously. He had a terrible conflict with the English ambassador, William Harborne.' Anthony almost choked on his wine. 'Are you all right, Anthony?' François asked, as Maria slapped Anthony on the back.

'Yes, yes, I'll be all right in a minute, carry on,' Anthony gasped, trying to catch his breath.

'Then when the king died, and Henry of Navarre became King, Jacques refused to acknowledge the new king. Jacques was tightly bound to the Catholic League. An ambassador that didn't serve his own king was of little use to the sultan, so they imprisoned him, and made me ambassador instead. I pleaded with him, Jacques, that is, to see sense, but he was so stubborn. I got on quite well with Sultan Ahmed, and negotiated a treaty that gave France great trading advantages. They also tasked me to negotiate restraint of the Barbary pirates. They had been causing havoc on the coast of Provence. I wish I'd had more success with that. I hadn't appreciated what a menace they are until yesterday. Are you better now, Anthony?'

'Yes, it's just that the coincidence overcame me. William Harborne and I met by chance in 1576. The Duke of Austria was chasing me across Europe, and he was persistent. When I crossed into Ottoman territory, I shook his men off. The innkeeper was himself amazed at the coincidence, because he hadn't had an English visitor for years, and he had two on the same night. William and I travelled onwards together and got to know each other very well. He took me to Constantinople, and we stayed there until 1580. Murad the third was the sultan then. A charming fellow on the outside, but he had all his younger brothers killed when his father died. From Constantinople I went to Florence, which is where I met my wife, Francesca.'

'So I assume Constantinople is where you learnt your Arabic,' François said.

'Yes, that's right. I had nothing else to do, except stay out of the Duke of Austria's way, so whilst William went about his negotiations, I took advantage of the Jewish interpreter we were assigned, and learnt Arabic. It stood me in good stead when I got to Florence. I went there as a secretary to the Duke of Tuscany's wife, but the duke had a fascination for alchemy, and some Arabic texts he couldn't read. So, I translated them for him. But tell me, what was your cousin's conflict with William? He seemed such a very reasonable man to me.'

'Oh, he was reasonable, but also highly intelligent and persuasive. My cousin rather inherited the conflict from his predecessor, another Jacques I'm afraid, Jacques de Germigny. France had had quite a long-standing treaty with the Ottomans and was recognised as the protector of all Christian people trading there. Your Queen Elizabeth was rather vexed that her ships could only trade in the Levant under the French flag. She required William to change that, and he used all his wits to achieve it. He worked on the Grand Vizier, lavishing fine English textiles, and manufactured goods on him, whilst at the same time fooling Germigny into thinking he was dull witted. Germigny eventually found out what was going on. One of William's ships entered the harbour of Chios, without permission, and he was forced to seek Germigny's help. He started looking into William's activities, but by then William had the Grand Vizier eating out of his hand.'

'So if William had already secured the treaty with the Ottoman's, why did your cousin have a conflict with him?'

'Well, King Henry was not happy that the English could operate under their own flag, and when your boss isn't happy, then it feeds down to you. But the main thing, by then, was that William was working hard on the sultan to go to war with Spain. He kept feeding him intelligence about King Philip's ambitions in Portugal; and with the proximity of the Portuguese colonies, particularly in the Persian gulf, that was a genuine concern. My cousin Jacques was closely bound to the Catholic league, so the conflict with William grew.' François drained his goblet and Anthony refilled it. 'Anyway, we've had enough conflict for a while. When we first met, I remember you saying that you had known the king's wife, Marie de Medici. So was it when she was a girl in Florence?'

'Yes, that's right, François. It's all such a coincidence, isn't it? Are we all just pieces on a board game? God rolls the dice, and we move around and bump into other pieces? Or is it fate? If Maria, I mean Marie, but she was Maria in Florence, if she hadn't been in a strop that morning, and her stepmother hadn't become exasperated with her, and if I hadn't been passing her room, then well,' Anthony took a long draft at his wine, 'I wouldn't have met Francesca, and Maria, my Maria, wouldn't be here now. I owe her everything. I do really. I took her on a walk to feed the ducks in the pond. Her brother had died, you see, what was his name? Philip I think. She was only seven then. Her

37

mother had died when she wasn't quite three. That's a terrible thing to happen, isn't it? So young, but old enough to feel it. While we were feeding the ducks, the most beautiful woman in the world was there, watching us. I mean no offence, Anne, you're very beautiful too, Anne, but my Francesca is something else. Well, it's in the eye of the beholder, isn't it, beauty I mean. But I had to leave Florence. It was because of Maria's wicked uncle, Ferdinando. He murdered Maria's father and stepmother with arsenic. I'd read all about arsenic in her father's Arabic books, you see. I could tell the symptoms. He knew I knew he'd done it, so it would have been me next. I had to leave the most beautiful woman in the world. Poor kid, she was about twelve, then I think. Is she well François? Is she a good queen? Little Maria de Medici I mean, not Francesca.'

'Yes, Anthony. She has three children, Louis, Elizabeth and Christine. Louis is seven now. Unfortunately, he has a speech impediment, a stammer. The doctors don't seem able to help very much. Both the queen and king are very worried about how he will rule when the time comes. Why was the Duke of Austria chasing you across Europe? That sounds like a good story, to lighten the mood.'

'He caught me in bed with his mother. She had been very young when she had him. She was a very attractive and kind woman. I wonder what happened to her.'

'That's one of your stories I haven't heard before, Papa.' Maria said, looking quizzically at him.

'Shhh! Don't tell your mother. It was long before I met her. I was destitute and with nowhere to stay, and she took me in. Where did you and Anne meet François? I think the wine is helping, don't you? Do you think it's helping, Anne?'

'Yes I do, Anthony,' Anne said, draining her goblet. 'I went to Rome with my uncle, Jacques Auguste de Thou. It was terribly exciting for me. First there was the journey, and when we got to Rome, the antiquities, the colosseum, the forum took my breath away. It was all so wonderful. My uncle is a historian and writer, so he made an excellent guide. He met François because he was looking for a printer, and François had set up his own printing firm while he was in Rome. He doesn't like to blow his own trumpet, but he is the first man to produce an Arabic typeface. My uncle introduced us, and we were attracted to each other at once.'

'They won't like that, the Arabs. Claligraphy, calligraphy, that's what they like, not type. What are you printing in Arabic, François?' Anthony slurred.

'It's a work in progress, but I'm going to print a bilingual Latin–Arabic edition of Cardinal Bellarmine's catechism.'

'Bellarmine? Why I've met Cardinal Bellarmine. What a small world it is. Will you do something for me, François?'

'What is it, Anthony?'

'Will you get a message to Queen Marie? Tell her how much I owe her. Tell her I'll do anything for her. If she's ever in any trouble, she's to call for me. Will you do that for me, François?'

'I will, Anthony. And I'll tell her there is nobody better to have at your side when the chips are down. Where shall I tell her to find you?'

'The Standen Vinyard, Frascati.'

CHAPTER FIVE

The cart rattled from side to side, up the rutted lane leading from the centre of Frascati to their vineyard.

'You haven't forgotten that you promised to teach us ciphers and lock picking, have you, Papa?'

'No, I haven't, Maria, but we're about to start the harvest. I'll teach you and Antonio lock picking and ciphers, if you'll take over teaching William languages, reading and writing.'

'Can't that wait? He's only four.'

'No, it can't. His mind's like a sponge at the moment. It's the best time to learn. I had the boat built for you, because you wanted it so much.'

'All right, Papa, I'll do it. Talk of the devil, here he comes,' Maria said, and Anthony reined in his horse. William ran up and climbed the spokes of the cartwheel and onto the footplate. Anthony lifted William onto his lap with his right hand and flicked the reins with his left.

'Papa, I saw you coming, so I ran and ran. Where have you been?'

'Oh, just sailing around in our new boat.'

'What's a boat, Papa?'

'Well, it's like a cart, but much bigger, and it floats on water. You know the wooden Duck that Antonio carved for you, that floats in your bathtub. Well, our boat floats on the sea.'

'What's the sea?'

'Can you teach him geography as well, Maria?'

'If I teach him to read first, then he can learn geography himself.'

'Well, you have a point. I learnt a lot from the Arabic texts in the duke's library, but I was an adult and interested. You'll be taking him sailing before you know it, and you'll want him to know the difference between the sea and the land, so just humour me. Focus on reading, writing and languages. Teach him wrestling when he's restless, and needs to get rid of some surplus energy, and try to take advantage of his interests. Just until we've got the harvest in, and I've taught you and Antonio lock picking and ciphers.'

'All right, Papa,' Maria said, just as they came to a halt outside the stable. Francesca was coming down the path from the villa, with Catherine clutched to her breast, in the crook of her right arm, and Anna walking along beside her, holding her left hand.

'You were longer than I expected. I thought you were only going to be away a week. Although, I suppose I should be happy it's only an extra three days. At least they did not lock you in the Tower of London this time, and you weren't fighting the Spanish. How is the boat?' Francesca asked, as Anthony jumped down and kissed her and Catherine before scooping Anna up in his arms.

'The boat is wonderful, quick and dependable. My, you've grown in less than two weeks. How old are you now, Anna?'

'I'm two years and four months and a million days.'

'I don't think you're a million days, sweetheart. But you are two years and two months, well done. Can you climb down yourself, William? Well done. What a clever boy. Look, here come's Antonio.'

'Hello, Son. How are the grapes looking?'

'Bursting with juice, Father. I think it's going to be our best harvest yet. I've cleaned the press and the barrels in readiness. Would you like me to unharness Lightning, and put him in the paddock?'

'Would you mind Son, it's been a bone-shaker of a ride.'

'I'll cook a chicken stew tonight, and you can tell us all about the boat, over a few flagons of wine,' Francesca said, leading the way to their villa.

'I think I might go easy on the wine tonight. I've had a bit of a headache today. I can't think why.' Anthony murmured.

Anthony was up early. His head was clear, and the sun was shining. He walked down, towards his fields of vines, and as he was approaching the stable, he heard a hammering sound. As he got to the open door, he saw Maria bending over something on a bench.

'What have you got there, Maria?'

'I found this piece of slate under that bale of hay in the corner. I've chipped off some ridges on one side to make it smooth. The other day, when I was walking in the hills, I found this lump of limestone. It's much softer than marble. When we were in Venice, I saw some kids writing on a slate with a piece of limestone, and I thought I could use this for William's lessons. See, you can write on the slate, like this.'

'Well done, that's brilliant.'

'But this is the best bit. If you take a cloth and rub over it, the writing's gone. It'll save on paper and ink. I've also thought about a lesson plan. When the weather is fine, we'll wander around the villa, and I'll ask him to name something, a tree, for instance. Then I'll ask him to write the name down on the slate. Next I'll ask the same question in English, and ask him to write it in English. We'll do the same in Spanish, Latin, German, and I'll also get him to count how many trees there are in a field. What do you think, Papa?'

'I'm very pleased to see you thinking about the lessons and planning them. Would you like to make a start on ciphers this afternoon?'

'Yes please, Papa.'

'Then I shall think about my lesson plan. We will begin after lunch. I'll let Antonio know.'

Anthony sat on one side of the dining table, and Antonio and Maria sat on the other side, facing him.

'My spying career got off to a very inauspicious start. They rather left me to my own devices, and I made some serious errors, which almost killed me. Sir Henry Norris realised his mistake and arranged some tuition for me. His secretary taught me about ciphers and codes. Then the orphaned son of a locksmith, who had turned to burglary for his living, taught me how to pick locks. He also taught me about following people without being seen, and how to avoid being followed yourself. Finally, an old soldier taught me combat and wrestling, which I have already taught to you.'

'So was that everything you needed to know, Papa?'

'Almost. There are a few more things, like how to make a cast of a wax seal, so that you can open a letter, copy it, and reseal it, so that nobody knows it's been read. We can cover that as part of ciphers, that's where I learnt it, from the secretary. There are also some things I learnt as I went along. For example, it's much easier to gain intelligence by physical means, such as intercepting correspondence and deciphering it, than by trying to bribe someone to give you information. I see bribery, or coercion, as like torture. The victim will give you the information he thinks you want to hear, even if it may not be the truth.'

'But how do you get your hands on the correspondence?' Antonio asked.

43

'Sometimes by picking locks, in the dead of night, to get into someone's study. Most of the time, I was just given the documents to deliver. I got a job as a dispatch rider, and when I was out of sight, opened the dispatches, copied, and resealed them. There's another method I've used a few times to eavesdrop on conversations. I was in a dark room one night and heard an owl hooting. It was so clear, I thought it was in the room with me. It seemed to be in the fireplace, but actually it was perched on the top of the chimney. I realised that if I could hear the owl, it could hear me. That led me to realise that if there isn't a fire lit, then a way of hearing a conversation taking place in a room is to find an empty room above or below it and stick your head in the fireplace. Anyway, let's make a start on ciphers. So tell me, what are ciphers?'

'A way of concealing messages, I suppose,' Maria answered.

'Very good. What other ways of concealing messages are there?'

'Invisible ink,' Antonio suggested.

'That's right. There are two fundamental ways of sending and receiving secret messages. One is to hide the medium which carries the message. For example, the ancient Chinese wrote messages on fine silk, scrunched it into a small ball, encased it in wax, and then the messenger swallowed it. With the passage of time, the message reappeared.'

'Argh, that's gross,' Maria exclaimed, and Antonio winced.

'I agree, I haven't had to resort to that method. The Persians used to shave the head of a servant and write on his scalp. Then they let his hair grow back and sent him off to the recipient. If the enemy stopped him and searched him, there would be no message to discover. When he reached the intended recipient, he would shave his head and show it to the recipient.'

'That's not much use, if it's urgent, and I'm not shaving

my head. You can try that if you like, Antonio.'

'Then, as Antonio has already suggested, there is invisible ink. The ancient Greeks used the milk of the Thithymallus plant as invisible ink. Once dry, it is invisible, but if you heat it, the ink turns brown. Urine will work too. So there are many ways of hiding a message. But if your enemy searches you and warms a blank page, or shaves your head, the message is revealed. Then, rather than concealing the medium by which the message is conveyed, that is the paper, the scalp or the ink, you can conceal the meaning of the message rather than the message itself. Julius Caesar used ciphers. He used a substitution cipher in which each letter of the alphabet gets moved a set number of places.' Anthony sketched out the cipher on a piece of paper.

a	b	c	d	e	f	g	h	i	j	k	l	m	n	o	p	q	r	s	t	u	v	w	x	y	z
D	E	F	G	H	I	J	K	L	M	N	O	P	Q	R	S	T	U	V	W	X	Y	Z	A	B	C

The lower-case letters, on the top are the alphabet, and the uppercase letters below are the cipher alphabet. As you can see, the cipher alphabet has been shunted to the right by three letters. The writer and the receiver agree three, which is the key. But it could be any number between one and twenty-five, as long as they agree on it beforehand. Now I will write a message for you to decipher,' Anthony said as he took up a quill once more, and wrote. 'What does this say?'

JRRG OXFN

'GOOD LUCK' Maria and Antonio said in unison. 'These ciphers aren't hard at all,' Maria said.

'Well, you had the cipher alphabet in front of you. Now I'll leave the room, and I want you to write me a simple message, using the Julian cipher. Don't tell me by how many spaces you have shunted the letters and don't let me see the cipher key that you make. How long do you think it will take me to decipher?'

'Years!' Antonio said.

'Well, there are twenty-five possible ciphers, so not years. But a few hours anyway,' Maria said.

'Then you get started. I'll feed the chickens and be back in half an hour.' When he had gone, Maria took the quill and a piece of paper. She dipped the quill in the ink.

'What do you think, Antonio? I've thought of a message. Where do you think we should start the key?'

'How about at Q?' He suggested. 'He's most likely to start at either end, I'd have thought.'

'Good idea,' Maria said, and began to write out the new cipher key.

```
a  b  c  d  e  f  g  h  i  j  k  l  m  n  o  p  q  r  s  t  u  v  w  x  y  z
K  L  M  N  O  P  Q  R  S  T  U  V  W  X  Y  Z  A  B  C  D  E  F  G  H  I  J
```

Then she wrote her message.

IYE GSVV XOFOB CYVFO DRSC MSZROB

'That's just gibberish, Maria. Let me see.' Antonio took the quill and worked his way across the message. Oh, I've got it. Right, let's crumple up the key, and my effort. I'll stick them in my pocket. Anthony returned ten minutes later and popped his head around the door.

'Are you ready for me yet?' he asked.

'Yes, Papa,' they said, grinning. 'Shall we groom the horses while you try to decipher it?' Maria asked.

'No, just give me a few minutes,' Anthony said as he picked up the quill and ran his eyes back and forth over the message. He counted with his fingers, 'Ah, I think I will. Never indeed, it's taken me just under a minute.'

'Never. You mean you've solved it?'

'Yes. It says you will never solve this cipher. Which is incorrect, I just have.'

'Have you been watching us, no you can't have. How on

earth did you do that, Papa? Is it magic?' Maria gasped.

'No, I just did some counting. The first thing that struck me was the number of Os. The most frequently used letter is E. So if e was O, then a had to be K. You started from Q.'

'That's incredible!' Maria whistled.

'No, that's cryptanalysis. There are some other tricks besides looking for the most common letter. For example, E can appear before or after almost any other letter, but T rarely appears before B,D,G,J,K,M,Q or V. The letter Q is almost always followed by U. So I shall make up some messages, and leave you to use these techniques. You go for a short walk and come back in ten minutes.' Maria and Antonio left, and Anthony wrote out a new cipher key and composed a brief message.

CN QIOFX VY KOYYL CZ SIO XCXHN ZCHX NBCM KOCNY YUMS

When Maria and Antonio returned, he presented them with it. He watched them counting.

'There are six Cs,' Maria said. 'I reckon C must be E.'

'There are five Ys,' Antonio added. 'And what two letter word starts with E?'

'Et, En, El, Eh. We don't know what language it's written in. Look, K occurs twice, and each time it's followed by O. Perhaps K is Q and O is U. And I agree Y is almost as frequent as C. So if I'm right about K and O and you're right about Y, then the forth word would be QUEE_. Queen, Queer,...' Within another few minutes they had solved Anthony's cipher. 'That's real magic, Papa. We did it.'

'You've done very well. I think that's enough for today. Tomorrow I'd like you each to take a piece of text, and tabulate the frequency of each letter. Try several languages and see what you come up with.'

'Reading the bible will never have been such fun,' Maria laughed.

◇ ◇ ◇

The following day, when Antonio had finished working in the fields, and Maria had completed William's lessons for the day, they sat at the dining room table poring over all of Anthony's books. Anthony left them to it and heated some water, ready to bathe William, Anna, and Catherine.

'What are they doing, Anthony? I've never seen them so studious,' Francesca asked, peeling some carrots.

'They're researching the structure of languages,' Anthony replied.

'They have inherited your fascination with language. That's all very well, but when are we going to find Maria a suitable husband? She's twenty now, and I'm despairing that she'll ever find the right man. Antonio still seems to be besotted with Greta. He's planning to visit her, at her parent's home in Turin, at the end of this term. I'm not sure it will work out. Why is she wasting her time studying medicine if she's going to marry and settle down?'

'She wants to help people, cure them of sickness, like her father. What's wrong with that?'

'Exactly, like her father. It's a man's job being a doctor. I don't see how it's going to work out for them, I really don't. What will Antonio do while she's curing folk?'

'Perhaps she could set up a practice here, and Antonio could run the vineyard,' Anthony suggested.

'There aren't enough people in Frascati to support a doctor's practice, and we're all quite healthy, here in the country.'

'In Rome then.'

'Talk sense, darling. A three-hour ride to work and the same home again. How is that practical?'

'I don't know, sweetheart, but it's for them to work out. You can't live their lives for them. We'll do everything we can to support them, but they need to decide for themselves.'

'You're right, of course, but it affects us too. You're not getting any younger, and the vineyard is hard work. I've been watching you; your old injuries trouble you.'

'Only when it's damp. There's plenty of life in the old dog yet. I'm going to see how they're getting on, while I can still walk as far as the dining room,' Anthony laughed, and Francesca threw a carrot at him.

'How are you getting on?' Anthony asked.

'It's fascinating, Father.' Antonio looked up from the books, quill in hand. 'The differences between the languages are as interesting as the similarities. E is the most frequently recurring letter in Italian, French, English and Spanish, but equal with I in Latin.'

'And in French, E is way out ahead. I've counted fifteen Es in every hundred letters in French, whereas in Italian it's only eleven,' Maria added. 'Another interesting thing is that although E and A are the top two letters in Italian, French, and Spanish; in English T takes second place.'

'Well, English is half German in origin. What have you found for German?' Anthony enquired.

'I don't see how it accounts for the English discrepancy,' Maria replied. 'E is even farther ahead with seventeen out of every hundred letters, but T is in sixth place with only six. I wondered about Greek, and the top letter there is alpha with eleven, followed by tau with eight, and epsilon with seven. Perhaps Greek has been more of an influence on English than German has.'

'I don't know, but you are arming yourselves with the tools to crack ciphers through frequency analysis. That has served me well. You should also know about codes.'

'What's the difference?' Maria asked.

'Well, in ciphers the letters are substituted, and in codes whole words are substituted. For example, the word queen might be substituted by apple, Rome might become cabbage, gunpowder might become queen. The problem with codes, from the user's point of view, is that both the encoder and the decoder need to have a code book. If several agents in the field use the same code, and if one of them is captured with the code book, then their enemy can decode their secret messages. The advantage is that without the code book, codes are virtually impossible to crack. There are, however, some ways of overcoming the problem of needing a code book. I have myself used a method in which I have written an innocent-looking letter, but if you look at, say, every ninth word, then those words make up the encoded message. In a simple form of this code, I might have dated the letter the 9th of September 1609, suggesting that every ninth word is the message. Sometimes I've put a tiny dot under a numeral in the year, to say that is the number to be used. They're quite fun to write because you have to be creative. I wanted to say Spain once, so wrote about a nephew's art works and used red and yellow to suggest Spain.'

'Can we start on lock picking soon, Papa?' Maria asked.

'I don't see why not. I'm planning to visit the blacksmith tomorrow anyway, so I'll get him to make you a set of picks each.'

Anthony was passing the dining room and heard Maria teaching William. It was raining outside, so that was why they were working indoors. He stopped to listen, but not wanting to disturb them, he stayed just out of sight.

'Qu'est-ce que c'est?' Maria asked.

'Une pomme,' William replied.

'Cos'è questo?' Maria asked, holding up a drawing of a dog.

'Un cane.'

'Well done, William. Let me see you write those words on your slate,' Maria said. 'Very good. Wie viele Äpfel halte ich?' Maria asked, putting down the drawing and picking three apples from a fruit bowl on the table.

'Sie halten drei Äpfel.'

'Sehr gut. Wenn ich dir zwei Äpfel gebe, wie viele habe ich?' Maria asked, passing two of the apples across the table to William.

'Ich habe zwei Äpfel,' William replied, picking up the apples and taking a bite from the reddest one.

'Dummkopf! Du hast zwei Äpfel, Wilhelm, aber ich habe nur einen. Quid est hoc?' Maria asked, picking a pear from the fruit bowl.

'Est unus piro'

'Bene factum!' Now let's try something in Spanish. 'Que es esto?' Maria asked, holding up a drawing of a bird.

'Un pájaro.'

'Is it a small bird or a large bird?' Maria asked.

'I'm not sure,' William replied. 'It looks small.' Maria took a fresh piece of paper and drew a much larger bird. She drew a comb on its head. 'That's a big bird.'

'En español, por favor, William.'

'Es un ave.'

'Bien hecho! Qué bien! Que tipo de ave es?'

'Es una polla,' William replied.

'You clot, William! Un pollo. Una polla is a vulgar word for what you keep between your legs and pee with. Don't be so thick!' Maria shouted. 'You're too stupid to be my brother.' Anthony sighed, and crept past the door, took his coat from a peg by the front door, and went to the stable.

A few days later, Anthony waited until he was alone with Antonio and Maria. 'I had you both a set of lock picks made yesterday by the blacksmith. He had a few old locks, that he let me have too. I suggest we start our lock picking lessons in the barn, where your mother won't see us. She didn't like me teaching you to wrestle, Maria, and I don't think she will like me teaching you to pick locks, either.'

'Excellent, let's get started,' Maria whispered, getting up from the table. They all went down to the barn. Anthony went over to a workbench in the corner and opened a drawer. He took out a screwdriver and started dismantling a lock.

'Can you both see clearly? This is a five-lever lock, see these are the levers. I'll put the key in and turn it slowly. Now, do you see how the notches on the key fit between the levers and how the projections on the key lift each lever, a slightly different amount, until these slots, or gates as they're called, in the levers, all line up.'

'Yes, I see,' Maria replied, and Antonio nodded.

'Well as we continue turning the key, this other projection, on the end of the key, engages with the bolt, and this projection on the bolt now slides through the gates on the levers, which are now all lined up, and the bolt retracts. The door is open.'

'Yes, but how do you do it without the key?' Antonio asked.

'Shut up, Antonio. He's going to show us, aren't you, Papa?'

'Yes, please be patient, Antonio. You need to know how a lock works before you can pick it.'

'Sorry.'

'Now do you see these other gates, on these two levers, here and here?' They both nodded, peering intently. 'Well, those are false gates. Locksmiths put those on to fool pickers. Now these are the tools of the trade. This is the pick,' he said, as he showed them a thin piece of metal about the same length as the key, but with its end bent at right angles, 'and this is a tensioner. They look similar, but they do different jobs. You insert them both into the key hole, like this. The tensioner you use to do the task that the end of the key was doing. It engages with the bolt and is what retracts the bolt. You keep up a gentle pressure on the tensioner. Then you feel for the first lever. Obviously, we can see it, but when the lock is assembled, you have to feel for it. Now, see how as I turn the pick, it lifts the lever. Did you hear that slight click?'

'Yes,' they both murmured.

'That was the projection just lining up with the gate in the lever, because I had that little bit of pressure on the tensioner. Now I'll move onto the second lever, see that's one with a false gate in it. It's not as deep as the true gate. If it were, it would be a gate. I can feel that's a false gate, but I've had a lot of practice. So I'm going to keep turning the lever with the pick, and there, I've got the true gate. Now for the third lever. There's the click. Now four, see there's the false gate, on four. Feel on and there's the true gate. Now I just have the fifth to go, and there you are. The lock is open. You both have a go with the lock dismantled, so that you can see what you're doing. You start with this lock, Maria. Antonio, you dismantle this one,' Anthony said, handing Antonio the screwdriver and a second lock. 'When you've got them both open, you can swap over. Although they're very similar, every lock is different.' Both Antonio and Maria could open their locks within a quarter of an hour. They swapped over and had the other locks opened in about ten minutes.

'You're both doing very well. Lock picking isn't easy, otherwise there would be no point in having locks. I'd like you to spend the rest of the afternoon continuing to work on the locks with the covers off. Being able to see what you're doing helps.'

'But we won't be able to see inside the locks when we're actually trying to pick one,' Maria said.

'No, you're quite right, but it's like practising scales and arpeggios on the lute. It needs to become second nature. As it starts to feel more natural, you'll find your eyes wandering and the picks become an extension of your fingers. You'll start to feel through the picks. It's going to take you weeks, perhaps months, to get there. Crouching over a lock, in the dark of night, you feel incredibly vulnerable. You need to get it open in twenty seconds. I got there, but it took months of practice.'

After a few weeks, they were both rapidly opening the locks without covers. Anthony then started them working on locks with the cover plates installed. He suggested they work at each end of the barn, so that they wouldn't be distracted by each other. Anthony took over William's lessons, while Maria and Antonio were working so intensely on the lock-picking practice. He looked in on them in the barn, every hour or so.

'How's it going, Son?'

'It's so frustrating, Father. I can get past the first false gate, but the second one gets me every time.'

'If you can get past one false gate, then you can pass any number. Take the cover plate off, and try a few more times, then screw it back on again.'

'Yes, Father.'

Anthony walked up to see how Maria was getting on.

'This is driving me insane, Papa.'

'Well, it isn't easy. It takes an immense amount of practice. As I said, the picks need to become an extension of your fingers. You need to feel through them.'

'Well I don't.'

'No, not yet. It's a knack. Keep practising,' Anthony said, before going to check on the vines. When he came back an hour later, they had both put the cover plates back on and were both still struggling. 'There was the click, Antonio. Now keep the tensioner on and feel for the second gate. Have you got it?'

'Yes, I've got the false gate, Papa. It's not as deep. I'm feeling forward, ah there's one.'

'Yes, I heard the click from here, so keep going. You're doing really well. You can do this.'

'I don't know, I think this might be it. No, it's deeper than the first false gate, but not as deep as the first true gate.'

'Right, so keep going. You're doing very well now.'

'This might be it. Yes, there's the click. Now I'm keeping the tension on and feeling for the next one, oh this is a deep one, yes, there's the click. Forward, there, false, forwards, click, another shallow one, forwards, click, it's open. I've done it, Father.'

'Well done Antonio! Now keep practising. When you can do it consistently, in less than a minute, we'll try you on some different locks. Then you can move onto locks set in a door.' He patted Antonio on the back and moved onto Maria. 'How's it coming along, Maria?'

'Argh! I just can't get past the second false gate.'

'Neither could Antonio, but he's got the feel for it now.'

'Yes, so I heard.'

'Well, if Antonio can do it, I'm sure you can, too. Keep practising. Try a few more times with the cover off. You just need to get the feel. Some people never get it, but you and Antonio are twins. I'm sure you will.'

Two weeks later Antonio, was opening seven lever mortice locks, padlocks and desk drawer locks, all set in situ.

'Well done, Antonio. Do you think you can get it down to twenty seconds in the dark?'

'I'll try, Father.'

'Good, let me know how you get on. Keep practising, it's a skill that needs constant practice. If I go a week without picking a lock, I make sure I spend a few hours on some locks, to get back up to speed.'

'I will, Father, thank you.'

'How are you getting on, Maria?'

'How do you think? Antonio's opening every lock you throw at him, and I can't even get my first one open. I just don't have the knack.'

'You do. You just don't know it.'

'No, I don't have it. I guess there are some things men can do that women can't do . It works the other way around too, so perhaps I shouldn't complain.'

'Maria, you can do it. There isn't a magic key in the balls that opens these locks. I have shown you and Antonio the same techniques. I've given the same demonstrations. I have, however, been conducting a small experiment.'

'What experiment, Father?'

'I have given Antonio encouragement, and I have not been quite so encouraging towards you. I sowed a slight seed of doubt in your mind by suggesting there was a knack, and saying that some people never get it. You did the rest.'

'Do you mean you wanted me to fail, Father?'

'No, I wanted you to learn a lesson, a very important lesson. You needed to learn it for William's sake, for Anna's and Catherine's, but most of all, for your own sake.'

'Well, I've been trying to learn, and it isn't coming,' Maria screamed, throwing the lock and her picks to the ground.

'The lesson is about praise and encouragement, not about picking locks. I was very pleased with the way you prepared William's lessons. You put a lot of thought and effort into it. But then I saw you call him a fool when he got something wrong. Yes, you need to correct mistakes, but children need encouragement and praise. There are lots of ways of thinking about it, carrot or stick, for example; and punishment can take many forms. But essentially a man, woman or child may alter their behaviour just enough to avoid punishment; but nobody can get enough praise. We'll move heaven and earth to get more.'

'So you sabotaged my lock picking on William's behalf,' Maria said, under her breath.

'No, I haven't sabotaged your lock picking at all. I simply haven't encouraged you quite as much as Antonio. Surely now you can see how powerful encouragement is, what a powerful tool it is. I know you want William to learn, and he is only four. You're doing really well with him. You just need to make kind corrections and continue with encouragement. You were encouraging him well, but then you blew it, when he made a few minor errors. Sleep on it, and I'm sure you'll catch Antonio up in no time.'

'What's wrong Maria?' Antonio asked.

'It's Father. He saw me telling William off during a lesson, and decided to teach me a lesson too. He says that praising a child when he gets something right is more effective that roasting them when they get it wrong. So he praised and encouraged you, and didn't encourage me as much, and now you can open locks in a flash, and I can't.'

'So I suppose that means he was right then.'

'Perhaps, but he could have left it until after I'd learnt to pick locks. Now I'm not sure I ever will.' Maria's head dropped, and Antonio put his arm around her shoulders. 'Why did it have to be me teaching William? Why couldn't you have done it?'

'You're better at it than I am. I enjoy growing the vines and getting ready for wine making, whereas you don't seem quite so keen on cleaning the barrels, and all that.'

'It's not that I'm not keen, I just think there are easier ways of making money. A hundred ducats we made, for a quick trip to Tunis and back.'

'Easy? It didn't sound so easy when you told me about the pirates.'

'Well, not easy, but it was exciting. Learning about ciphers was wonderful, think how valuable we will be, with that skill, and lock picking; but I'm not sure I'll ever master that now.'

'Let's work on some together. It took me ages, but if you do it repeatedly, with the cover off, so that you can see what you're doing, and then squint a bit, so that you have to feel your way, I found that helps.'

Over the next few weeks Antonio worked on lock picking with Maria. On the 10th of August there was a great feast to celebrate their twenty-first birthday. The following day she was overjoyed when she picked her first lock with the cover plate on. Refilled with confidence, the she picked the other types of lock, that Antonio had already mastered. Then there was a long break, as everyone worked to harvest the grapes, press them, and start the fermentation.

Maria found Anthony in the dining room teaching William Greek.

'Papa, I was wrong, and you were right. It was hard to see that at first, because I wanted to learn lock picking so much. I was so angry that you had to make me learn my lesson in a way that thwarted my ambition. I realise now that I wouldn't have learnt it any other way. I think I'm ready to teach again.'

'I'm glad. Have you made any progress with lock picking?'

'Yes, Antonio helped me. I'm as good as him now.'

'Well, we were just about to read some Aristophanes comedies. Would you like to take over?'

'With pleasure. How do you think I should deal with the, you know, the innuendo, the saucy bits?'

'I should answer questions honestly, someone has to, some time,' Anthony replied, leaving Maria and William to it.

The rest of 1609 and the first weeks of 1610 passed peacefully at the Standen vineyard. Maria had taught Antonio to sail, and they had explored the Italian coast as far north as Genoa. It had taken them two and a half days to sail from Ostia to Genoa, and Antonio was excited to discover that it was only a two-day walk from there to Greta's family home, on the outskirts of Turin. He persuaded Anthony and Maria to drop him off there for the Christmas vacation, and collect him when Greta returned to Bologna University. Maria's classes expanded to include Anna, although Catherine was a little too young. The vintage of 1608 seemed to be promising, and their 1607 wine had sold out. William's education was going well, and his wrestling skills made him more than a match for boys of his own age, and even a little older. One day, in late

January, a messenger called. From a satchel, slung over his shoulder, he took out a letter, which was sealed with the French royal coat of arms. Anthony opened it and read.

7th January 1610
Dear Sir Anthony,
I recall with fondness the great help you gave me as a child. We could use it now, since we are struggling with the dauphin's education, specifically in terms of his stammer. There's a danger the doctor will amputate half this foe, that is his tongue. No council within France has an alternative. We urgently court your assistance, please come.
Yours sincerely
Marie

'Will there be a reply, sir?' the messenger asked.

'Just tell her majesty that I will come as soon as I can. Have you ridden all the way from Paris?'

'Yes, sir, with several changes of horse. It's taken me eight days. She said it was most urgent. Will you be returning with me, sir?'

'No, but I will not be far behind you. I will just need to get some affairs in order, before my departure. Will you take some refreshment, before you return?'

'Thank you, sir, but I will change horses in Rome, and will take some refreshment there. As you will follow on later, sir, they instructed me to give you this.' The messenger reached into the satchel and passed another letter to Anthony. 'It's a warrant stating that you travel on the king's business, sir. If you require accommodation, goods or services within France, show it. The crown will recompense reasonable expenses which tally with your account, which you are to provide to the chancellor. Good day to you, sir.'

'Good day,' Anthony said as he closed the door, deep in thought.

'What is it Anthony, who was that?' Francesca asked.

'A messenger from the queen of France.'

'The little girl I thought was your daughter?'

'Yes that's right. She needs my help now, the dauphin has a stammer.'

'Well what does she think you can do about it?'

'I don't know, but I have to go,' Anthony said. Francesca thought for a while.

'Well we should treat it as an opportunity. You must take Maria with you. The French royal court, my, there are bound to be lots of eligible, rich young men there. Yes, you must take her, but you should buy her the latest fashions, as soon as you get to Paris. Promise me you will.'

'Yes, very well, darling. I'll talk with Maria now.'

Maria was nowhere to be found in the house. He found her in the barn, practising her lock picking.

'Maria, we're going to Paris.'

'Whatever for, Papa?'

'I've just received this letter, from the queen of France,' he said, passing it to Maria. She took it from his hand and read it.

'When did you learn to cure speech defects, Papa? I know your talents know no bounds, but this is a bit of a stretch.'

'Do you remember when I was teaching you ciphers, and I mentioned the letters I wrote using the date to show which words to read within an innocent-looking letter?' Maria nodded. 'Read the date.'

'7th January 1610.'

'It's the 20th today, and the messenger just told me it's taken him eight days to get here from Paris.'

'So what was he doing with the other five days?' Maria asked, puzzled.

'Try reading every seventh word.'

'The a since —'

'No, leave out the Dear Anthony.'

'Help we are in danger, foe within court, good lord! Can

it be a coincidence?'

'I don't think so. My guess is that François was good to his word and sent my regards to Marie, with some account of how we fought off the pirates. Perhaps she has nobody she feels she can trust in court, and has sent for me.'

'Yes, I see. But you said we are going to Paris.'

'Your mother sees an opportunity for you to find a suitable husband, and I could use your help.'

'You have it, Papa. Eight days' ride, you say.'

'Yes, but with fresh horses every day…'

'Papa, we could sail to Nice in a day and a half. From there it would be only half the distance.'

'Yes, that's an excellent idea. But I think it would be better to sail to Marseilles. Nice is in Savoy, and I have a warrant giving us the king's protection within France. I would feel much better leaving Maia with a French harbour master, having shown him our warrant.'

'That makes good sense, Papa.'

CHAPTER SIX

Antonio took his father and twin sister to the harbour in Ostia, on the cart, together with provisions for their journey. Anthony did not know how long they were going to be away, and didn't want to leave his carthorse in the stable at the boatyard, for an indeterminate length of time. Once they had transferred the provisions onboard, they bade Antonio farewell, and got Maia ready for the voyage. They cast off in the early afternoon, and once clear of the harbour, headed west-south-west towards the straits of Bonifacio. They had to put in several tacks, as the wind was from the west for most of the first day at sea.

'We should reach the straits between Corsica and Sardinia, mid-morning tomorrow,' Anthony said. 'That will be perfect, because I have no intention of trying to navigate that strait in the dark. If the wind drops, and we're not going to get there with enough daylight to traverse the strait, then we will anchor off one of the islands until daybreak.'

'How long will it take us to get through the strait, Papa?'

'From passing between the islands of Razzoli and

Lavezzi, at the eastern end of the strait, and clearing Cape Testa at the western end, is ten miles. It depends how many tacks we have to put in, because the straits will funnel the wind, and we'll either have it behind us, or bang on the nose. Do you want to take the first watch overnight, or shall I?'

'I'll take the first watch, Papa. Last time you fell asleep, and didn't wake me. I'll wake you, after I've turned the hourglass for the third time.'

'Very well, I'll make a start on the stew. Call me if anything looks amiss.'

Anthony took the watch between dinner and dusk. Maria woke him after three hours on watch, then he woke her at midnight. They had each taken one more watch, before the first of nautical twilight revealed the horizon, and the mountains of Corsica, looming ahead of them. As predicted, they reached the eastern end of the strait around mid-morning.

'I think we're in luck. The wind is in the east, Papa.'

'Yes, and it's time to shorten sail. We'll put the third reef in the main, and take the jib down, just leaving the staysail up.'

'Why, Papa? There's not that much wind? We've carried full sail in much, much more wind than this.'

'You'll see,' Anthony replied, as he let out the main halyards and tied the reefing lines, leaving the mainsail with a little over half its normal area. He tightened the halyards, then took down the jib.

'I don't understand. We're slowing,' Maria complained.

'Any minute now, look at the wavelets ahead,' Anthony said as the wind behind them accelerated, and Maria struggled with the helm, as Maia raced through the strait. 'The islands funnel the wind between them, and it accelerates as it passes through the narrow gap. This is notoriously the windiest place in the Mediterranean, this side of Gibraltar. Are you happy for a few minutes? I'm just going below to check the chart.'

'Yes, I'm fine. Now I know what's happening, it's quite exciting. I was just taken by surprise, that's all,' Maria shouted above the howling wind. When he came back on deck a few minutes later, Anthony pointed, then cupped his hands to call to Maria.

'Over there to starboard, we are just passing the great city of Bonifacio.'

'Where? I can't see a city,' Maria called back, puzzled.

'The chart shows a gap in the cliff. The channel then turns a right angle to starboard and leads to the city. I've heard that you have to be within a cable of the entrance, to have any chance of seeing it. It's a very well-hidden city, from seaward.' Even with deeply reefed sail, Maia made over ten knots as they charged through the strait. An hour after they put the reef in, and as they passed Cape Testa, off their port side, the wind dropped as quickly as it had risen. Anthony went to the mast and shook the reefs out. 'Steer north-west from here, one hundred and eighty miles to go.'

They tied Maia up in the harbour of Marseilles, just after noon the following day. When they had tidied the boat up, they went looking for the harbour master's office. When they found it, there was a sign saying that it was closed for lunch and would reopen at three o'clock.

'We may as well get some lunch ourselves,' Anthony suggested. They found a pleasant restaurant on the harbour front, and the waiter recommended Bouillabaisse, a local speciality fish stew, served with bread. They ordered that, and some wine to go with it. When it arrived, they ate and drank in silence. 'Well, I don't think the wine is up to our standard, but the stew was excellent. I shall ask the waiter for the recipe,' Anthony said, licking his lips. The waiter cleared away the dishes before bringing out a selection of pastries for dessert. They made their selection, and the waiter said that he would write down the recipe for the Bouillabaisse, stressing that almost any fish could be used. It was whatever was left over, at the end of market day.

Anthony paid the bill before remembering the warrant, then they made their way back to the harbour master's office.

The harbour master's door was a double hung, Dutch style of door and the top half was open. They could see the harbour master sitting in his chair, his feet on the desk and snoring. Anthony knocked on the door, and he awoke with a start.

'What's that?' he snorted.

'May we come in, sir? We arrived during your lunch break,' Anthony explained.

'Yes, of course, come in.' He put on a display of tidying the papers on his desk. His paunch marked him as a man who enjoyed a good lunch, and his red cheeks suggested he liked to wash it down well. A scar on his left cheek showed he had seen some action. Anthony thought he might be in his early fifties, but possibly younger. 'So you arrived today, you say, how so, sir?'

'We are on the king's business, sir,' Anthony said, handing him his warrant. 'We have tied up our boat, astern of the brigantine, Brise de Mer, I think her name was. Can we leave her in your safe keeping until we return from Paris?'

'I see. How long will that be?'

'We don't know, as long as His Majesty requires us.'

'Well, we'd better take a look at her then,' the harbour master said, getting unsteadily out of his chair, 'lead on!' Anthony and Maria preceded him out of the office and over to the quayside. They stopped beside Maia. 'So, is this your boat then, sir? She's a beautiful vessel. The king must pay you well. If the king's paying, would you like me to have her lifted out and her bottom cleaned?'

'That won't be necessary. She's very new.'

'Well, His Majesty won't know that, if you don't tell him, sir,' the harbour master suggested, winking and tapping his finger against his nose.

'No, that really won't be necessary. Just keep a good eye

on her, please.'

'Well, if you say so, sir. Let's get back to the office. You'll need to fill out a form.' The harbour master led them back. 'Sit down, sir, mademoiselle,' he said as he rummaged in his desk drawer for the form. 'There you are. It's all self explanatory. Boat name, tonnage, your name and address, home port, any dangerous cargo, wines and spirits, etc. etc.,' he said, watching Anthony completing the form. 'How much gunpowder, sir?'

'A two-gallon cask, about a third empty.'

'That's quite a lot of gunpowder to have got through, for a new boat, sir,' the harbour master said, raising his eyebrows.

'We had an encounter with Barbary pirates on our maiden voyage.'

'They are a pestilence, sir. How much brandy, sir?'

'A gallon barrel, about two pints short.'

'Ah, now if you're away for a while, there might be some evaporation, sir, it does happen. You'll have to leave the boat keys with me, sir, in case of emergencies.'

'We will take off what we need for our journey and lock up before bringing you the keys. Can you tell us where we can buy some horses?'

'Certainly, sir, there's a livery stable near the cathedral. I'll draw you a map, sir, while you're getting your things.'

Anthony and Maria went back to Maia. 'I'm glad I had these rifle holsters made at the saddle-makers. I don't trust that harbour master. If he finds our rifles, he may be tempted to sell them. At least we can take two with us,' Anthony said, as he began packing the saddle bags with provisions for the journey. He threaded a pistol holster onto his belt and handed another holster to Maria. 'We'll take the flintlock pistols with us too.'

'Why not take the key to the gun locker with us? Just give him the rest?' Maria suggested.

'Why didn't I think of that?' When they had completed their packing, Anthony locked up, and they headed back to the harbour office. 'Here are the keys,' he said, putting the bunch of keys on the desk. The harbour master picked them up and opened a cabinet fixed to the wall behind his desk. He hung the keys on one of two dozen hooks in the cabinet, then wrote Maia on a scrap of paper and impaled the paper on the hook.

'Here's a map showing you where the livery stable is, sir. It's about a quarter of an hour on foot. Tell Pierre I sent you. You'll get a good price, sir.' And you'll get a good commission, Anthony thought to himself. It was a pleasant walk to the livery stable, in bright sunshine.

'Are you Pierre?' Anthony called out to a stockily built young man, with long, thick, black hair who was grooming a grey stallion.

'No, that's my father. He's out of town. Can I help you? My name's Jaques.'

'We need two good horses. We don't know for how long, since we are on the king's business. Our boat is in the harbour here, so we will have to return when the king says that we can.'

'I see. Do you have a warrant?' Anthony took the warrant from his pocket and passed it to Jaques. 'Yes, that's all in order. You can have this grey. His name's Éclair, and there's a bay mare that he gets along with, over here. Her name is Lièvre. I suppose you'll want to charge them to the warrant. I'll just have to take a few details.' Anthony followed Jaques through to the office, where he filled out another form. Then Jaques saddled both horses and fitted their bridles. 'Would you like me to strap those on for you?' Jaques asked, pointing at the saddle bags and rifle holsters.

'Yes please,' Anthony replied, as he and Maria passed them over.

Ten minutes later, they were trotting out through the city gates and heading north on the Lyons road.

They entered Paris after five days of riding. The evidence of construction work was everywhere. Wide new avenues were being built, and a new bridge spanned the Seine.

'Now we have to find a dressmaker, I promised your mother,' Anthony said, peering at each shop that they passed.

'Nonsense, Papa. We haven't sailed and ridden hard to get here, only to tarry for a few days while somebody makes a dress for me. Do you think the queen's message to you implied some urgency?'

'Yes, of course it did.'

'Then we shall go directly to her. Our appearance will show our diligence in complying with her wish. If, on the other hand, I appear wearing a ballgown, in the latest fashion, what will she presume?'

'You're right, of course, the Louvre it is.'

When they arrived at the Louvre Palace, Anthony showed the sentry his warrant. They were told to proceed to the main guardhouse. On arrival at the guardhouse, Anthony again showed the duty officer his warrant and asked that the queen be informed of his arrival. A quarter of an hour later, a groom took their horses to the stables, and a servant led them to the queen's salon. They walked the length of a magnificent hall, weaving around artists and their easels, their models, and sculptors.

'Goodness, it's busy in here,' Maria remarked.

'Yes, mademoiselle. The king is a great patron of the arts. Anyone who can wield a brush, or a chisel, is welcomed by him here to practise their art. He has a good look around when he's not otherwise busy, and buys quite a few of them,' their escort explained. They continued through endless corridors, with high ceilings from which hung giant chandeliers. There was scarcely any space on the internal walls to fit any more paintings. Eventually, they reached the queen's chambers. Their escort knocked on the door, then opened it, and stood aside for Anthony and

Maria to enter. Queen Marie was seated, and wearing a voluminous full-length, blue-silk dress, embroidered with fleur-de-lis in gold thread. A ruff topped the dress. Marie's face was plumper than Anthony remembered, and there was a sadness in her eyes. She had with her a man and a woman. They both stood up as Anthony and Maria entered the room. The man was around five-feet-six. He had a waxed moustache, and the tips pointed upwards. His beard was also trimmed to a fine point. He had brown eyes that seemed inquisitive. His long nose undulated to its tip, in front of the philtrum of his lip. The woman was a couple of inches shorter. She also had a roman nose, but a petite mouth. Her eyes were striking, just a fraction of an inch wider apart that you might expect. Anthony estimated they were of a similar age, perhaps forty. They were both very finely dressed. Anthony bowed, and after he poked Maria in the ribs, she curtseyed.

'Sir Anthony, thank you for coming so soon. My messenger said that you would follow him in a few days, and yet you arrive on the same day. He must have tarried en-route. I will have words with him.' It surprised Anthony that she addressed them in Italian. Perhaps it was to make Maria comfortable. He flipped back into her native tongue.

'It is not his fault, Your Highness. We sailed a good part of the way, and have ridden only from Marseilles,' Anthony explained.

'Well, I am glad you have come. Please sit down. Be a dear and bring over those chairs for my guests, would you, Concino?' The man smiled and walked across to the wall on Anthony's right, where a row of six ornately gilded chairs stood, with their backs to the wall. He took one in each hand and brought them over to where Anthony and Maria stood. He put them down, facing the queen. 'Thank you, Concino, now please all sit down. Concino, Leonora, let me introduce Sir Anthony Standen. I take it this is your daughter, Maria?'

'Yes, Your Highness. I apologise for our attire. It has

been a long journey. My wife insisted I buy Maria a fine dress as soon as we got to Paris, but Maria insisted we come directly here, to render such service as we can.'

'Thank you, my dear,' she said, smiling at Maria. 'I will have my dressmaker rustle you up some gowns. I envy your youthful figure. You will be the greatest beauty at court. Sir Anthony, Maria, this is my lady-in-waiting, Leonora, an old friend from Florence, and her husband, Concino Concini. They both came with me to France, and have been my greatest comfort in this strange land. I remember your last visit, Sir Anthony, when you brought news of King Jame's ascension. I fear I was not as welcoming as I should have been.'

'I understand, Your Highness. You were coming to terms with thinking in French, and the king's mistresses galled you.'

'You still have a sharp memory, Sir Anthony. He has only forty-five mistresses now, eleven have either died or moved away. The brats are everywhere, eleven mingle with the six I have borne him. Anyway, I digress. I was so pleased to receive the letter from François Savary de Brèves. It brought back such powerful memories of you, and Florence, and my dear father. You were very kind to me, and wise.'

'Your Highness, your message spoke of a problem with your son's speech, and of another matter. How can we help?' Anthony asked.

'The dauphin, Louis, does indeed have a speech impediment. He also has a malformation of the teeth, several of which seem to have grown together. We have tried everything for him. The physicians have bled him, treated him with valerian to sedate him, and now they suggest that removing half his tongue may help. Dear Leonora has attempted to exorcise his demons, but despite her prowess, he stammers still. I remember how kind you were to me when I was distressed, and how calming that was. When poor Louis is trying to form a sentence, he struggles so, and the more agitated he becomes, the more difficult it is for him to speak. People try to put words into his mouth, and he hates that. I persuaded Henry that we should give you a chance before we let the surgeon loose on his tongue.'

'I will do my best, Your Highness, although it is not a problem I have encountered before. I recall reading of it in one of the Arabic texts in your father's library. I will think about it. What of the other matter?' Anthony asked, glancing at Concino and Leonora.'

'You may speak freely in front of my friends, Sir Anthony. They are my most faithful companions. Yes, that worries me. Henry makes light of it, but there have been nineteen assassination attempts, that I know of. There have been shots fired from the crowd, arrows from a rooftop, attempted poisonings. Only twice have we caught the culprits. The first was a boatman from Orleans, Pierre Barrière. Fortunately, he had confessed his intended regicide to a Dominican priest, who overcame the sanctity of the confession, and warned the palace guard. We broke him on the wheel in 1593. The second was Jean Châtel, a nineteen-year-old clothier's son. As Henry entered the Hotel de Bouchage, in 1594, on his way back from Picardy, and bent over to accept the obeisance of two courtiers, Châtel sprang out of the crowd and stabbed at him, cutting Henry's lip before he could be restrained.'

'1593 and 1594, you say, that was over fifteen years ago. I assume there have been more recent attempts, Your Highness.'

'Oh yes, those were the only two who we caught. The most recent attempt was an arrow fired from a roof top, the week before I wrote to you. He had gone by the time the guards got up onto the roof.'

'So there have been nineteen attempts over fifteen years. Has there been a pattern, Your Highness?'

'There have been peaks and troughs, if that's what you mean. You will know, I'm sure, that in July 1593 the bishops assembled in St. Denis to receive Henry's abjuration, that is his sworn oath renouncing the heresy of his Protestantism. You might expect that would have angered the Protestants and pleased the Catholics.'

'Yes, Your Highness, I can see that.'

'Well, it did, in part. Some Catholics came across to Henry's side at once. Nicolas de Neufville, who had worked for the Catholic League, he joined Henry as adviser on foreign affairs and second minister under Sully. You might also expect that Pope Clement would have immediately absolved Henry of his sins and retracted his excommunication, but, oh no, it dragged on and on. Philip of Spain and the Catholic League lobbied hard to block his acceptance into the Catholic faith.'

'I suppose Philip couldn't accept that he'd lost the opportunity to put his own man on the throne, Your Highness.'

'Yes, it probably was sour grapes, but Pope Clement and his nephew, Cardinal Aldobrandini, were desperate to escape the domination of Philip, so negotiations dragged on.' Anthony thought that, from the corner of his eye, he saw Maria bite her lip when Aldobrandini was mentioned. 'Meanwhile, Henry was crowned in February 1594, yet it was not until September of the following year that he was absolved and reconciled with Rome. Henry's early years on the throne were marked by priests preaching against him. He had to have several banished. The Catholic clergy demanded that Henry re-establish Catholicism as the sole religion in France, and that all church property seized by the Huguenots be restored.'

'What did he do, Your Highness?'

'He promised to restore religious conformity, whatever that means. It seemed to cool things down a bit for a couple of years, which probably made the Edict of Nantes an even greater shock.'

'The Edict of Nantes?'

'Yes, it granted freedom of conscience and places of

security to the Huguenots. Then things really kicked off. Pope Clement apparently said "this crucifies me" as well as "freedom of conscience is the worst thing in the world." The Spanish ambassador asked Pope Clement to restore Henry's ex-communication. Guillaume Rose, bishop of Senlis, preached against the edict and said that he would join a new league. Henry had him called before the Parliament of Paris.'

'What did they do, Your Highness?'

'Practically nothing. He was forbidden to preach for a year. Henry worked hard to bolster his support. He allowed the Catholic nobles to ban Huguenot worship in their lands. That worked quite well, but the main opposition was in Paris. A rumour went around that the Huguenots would use their new legal status to mount a revenge for the St. Bartholomew's Day Massacre. The Jesuits and the Capuchins led the opposition to the edict. A Capuchin priest, Jean de Brulart, exercised some influence over the magistrates, preaching that any judge who consented to registration of the edict would be damned.'

'What influence did he have, Your Highness?'

'His brother is Nicolas de Brulart, president of Parliament and one of Henry's councillors. Henry had to get him to chastise his brother. Anyway, the Edict of Nantes became a focus for Henry's opponents. There have been many more attempted assassinations since he issued it.'

'But all the opposition seems to have come from priests, Your Highness. What makes you think the danger is within court?'

'They always seem to know where he will be. We have been cautious about advertising royal appointments, yet still these attacks happen. I'm sure there must be someone at court who is behind it.'

'What motive could they have?'

'Perhaps they have religious motives, or they covet the crown themselves. I suspect the latter. If we install you here to work with Louis on his stammer, I thought you might snoop around and find out what is going on. Do you think you could do that?'

'I'm sure we can, Your Highness.'

'Excellent. Before we introduce you to Louis, we must get you settled in.' The queen clapped her hands and a liveried servant entered. 'Take Sir Anthony and his daughter to the guest accommodation. Do you have much luggage with you, Sir Anthony, Maria?'

'Only the clothes we stand in, and a few personal items on our horses in the stable, Your Highness,' Anthony replied.

'Marcel, send for Gaston, and have him measure them for some court clothes. Make any arrangements for baths that they may wish. Ask Gaston to provide them with at least one change of clothes from whatever he has until he can rustle up something bespoke. When they are refreshed, bring them to me, together with Louis,' the queen ordered.

They gave Anthony and Maria adjoining rooms in the guest accommodation. They both had fine views of the Seine, comfortable four-poster beds, large walnut wardrobes and matching cabinet, table and chairs. Anthony lifted the lid of another cabinet and found it to house a chamber pot, with a comfortable red-velvet seat above. There was a knock at the door, and Marcel and another servant brought in a tin bathtub. A further six servants followed them, with large jugs of steaming water, which they poured into the bathtub.

'There is a bar of soap in the top drawer of the cabinet, sir,' Marcel explained. The other servants left, but before they could close the door behind them, an exquisitely attired man in his early thirties appeared.

'Sir Anthony, I assume. I am Gaston, the queen's dressmaker,' he announced, his eyes running over every muscle of Anthony's body, as he paced around the room, examining him from several angles. 'I shall just take a few measurements,' he said, holding a tape against his inside leg, checking the tape, then putting it around his waist and chest. 'My word, you are tall, Sir Anthony, and in fine shape for a man of your age. I will have some clothes that will fit passably well with you in twenty minutes. I will deliver bespoke costumes within a week,' Gaston said before leaving, followed by Marcel. Anthony closed the curtains, took the soap from the drawer, undressed, and took his bath.

He was towelling himself dry when there was another knock at the door. He wrapped the towel around his waist and opened the door. Marcel was carrying some clothes and shoes.

'Thank you, just put them on the bed, could you?' Anthony said. Marcel did as requested.

'Is there anything you wish to remove from your clothes before I take them to be laundered, sir?'

Anthony removed his purse from his own doublet pocket and handed his old clothes to Marcel, who then left and closed the door behind him. Anthony donned the yellow silk nether-socks, and the blue breeches, followed by a yellow silk shirt and a blue waistcoat and matching, padded-worsted coat. Finally, he tried on the buckled shoes, which fitted perfectly. He was examining himself in the mirror when there was another knock on the door. He opened it and Marcel and Maria were standing there. She was wearing a red dress which the hoops of a farthingale gave the appearance of a church bell. Her bodice was buttoned in front and tapered to a point at the waist. The sleeves were lavishly embellished with lace.

'You look stunning, Maria,' Anthony gasped.

'Thank you, Papa. I don't think I could wrestle or pick grapes in this, but I suppose I'll get used to it.'

'Her Highness will receive you in her salon now, and the dauphin has joined her,' Marcel advised, leading them back to the queen's quarters. Marcel knocked and opened the door when he heard the queen instruct them to enter. Anthony and Maria went in. The queen was now alone with her son.

'Sir Anthony, Maria, please come and meet the dauphin. Louis, this is Sir Anthony Standen. I knew him when I was about your age, a year older now I think about it. I was ten. He was very kind to me, and is brilliant at languages. He and his daughter Maria are going to work with you on your stammer. You had better learn from him and improve, otherwise the surgeon will cut out half your tongue. You don't want that, do you?'

'No m...m-other. I do not. S...s-ir Anthony, do you have experience of s... s... a defect like I have?' Louis asked.

'No, Your Highness, I have not, although as your mother has said, I have spent my life studying language. We will work together, and I hope we will make good progress. I already have a few ideas that I think we can build on.'

'Excellent!' the queen exclaimed. 'Louis, take Sir Anthony and Maria back to your day room, and you can start straight away. Sir Anthony, the king is away, but he will be back tomorrow and will want to meet you. François's account of your exploits intrigued him. You will have about an hour with Louis before they will collect you for dinner, where you will meet some other courtiers currently in Paris.'

Anthony and Maria walked a pace behind Louis, along the corridors of the Louvre Palace which were adorned with paintings and tapestries, landscapes, portraits, biblical scenes and French battle successes. When they reached Louis's room, a servant standing outside opened the door and bowed as Louis passed him. It was a large, light, and airy room. In front of the fireplace, two armies of intricately carved, wooden model soldiers confronted each other, with a wooden castle off to one side. One army was painted in red and yellow uniforms, the other in either blue or red. There were two tables, a small, low, round table with chairs around it of varying sizes, presumably designed to accommodate the nine-year-old Louis, as well as younger children and adults. The larger table was rectangular and the normal height for a dining table. The chairs were again designed to accommodate adults on the side nearer the window, whilst the chairs nearer the door were high chairs with additional stretchers between the legs to allow a child to climb to the seat.

'Please make yourselves comfortable,' Louis said, climbing to a seat at the dining table. 'My s...s-isters, Elizabeth and Christine, are in the room next door. Nicholas and Gaston are with our governess, and Henrietta is with the wet nurse. Do you really b, do you really believe you can help me, S...s-ir Anthony?'

'You may call me Anthony, Your Highness. I hope so. Certainly I draw encouragement from the approach that the medical profession has taken. Although I am not a physician, I cannot see how blood letting, sedation or surgery may help. I have noticed that there are some sounds that cause you difficulties, s and m, for example. I have also noticed that you find an alternative that is easier. You were going to ask me if I had experience with stammers and cleverly switched to defects.'

'Not quite correct, Anthony, I was g...g-oing to ask of your experience with s, with s...s-peech defects. However, you are otherwise right.'

'I also find you calmer now, with us, than earlier, and your speech is more fluid as a result. I suspect that stress is a factor. I remember when I was young, and learning a new language, searching for alternative ways of expressing my thoughts, when the words I was reaching for remained stubbornly outside my grasp. Some people would butt in and say what they thought I was trying to say, which might, or might not have been, what I was reaching for. Others would ignore me and start off on a different line of conversation. Eventually, I found that those people weren't worth talking to anyway. Can you sing, Your Highness?'

'Yes, I can talk to melodies, with no trouble.'

'Can you do it with the troublesome sounds? Could you sing something like, I sing to the stars, and they shine on me.'

'I can try. I sing to the stars, and they shine on me.' Yes I can.

'Excellent, Your Highness, there is something we can work on. It might seem affected at first, but poetry and the best prose have a rhythm, like a song. People enjoy the rhythm, and you may find that the rhythm carries you through the difficult sounds. It might be like a dance, when I miss a step, but the rhythm of the music helps me get back in time again. What do you think, Maria?'

'I don't recall you ever dancing, Papa, but your argument makes sense.'

'Thank you, Anthony, you have b...b-een very helpful,' Louis said smiling. There was a knock on the door. 'Come in!' Louis said. Marcel opened the door.

'Dinner will be served soon, Your Highness.'

CHAPTER SEVEN

Marcel accompanied Louis, Anthony, and Maria to the small dining room. On the way, they collected the Princesses, Elizabeth, and Christine, from their rooms. He explained that Prince Nicolas and Prince Gaston, at three and two years of age, had already eaten and were being put to bed by their nurse. Princess Henrietta, at less than a year, was already in her cot. They heard the hubbub of conversation as they approached the open door of the small dining room. It may have been known as the small dining room, but the dining table, which was laid for twelve, occupied less than half the room. Four liveried servants were circulating with gilt trays, carrying full wine glasses, amongst the seven other diners. Anthony could see Queen Marie talking with a tall handsome man, about Anthony's age, at the far side of the throng. An attractive woman of about thirty saw them and came over to them.

'Your Highnesses, Prince Louis, so you have met your new tutor. Will you be making a start tomorrow?'

'We have already begun, and things are p…p-rogressing very well indeed, thank you, Jeanne. Anthony, this is Jeanne de Harlay, the daughter of our g...g-overness, Françoise de Montglat.'

'Sir Anthony, I am delighted to meet you. The queen has told us all about you, and you too, Maria.' Jeanne said, as they shook hands. 'You seem to have effected a remarkable improvement already, and this is my mother, the royal governess,' she added, as Françoise came over to greet them. After further introductions, Françoise and Jeanne shepherded the royal children away as Queen Marie approached. As Marie arrived, Anthony and Maria took glasses from a waiter.

'Anthony, you must meet Pierre-Olivier, you have so much in common,' she said, taking his arm and leading him towards two men. Anthony thought Marie was speaking French confidently, which pleased him. He had been worried that if she spoke Italian too often around court, it might mark her out as too much of a foreigner. She should blend in as far as a queen can. Anthony remained a pace behind Marie, studying the two men as they approached them. One was older than the other, late-sixties compared to late-thirties. The older man was grey-haired, with a neatly trimmed moustache and beard. He had penetrating brown eyes, and Anthony thought he saw sadness in them. The younger man also had brown eyes, but his hair was brown and long. His beard was trimmed, but not so neatly, and his moustache was waxed to an upwardly pointing tip on either side of a generous mouth. His eyebrows were odd, shaped like chevrons which rose to a point, just outside the apex of his eye socket, before sloping down again. 'Pierre, Nicholas, may I present Sir Anthony Standen? Nicolas is Secretary of State. Pierre,' she said, turning to the younger man, 'Sir Anthony has travelled widely, isn't that right, Anthony?'

'Well, I have travelled as far north as Stirling Castle, as far west as Cape Finisterre, only recently as far south as Tunis, and as far east as Constantinople. I have even crossed the Bosphorus, so technically I have set foot in Asia. Have you travelled far, Pierre?'

'I have just completed a circumnavigation, in fact. His Majesty wishes me to write an account of my travels.'

'Good heavens, well, that puts me in my place.'

'I am sorry, Anthony, that was cruel of me,' Marie chuckled. 'You must ask Pierre all about Taoism. I remember how you comforted me when I was grieving, and I think you'll find it interesting. You will be almost opposite each other. I have seated you that way.'

'Aren't Concino and Leonora joining us?' Anthony enquired.

'Sadly not. Leonora has had one of her fits again, and Concino is staying with her. He is such a dear.'

'I'm sorry to hear that. What sort of fits does she have?'

'She has convulsions and seizures. They are rare, but are most disturbing when they she has them. She sometimes sees apparitions as well. They say that demons possess her, but that she has gained some control of the demons through equivalent powers. That is why I asked her to try to exorcise poor Louis's demons, sadly to no avail. Now please excuse me, Jean Louis was in the middle of a most amusing story.' Marie then returned to the tall man she had been talking to.

'I thought only Sir Francis Drake had completed a full circumnavigation,' Anthony said, turning back to Pierre.

'Some of Magellan's men have as well. I am the first Frenchman to have done it, although, from what I have learnt of the Pacific Islanders, I wouldn't be surprised if they had not been making such epic voyages millennia ago.'

'Have any women done it yet?' Maria asked, having sidled over to them.

'Women! Good lord no, of course not. The oceans are not a boating lake, you know.'

'May I introduce my eldest daughter, Pierre? Maria, this is Pierre. I'm sorry I didn't get the rest of your name.'

'Pierre-Olivier Malherbe, at your service, Maria, enchanté,' he said, reaching out for her hand and bending forwards to kiss it.

'So I could be the first. How exciting,' Maria sighed, just as the dinner gong boomed. They all moved towards the dining table. Anthony found his place card and stood behind his chair as the others did. Grace was said and after the queen had taken her seat, followed by the dauphin and the other royal children, everyone else sat down.

The waiters served a trout mousse, with a horseradish-cream topping. They removed the wine glasses and replaced them with fresh glasses, pouring a Sauvignon blanc to go with the trout. Anthony looked around the table. There were six diners on each side of the table. He was sitting next to Jeanne, who was at one end of the table. Opposite her was Pierre. Françoise, the governess, was seated to Pierre's right, and next to her was the dauphin, Louis. The queen was to Louis's right, and Jean Louis, the man who had apparently been telling such an amusing story, was on the queen's right-hand side. Maria was sitting at the far end of the table, to Jean Louis's right. Opposite Maria was Nicolas, and to his right was the Princess Christine. There was a very condescending-looking fellow, to whom Anthony hadn't yet been introduced, sitting to the right of Princess Christine. The condescending fellow had Princess Elizabeth to his right, and Anthony had Princess Elizabeth to his left. Anthony wondered what the condescending fellow had done, to be seated between an eight and a four-year-old princess, and opposite the queen. He turned to his right and whispered to Jeanne.

'Who is the fellow between the princesses?'

'That is Roger de Saint-Lary de Termes. His father was governor of Metz. Jean Louis introduced Roger to the last king's court, and he became quite a favourite, becoming master of horse. He kept his position, under our good king, and become governor of Burgundy, after his role in uncovering the Biron conspiracy,' Jeanne whispered back.

'What was the Biron conspiracy?'

'That was eight years ago. Charles de Gontaut, duc de Biron, fought for Henry the Third against the Catholic League, and became known as the thunderbolt of France. He survived the succession of our Good King Henry, who made him Admiral of France. For some reason, they say that after the Treaty of Vervins, he started intrigues with both Spain and the House of Savoy. Whatever happened, they beheaded him in the Bastille in 1602. As an Englishman, you must be an admirer of William Shakespeare, Sir Anthony.'

'The name is familiar. I think Anthony Bacon may have mentioned him.'

'Oh, you should try to see his plays. I only bring it up, because they say that Biron was the inspiration for Berowne, in Love's Labour's Lost.'

'Sir Anthony, you are interested in Taoism. Her highness led me to understand,' Pierre asked.

'Oh, erm, she did, didn't she?' Anthony said, looking up and across the table. 'I'm afraid I don't know why. I haven't heard of it. What is Taoism?'

'It is the dominant belief system in China. Tao translates as way, which concerns the ultimate creative principle of the universe. It evolved around the time of Christ, and concerns unity and opposites. Yin and yang represent the opposites, and might be light and dark, hot and cold, motion and stillness, for example. Although they are opposites, they fit together perfectly. Yin cannot exist without yang, and vice versa.'

'In that case, I do understand why her highness brought it up. What does Taoism say about God?'

'In Taoism, there is no omnipotent being beyond the universe,' Pierre whispered across the table.

'So there are no deities.'

'Oh no, Sir Anthony, there are many deities, but they are master philosophers who have revealed the mystery of the universe, rather than the creators of the universe. They are revered for their wisdom, rather than worshiped as gods.'

'That is fascinating, Pierre. How long did your circumnavigation take?'

'I departed Honfleur in 1582, and returned last year, after twenty-seven years,' Pierre said wistfully.

'Which countries did you find most interesting?' Anthony asked.

'All of them, in their own ways. I suppose China and India were the highlights. I learnt much about myself in India. Their skills in meditation are unparalleled. At first I had to be induced into the meditative state, but with time, instruction and practice, I could achieve it myself.'

'By meditative state, do you mean contemplation, like being at prayer?' Anthony asked.

'Not quite like that, no. It is a much deeper state of trance. It is being in a deep sleep, but able to direct one's dreams, to be able to explore long lost memories, and suppress pain, perhaps even cure ailments.'

'Well, I should certainly like to learn more about that. My bones have been painful recently. I was very badly beaten when I was young.'

'Well, why don't you come to visit me when you can get away? I have taken rooms in a house on Rue St. Honore, at number sixteen. Do you know where that is?'

'I do. It is close to there that I received the beating.'

'Excellent! I'm sure we will have much to discuss,' Pierre replied, as the fish plates were taken away, and the plates set for the main course.

After dinner, Anthony and Maria walked back to their rooms.

'Come inside for a few minutes before you retire. Let's discuss what we each discovered at dinner,' Anthony suggested. They went into Anthony's room and sat on the chairs at the small table. 'Did you hear anything interesting?'

'Possibly, Papa. I was sitting next to Jean Louis de Nogaret de La Valette, duc d'Épernon. He was the fellow the queen was talking to when we arrived; the one who had been telling an amusing story. He was polite to me, and looked me over, if you know what I mean, but he spent almost all of his time talking to the queen. He did a lot of whispering in her ear. I wouldn't be the least surprised if they were having an affair.'

'Surely not, it would be too great a risk for her.'

'Perhaps, but if the king has forty-nine mistresses, why shouldn't she have affairs too? I was sitting opposite Nicolas de Neufville, Seigneur de Villeroy. He spoke with me all evening. I suppose with a four-year-old princess to his right, even I was better company. He has served as Secretary of State for three kings now. Charles the Ninth, Henry the Third and the current King Henry. There's no love lost between him and Jean Louis. Apparently, while serving the former Henry, Jean Louis accused him, in front of the king, of misdirecting funds for his own use. Jean Louis said that if the king were not present, he would fight him.'

'Good heavens! What happened?'

'I don't think he can have much backbone. Apparently, he wouldn't leave his room for two days, and when he did, he asked the king if he could leave court. The king refused and insisted that Nicolas had his full confidence. His reputation was untarnished because everyone at court hated Jean Louis. Also, Catherine de Medici, the king's mother, was very fond of Nicolas. She often sought his counsel.'

'That is interesting. Catherine was the power behind the throne for all three of her sons, Francis, Charles and Henry. When I got mixed up in the War of the Three Henrys, it was Catherine and her Flying Squadron of young, female, aristocrat spies, that got me locked up for over a year in Bordeaux. You know the sour faced fellow sitting opposite the queen?'

'Yes, but I didn't speak to him,' Maria replied.

'He is Roger de Saint-Lary de Termes. He was introduced to the previous Henry's court by Jean Louis, so they are probably friends. Henry promoted him to master of horse, after uncovering a Catholic plot.'

'That reminds me. When we got up from the table, Jean Louis and Roger left the dining room together. I was a few paces behind them, so I heard little. They were talking about Julie and Rudolf, and Henry's ambition.'

'Henry's ambition, I wonder what they meant by that.'

'Isn't it obvious? Henry has this Julie, or it may have been Julia or Juliet, I can't be certain, earmarked as his next mistress. Perhaps she's currently with someone called Rudolph. What did you discover, Papa?'

'Not as much as you, Maria, apart from what I've told you about Roger. I found Pierre quite fascinating. He has invited me to visit him.'

'Why do you want to visit Pierre? I don't see how he can be involved, if he's just got back from sailing around the world.'

'You're quite right. I'm just interested in what he has to say. I feel drawn to him somehow.'

'So do I, I'll come with you. When are we going?'

'One of us should be available to help Louis. You saw the improvement he's making. We just need to help him with getting a rhythm to his speech, and finding alternatives to the words with sounds that he struggles with. It won't do you any harm to befriend the next king of France.'

'Yes, you're right,' Maria murmured, stroking her chin. 'He could be a very useful client.'

'Just promise me you won't call him a clot.'

'No, Papa, I've learnt that lesson.'

The following morning, Anthony walked along the Rue St. Honore. It was almost exactly as he remembered it. He walked past number sixteen and continued to number twenty-six. The brass plaque by the door declared that it was still the English embassy. He stood outside for a few minutes, thinking about Sir Henry Norris, who had set him on his journey to becoming a spy, and his secretary, Robert, who had taught him ciphers in that very building. Walsingham, the great spymaster; his wrestling instructor, Harrison, and the old thief, Pollard, who had taught him to pick locks, they all flashed through his mind, and he smiled. Then he turned and went back to number sixteen, climbed the steps to the front door, and knocked on the brass knocker. He looked around and noticed that the building opposite had a sundial fixed to the wall. The shadow showed eleven o'clock. He heard footsteps approaching from inside, then the door was opened by a middle-aged woman. She was slender and of average height.

'Is Pierre-Olivier Malherbe in?' Anthony asked.

'Yes, I heard him come back about an hour ago. His rooms are on the second floor,' she said, standing aside to let Anthony in.

'Thank you, madame,' Anthony said, and climbed the stairs. On the first-floor landing, he saw that there were several doors. The staircase continued upwards at the end of the landing. The layout was very much as Anthony remembered the English embassy. He continued up to the second-floor landing. The first door opposite the stairwell would open onto a room equivalent to the reception room where he had posed as a Venetian wine waiter, to entrap the Spanish ambassador all those years ago. A brass plate on the door read Pierre-Olivier Malherbe, so he knocked. The door opened.

'Sir Anthony, I'm so glad you could come. May I take your coat?' Anthony removed his top coat and handed it to Pierre. 'I'm sorry about the mess. I'm trying to assemble my thoughts for the history of my travels.' There was a large dining table in the middle of the room, with papers strewn all over it. There was a fireplace against the external wall, but no fire was lit. The long, internal wall of the room was lined with bookshelves. The books were arranged so that the larger books were on the lower shelves and the smaller ones near the top. There was a chair in front of the shelves, with a footprint on the seat. Sunlight streamed in through the tall windows at the far end of the room. 'It's quite warm for April, isn't it? I didn't think I'd light a fire. Are you warm enough?'

'Oh yes, I'm just right,' Anthony replied, marvelling at the artefacts on the table.'

'I'm sorry about those. They are shrunken heads from Peru. Let me clear some of these things away, and make space. Do sit down,' he suggested, picking up a pile of papers from an armchair. 'Would you like some wine? Or perhaps you'd like to try some Chinese tea? It's a drink made with dried leaves.'

'I'll try it.'

'Excellent, I'll just pop down to Madame Dufour's kitchen for some hot water. I won't be a minute.' Whilst Pierre was away, Anthony examined the papers strewn across the table. There was a large book open. On the recto was a diagram which caught his eye. In the middle of the diagram there was a circle. The circle enclosed what looked like two tadpoles, curled around each other, filling the circle. One tadpole was white, the other was black. In the middle of the thickest part of the white tadpole, there was what looked like a black eye, or teardrop perhaps. To its right, in the thickest part of the black tadpole, there was an equivalent white eye. The image was surrounded by eight branches of strange symbols, set regularly, as if like the hours on a clock-face. The verso was covered by similar symbols, set regularly on the page, like text, but not a text that he recognised. The door opened and Pierre came in carrying two small porcelain bowls on a small tray. 'Here, try this. I drink it in preference to wine these days. Be careful though, you might want to let it cool down a little. I see you have discovered the Bagua.'

'Thank you,' Anthony said, taking the bowl in his right hand. 'Bagua, do you mean this diagram?'

'Yes. The black and white elements of the circle represent the yin and yang, opposites yet bound together. The eight symbols represent the fundamental principles of reality. Why did the queen suggest we discuss Taoism?'

'When she was a child, I was assisting her father with his alchemy by translating some Arabic texts for him. One day I was passing Marie's room; her stepmother couldn't console her. One of her brothers had died. I took her for a walk; she was angry at God. It reminded me of when I was a child, and the questions I kept asking myself, which was who created God? And how can anything always have existed? I know a chicken comes from an egg, and an egg comes from a chicken, but where does the very first egg come from? The theory I came up with was, what if everything came from nothing? What if nothing is made from an equal debit and credit, positive and negative, yin and yang, if you like, and it explodes? Perhaps everything in our universe is made up of pieces of credit, and there is another debit universe. God is everything and nothing. Am I making any sense?'

'Yes, that is very similar to Taoist belief. Are you sure you haven't studied Taoism?'

'Yes, I'm sure.'

'Then in the sense of Taoism, you are something of a deity yourself, a minor one, of course. You haven't written it down, I suppose.'

'No.'

'I shouldn't here. You'd get away with it in China, but they would burn you in the west. I'm thinking very carefully about what I should include in the account of my travels, and what I should leave out. Anyway, you wanted to learn about meditation. How are you enjoying your tea?'

'It's very refreshing, although still rather hot,' Anthony replied, taking another sip.

'Why don't you put it down on the table and take a seat in this armchair? Was it your leg you said was causing you pain?'

'Yes, the right one mainly,' Anthony replied, as he sat down. Pierre picked up a small round mirror and leant over him, holding the mirror above him.

'Look into the mirror and relax. Watch the mirror as it moves to the left, and then to the right. To the left and to the right. Keep watching the mirror as it moves left and right. Imagine you are standing at the top of a flight of ten steps. I am going to count slowly from one to ten. Each time I count, you will imagine yourself stepping down to the next step. At each step, you become gradually more relaxed. Your eyes feel heavier. Ten. You are feeling more relaxed. Nine, your eyes are closing. Eight, you can hear only my voice, Seven, the staircase is darker, but you are perfectly safe, you cannot fall. Six, you are in complete control, but relaxed and confident. Five, your arms feel heavy. Four, your legs feel very heavy, but you take the next step with ease. Three, your eyes are closed. Two, you feel warm and comfortable. One, there is a door in front of you. You reach for the handle and open the door. In front of you is the happiest place you can possibly be. You step into it. Ten, and open your eyes, you are awake.' Anthony opened his eyes.

'How long have I been asleep?' he asked.

'You haven't been asleep at all. You have been in a trance,' Pierre said, smiling. 'We have been talking, and I asked you to draw me something. Do you remember that?'

'No, not at all. I remember you counting down from ten. You got to about four and then I heard wake up. If I wasn't asleep, how could I wake up?'

'A good question. I can't explain it, but I think of it as a trance is when your conscious mind goes to sleep, but your unconscious mind wakes up. You can still talk, like a man talks in his sleep, and you can walk, as some people walk in their sleep. But your subconscious mind is in charge.' Pierre reached across to the table and picked up a sheet of paper. He handed it to Anthony. 'Do you recognise this woman?' Anthony sat bolt upright in the chair.

'It's Francesca, my wife. How long have you known her? When did you draw this?'

'I didn't. How could I? I asked you to draw the most

beautiful thing you could think of. I confess I wasn't expecting such magnificent penmanship. It took you about an hour. You are a lucky man. Your wife is very beautiful.' Anthony reached across to the bowl of tea. He took a sip, and it was stone cold.

'I have only drawn her from memory once before, on a hillside overlooking A Coruña, in 1588. This time I have drawn her as she was the week before last. It's quite incredible. How could I draw this and not remember doing it? Is this something anybody can learn to do? Could you teach me to put someone in a trance?'

'Well I did. I don't see why you wouldn't be able to. Some people are very difficult to get into a trance, you were very easy. How is your leg now?' Pierre asked. Anthony stood up and walked around the room.

'Why it is much better, there is no pain at all.'

'The pain relief will only last a few weeks, unless you have further sessions. My landlady, Madame Dufour, is very good at being induced. She has found it helps her bad back. If you like, and if she agrees, I could teach you, using her as a subject. She won't mind, free medicine she calls it.'

'That would be wonderful; but I had better be getting back to the palace. Perhaps I could call around in a few days?'

'I have some business to attend to, but I will ask Madame Dufour if she is happy to be your subject. I will drop a note into the palace for you, letting you know when would be convenient.'

'Thank you, Pierre,' Anthony said as they shook hands. He put on his coat and left. As he closed the front door behind him, he looked across the street to the sundial. It was two o'clock in the afternoon. He had been at Pierre's for three hours.

Maria heard her father return and opened the connecting door.

'How was your meeting with Pierre, Papa?'

'It was quite extraordinary,' he said, pulling his sketch from the pocket of his doublet and handing it to Maria. 'He put me into a trance and I drew this.'

'Mother will be pleased. I didn't know you were such a talented artist. Anyway, how are we going to work out who is behind the attacks on the king?' She asked, putting the sketch down on the table and sitting down. Anthony pulled a chair out and sat facing Maria.

'I'm not sure. It's not at all like the last time. We had definite dates of the attacks and could check whether the suspects had alibis. With this, whoever is planning the attacks is clearly paying someone to do the dirty work.'

'Like Pierre Barrière and Jean Châtel, yes I see, Papa. But they must have known they faced certain death. Surely no amount of money would induce someone to take that risk.'

'Hope, however slender, is a powerful drug. What I wonder is how whoever is planning this found Barrière and Châtel, and all the others who escaped. He must have a network of conspirators always on the lookout for potential assassins.'

'Or she, Papa.'

'I think that's unlikely, but we can't rule out the possibility. But, there's no point looking for alibis, so we have to look for motive and means.'

'What do you mean by means, Papa?'

'I'm thinking of co-conspirators. How is our man communicating with his network, whether that network be the Catholic League, or the Huguenots? Is he giving the orders, or is he a middle-man?' Maria kept her gaze on Anthony as he turned his head to stare out of the window. She wanted to fill the silence, but waited. Eventually, he turned back to face her. 'I think we have to start with motive. I will interview all of our suspects and ask them who they suspect. That way I may put them at ease, whilst also gathering intelligence on the other suspects. If I can find some opening, I'll try to bring the possibility of their own involvement into the conversation.'

'Are we agreed on who our suspects are, Papa?'

'I assumed that Marie had organised the dinner so that we could meet all the potential suspects. But you make a good point. There may be others that could not attend. I'll speak with her and see if there is anyone else she can think of.'

'So then we need to decide which suspects you question, and which ones I take.'

'No, I'll do all the questioning.'

'But, Papa, I want to be in on this too.'

'You will be. If I unsettle the suspect, he may try to contact his network. I can imagine our man looking out of his window, watching me walk away, before making his move. Perhaps he'll write a ciphered message, or go himself to meet someone. If we get you a disguise, and you keep the suspect's quarters under observation after I leave, then you may find out who they communicate with.'

'Excellent idea, Papa. Let's get started straight away.'

'Hold your horses. We need to fix you up with a disguise, and I also need to teach you the arts of surveillance.'

'What was that? Sir what?'

'Surveillance, following without being observed. We will need to get you some sort of disguise, turn you into someone that nobody will give a second glance.'

'I get a lot of second glances, Papa, mainly from men.'

'Yes, we need to disguise your curves, perhaps some padding, and a false beard. We could make you up as a beggar.'

'I'd need quite a lot of padding around the middle, unless we bind my breasts too, and you don't see many fat beggars.'

'We could dress you in a monk's habit. There are plenty of fat monks.'

'What excuse would a monk have to be hanging around on the street watching a house?'

'Yes, you're right, of course. What about if you become a beggar, but have a stoop? That would disguise your womanly attributes. We should get you a crutch, too. I'll find the nearest theatre and hire a make-up artist.'

For the rest of the week following their arrival in Paris, Anthony and Maria spent the mornings working with Louis on his stammer. Anthony tried to pass the onus of the therapy to Maria, who seemed to be developing a genuine liking for the dauphin, and who was as quick as Anthony to perceive what was working and what was not. While Maria was working with Louis, Anthony went looking for Gaston. He found him working on a magnificent gown for the queen.

'Gaston, I'm sorry to disturb you, but could you let me have my daughter's measurements please?'

'Sir Anthony, I will be more than happy to make another dress for your daughter. What sort of dress would she like?'

'I'm sure you're too busy with this wonderful gown, I, er...'

'Not at all. I have assistants who can help.'

'No, really, it's just that when we get home, Maria wants to put on a little play for the other children. She's written a story about a beggar, and want's to get a costume made. The fabrics you work with would not fit the part at all. I thought I'd find a theatrical costume maker and see what they could do for us.'

'My assistant Jaques used to work with a theatre company. Jaques, come and meet Sir Anthony!' Jaques peered at Anthony from behind a mannequin, and came over. He bowed. He was a short man in his mid fifties, Anthony guessed. 'Jaques made Maria's dresses while I was working on your clothes. Now, what exactly would she like? A beggar you say.'

'Er, yes. Her story involves her playing the part of a crippled man, fallen on hard times.'

'I have a friend, still working for the theatre, who does all the wigs and make up, Sir Anthony. I'm sure I could soon have your daughter looking the part.' Jaques said.

'This will be just between us, I hope. I wouldn't want Her Majesty to think we were slacking in our duties to help the dauphin.'

'Of course, Sir Anthony. It's no trouble at all. When would it be convenient to take your daughter to the theatre?'

'Why would she have to go to the theatre?'

'If a job is worth doing, it is worth doing well, Sir Anthony. Francis, my friend who does the make up, will need to trim some of your daughter's hair to make her beard. Only by using her own hair will it look authentic. He will need to fit her for her false beard and moustache so that it will fit perfectly. It is a delicate process. He will use some fine netting and attach each hair to the netting by knotting the hair through it. He will also show you both how to apply the facial paint, and how to attach the beard, so that when they deliver it to you, you know how to apply it.'

'Yes, of course. I suppose we could go this afternoon, if that's convenient for you. Is it far?'

'Just a short walk, Sir Anthony.'

Anthony went from Gaston's workshop to the queen's apartments. Marcel was just leaving as he approached. He asked if he could have another audience with the queen. Moments later, he was ushered in. Marie was playing cards with Leonora Concini.

'Sir Anthony, how are you settling in? You and your daughter do seem to be helping Louis. He likes you both very much.'

'We are doing our best, You Highness, and I'm sure we can help him. It is the other matter that I wish to discuss.' Anthony said, glancing at Leonora.

'Sir Anthony, don't be tiresome. I told you that Leonora is my dearest confidante. We can speak freely with her. Now what is it you wish to ask?'

'Well, Your Highness, are there any members of court who might be responsible, but were not at the dinner you arranged when we arrived?'

'I see. Let me think. Hercule, duc de Montbazon, was out of the city, but he's back now. It couldn't be him. He fought with Henry and is one of his dearest friends. He's master of hounds and governor of Paris. Then there is Charles d'Albert. He's very good with Louis. He's teaching him hunting and falconry. But he's far too young to have had any involvement in the early attempts. I wondered about Henri, Prince de Condé, but he fled to Brussels.'

'Fled, Your Highness?'

'Yes, Henry was terribly annoyed. Henry is Henri's godfather, and until Louis was born, Henri was his heir. Last year, Henri married Charlotte Marguerite de Montmorency. Henry encouraged him, because he fancied Charlotte himself, and wanted her nearby. But Henri is totally in love with Charlotte and wouldn't play along with Henry's scheme. Instead he fled with her to Brussels. Henry's talking about invading Flanders over it, but I think it's all bluster. It's not as if he doesn't have enough mistresses already. Anyway, I think he may have moved to Milan now, that's what I heard. So you can't snoop on him.'

'Is there anyone else you can think of, Your Highness?'

'No, I don't think so.'

'In which case I will leave you to your game, Your Highness, Signora Concini.' Anthony said, bowing, before turning to leave. He stopped and turned back to the queen. 'There is one thing more, Your Highness. The potential suspects are nobility, and may be reluctant to speak with me.'

'When you desire an appointment with a member of court, or indeed anyone else, inform Marcel. He will arrange an appointment with my authority.'

'Thank you, Your Highness.' Anthony said as he bowed and left.

Jacques led Anthony and Maria north east from the Louvre. They passed through the bustling Les Halles market and along the Rue Française. At the junction with Rue Mauconseil, Jacques stopped.

'Here we are. The Hotel de Bourgogne. The theatre of Paris. The brotherhood built it in 1548.'

'The brotherhood?' Anthony murmured.

'That is how they were known, the Confrerie de la Passion, they called themselves. They were a group of artisans and merchants who staged mystery plays, bible stories and farces. It is now owned by the great actor, Valleran le Conte. Are you alright, Sir Anthony? You look rather pale.'

'It's just a memory. I've been here before. That would have been in 1567. I was going to take a girl to see a play here, but something happened.' Anthony slapped his arms across his chest, as if he was cold. 'Anyway, that's another story. Let's go in.' Jacques knocked on the door. They heard footsteps approaching, and the door opened.

'Monsieur Valleran, we have come to see Francis.'

'Welcome Jacques, monsieur, mademoiselle. Please come in.' Valleran said, as he led them inside. Anthony and Maria gazed around. They were in a hall around ninety feet long by forty feet wide. At the far end was a stage. To their right, there were boxes, separated from the main hall by waist height timber screens. In each box there were several chairs. The main hall had two rows of benches, either side of a central gangway. The hall was well lit by windows beneath the high roof. Valleran led them towards the stage. There was a narrow passageway to the right of the stage and a door which led backstage. 'Francis, you have guests. I will leave you now. I must go and see Alexandre, and find out how he's getting on with the new script.' Valleran bowed and left.

'How can I help you, Jaques?' Asked a short, plump, middle-aged man as he stood up from behind a workbench in the corner of a room lined with rails, from which a multitude of colourful costumes hung.

'May I introduce Sir Anthony and his daughter Maria? They are friends of the queen. Maria wishes to perform a play for her siblings which requires her to become a beggar man. I will make her a costume, but she will need a false beard, moustache and make up. You can charge it all to the queen's account.'

'It will be my pleasure. Would you sit here, Maria, and we shall get started.' Francis said, pulling out a chair. He then opened a cupboard and took out a roll of fabric and a pair of scissors. He cut out a square of the fabric. After opening the drawer, he picked a needle and cut some thread. Francic threaded the needle as he walked over to the window. 'I'm going to place this gauze over your mouth and chin, Maria. Then I shall make some cuts in the gauze, and put some stitches in, as I shape the gauze to fit your face.' Francis started with some large vee shaped cuts, and progressively smaller cuts as he moulded the gauze to Maria's face.

'What is gauze, Jacques?' Anthony asked.

'It's made from silk, with a loose, open weave. They make it in Gaza, which is in Palestine, and that's where it gets its name from.'

'Now I think of it, qazz is Arabic for raw silk. Perhaps that is where Gaza gets its name from.' Anthony added.

'I didn't know that, but it would make sense.' Jacques replied. Anthony watched, fascinated, as Francis snipped at the gauze, added a stitch here, and a stitch there, before trying the gauze against Maria's face again.

'What's the new play, Jacques, the one that Valleran has gone to see about?'

'It's the Elegy of Lady Fiammetta, based on the book by Giovanni Boccaccio. Alexandre has been writing it for months now. It sounds like a great story, but I think we should stick to farces. That's what the audiences want. They have enough tragedy in their daily lives; they come here for laughter.'

'Yes, that's a perfect fit, Maria. I'll just mark the outline of your lips, so that I can cut out that section of gauze. Next I'll harvest some of your hair for the beard, then we can move on to the make up.' Francis said, putting down the gauze, and picking up the scissors again. He collected the hair in a wooden bowl, which he put on the bench. Then he went to the cupboard and took out several jars. 'This is soot, and the other powder is ground chalk. I'm mixing them with a little water to make a paste. Now I'll take a brush and apply some to Maria's face.' After a few minutes he stood back. 'There, what do you think, Sir Anthony?'

'It's very good. She looks pale and dirty. You've certainly aged her, but there's something not quite right.' Jacques and Francis exchanged glances. 'I know what it is. Her skin is still perfectly smooth. What if you added the powders to some lard rather than water? That would make it more textured, don't you think? You could add lines in her face.'

'Lard? I've never heard of such a thing.' Francis exclaimed. The face paint works perfectly well, and I don't think the actors would want lard smeared over their faces.'

'Yes, but the audience don't get close enough to see the lines, do they?'

'Well, I can't see it catching on, but you try lard if you want to.' Francis said. 'I'll show you how to stick the beard on when I've finished making it.' Francis said, going to the cupboard and taking out another jar. 'This is spirit gum. It's a mixture of tree resin and alcohol. Just paint it onto Maria's face, where the beard and moustache will go, then apply the false beard. As the alcohol evaporates, the gauze becomes glued on by the resin. When you need to remove it, apply some alcohol, brandy is best. That will dissolve the resin. It will be a lot less painful than just pulling it off.'

'Thank you, Francis. How long do you think the beard

will take to make?'

'We don't have another performance until Saturday. I can send it over by Friday.'

'Perfect!'

'How can we progress the investigation while waiting for my false beard, Papa?'

'You remember I said that I need to teach you about surveillance, the art of following and observing someone, without being seen yourself. The same reformed criminal who taught me lock picking taught me surveillance. Before we start practicing the art, we need to discuss the theory. I will have questioned the suspect, and if the suspect questioned is the guilty party, then he might be alarmed. He might try to meet an accomplice or send a message. You will wait, in disguise, and if he makes a move, or sends a messenger, you will follow him or the messenger, without being seen yourself.'

'It seems perfectly easy, Papa.'

'It isn't, believe me. I was observed once, and they nearly killed me. Now the first things to think about are pinch points.'

'You mean like a narrow alley, Papa?'

'Yes, it might be an alleyway. When we practice, you'll try to follow me, without me noticing you. If I walk down the alleyway, a few yards and stop. I can wait and see or hear if anyone has followed me into the alleyway. So you need to anticipate me stopping and looking round or listening for your footsteps. Remind me to get some sacking to tie around your boots, to muffle your footsteps. A bridge is another pinch point. I can stop on the bridge, peer down the river, then glance behind and see if anyone behind me has stopped too. Although I'm trying not to be observed, I'm also discretely observing everyone around me. I look at their faces, their shoes, their clothes. I visit at least three places before my intended destination and if I've seen the same person at more than one of the places, I assume I'm being followed.'

'But you've been alarmed, you'll go straight to your accomplice.'

'Yes, you may be right, Maria. But I'm teaching you the theory as it was taught to me. You need to learn about surveillance, both to anticipate what a wary suspect might do, and also to protect yourself from being observed. It's possible that the suspect might instruct an accomplice or servant to follow him at a distance, along a pre-arranged route, to check that he isn't being followed.'

'That seems unlikely to me, Papa.'

'I'm not at all sure. Whoever is behind these attempts has remained undetected so far. He has to be clever and very careful. Now where was I?'

'You visited three places before your destination, Papa.'

'That's right. The other thing he taught me was to hone my senses, like with lock picking. That feeling that the pick is an extension of your fingertip, that enhanced sense of feel. You need to use all your senses. When you're in that dark alleyway, can you hear footsteps, breathing? Can you smell anyone?'

'Smell anyone?'

'Yes, try it. I'm not suggesting you go around sniffing people. Just close your eyes occasionally and find out what you can sense with your ears and nose. A chef, for instance, has a distinctive smell. A clerk may smell of ink. Anyway, let's go out and practice.'

Anthony led Maria to the English embassy on Rue St. Honore. The sun would set within the hour, and the street was emptying.

'Maria, you sit cross-legged over there, as if you are begging. I'll be standing by the steps of the embassy, as if I've just left. I'll set off walking, and you try to follow me without being observed.'

'All right, Papa.'

Anthony set off at a brisk pace. When he passed the

Louvre, he turned left, heading into the Les Halles market. He entered a grocery shop on his left and bought an apple. Through the window he saw Maria turn the corner and stop. He watched her run to the next junction and peep around the corner. She stood for a few moments, then walked back towards the shop. Anthony left the shop, pretending not to notice her, and continued strolling through the market, munching his apple. At a bakers shop, he stopped and looked in the window. He could see Maria's reflection, standing about fifty yards behind him. At the next junction he stopped as a horse and cart approached from the street to his left. He turned left, let the cart pass him, then ran alongside the cart as it continued over the junction. He then stopped and concealed himself in a doorway. He watched Maria looking all around her. He pressed himself further into the darkness of the doorway as she passed him on the other side of the street. Then he followed her. As she approached the next junction, he ducked behind a market stall. He watched her look in each direction at the junction, then back towards his hiding place. She continued in the direction of the theatre, and Anthony followed her. When she arrived at the theatre, he waited as she went inside.

'How is Francis getting on with your beard?' He asked as she re-emerged.

'So I was right, this is where you were heading.' Maria said.

'No, I followed you for the last half mile.'

'How did you get behind me?'

'By ducking behind a horse and cart as it crossed the road. I then hid in a doorway before following you. I also saw your reflection in the bakery's window. Don't look so disappointed, I've had a lot of practice.' Anthony took Maria back over the route they had taken and pointed out where he had hidden and how he had observed her. 'We'll continue tomorrow and I'm sure that by the time you've got your disguise, you'll be better than I ever was.'

Anthony was looking forward to his next meeting with Pierre, not only because Taoism fascinated him, and how it chimed with his own beliefs, but to learn more about induction into the meditative state. He had been induced to do something, that he had absolutely no recollection of doing, yet he had clearly done it. The fact that his leg, which had been troubling him, now felt much better, was a tremendous bonus. On Thursday, Marcel brought to him a note from Pierre, which confirmed that he was free from ten in the morning on Friday, through to two in the afternoon, and that Madame Dufour was happy to serve, once more, as the patient. Anthony slipped the note into his coat pocket. It surprised him to feel so excited. He felt a kind of anticipation that he hadn't felt since he picked his first lock. He was snapped out of his reverie as Maria came rushing into his room.

'Oh, Papa, excellent news. We expect the king back on Monday, and Louis is making significant progress. We are working on a poetic speech that we both hope will impress him. Isn't it wonderful?'

'Why of course, Maria. I'm glad that you are so intent on Louis's progress, but why such fulsome joy for the return of the king?'

'I saw the sense in making a good friend of the dauphin, but he is only eight years old. It will be many years before he is king, so it's a long-term investment. But if I can impress the king, there may be profitable work to come from it much sooner, while I am still young. Don't you see, Papa?'

'Well, yes, I mean no. What is this obsession with wealth? You were the same when François and Anne needed transport to Tunis. You made the deal for a hundred ducats. Why are you chasing after a fortune? Your mother wants us to find you a noble husband but…'

'Oh, Papa, mother was quite happy looking after us, raising us, and part of me wants that too. But another part of me wants more. You're a fine one to berate me for seeking my fortune, since by your own account you were always making and losing your own.' Anthony opened his mouth to shout Maria down, but the words stuck in his throat.

'You're right, I'd be a fine one to chastise you for seeking your fortune. It's true, I was forever chasing and losing a fortune, before gaining and keeping one. I was trying to prove something to my father, which was a fool's errand. If you have any respect for me, and I hope you do, then know this. The only joy in finally securing my small fortune was to find Francesca again, and you and Antonio. Love is everything, not gold and silver. What is it you really want?'

'I don't know, Papa, but I want to find it myself. I want independence. I don't want to be shackled to some duke, or other man, however wealthy and handsome he may be. I'm not a case of fine wine to be traded then consumed, and my empty flagon thrown aside, as the quest for a fresh wine starts. My goal may lie at the end of the rainbow, across an ocean perhaps, but I want to find it myself. Will you help me, Papa?' Maria begged, squeezing her words out between sobs. Anthony pulled her close to him and wrapped his arms around her.

'I don't think I've seen you cry before. You're always so strong. At the end of the fight for our lives, with the pirates, Anne broke down having killed a man for the first, and almost certainly the last time. You were unmoved, although it was your first time too, and you must have killed a dozen or more. Of course I'll help you, I'm your father.'

CHAPTER EIGHT

Anthony was shown into the governor's office. Hercule, duc de Montbazon, looked up from the letter he was writing, put down his quill, and indicated that Anthony should sit in the chair in front of his large walnut desk.

'Sir Anthony, I am intrigued that you wish to speak to me. How can I help?'

'Your Grace, Her Highness is very distressed by the number of assassination attempts against the king. She has asked me to make some enquiries, and as one of the king's greatest friends, for many years, I thought you might have some thoughts on who might be behind them.'

'Behind them, you say. My assumption has always been that they are just religious lunatics. Do you think there is some evil mastermind directing them in some way?'

'If they were simply lunatics, how is it that they know where the king is going to be?'

'Perhaps it's just chance. One of these lunatics is in the street one day. The king approaches in his carriage, the fellow pulls out his knife, and takes the guard by surprise.'

'Is France so full of lunatics with no care for their own

lives? I understand the first two attempts were in 1593 and 1594.'

'Yes, that's right, Barriere and Châtel, if my memory serves me well. They were Catholics. At the time, I thought it was odd, because Henry had just converted to Catholicism. I would have thought that the Protestants might have felt more sold out.'

'I understand that the Catholic League tried very hard to prevent the king from becoming Catholic. Have you any idea why they might do that?' Anthony asked.

'I can only assume they somehow knew of Henry's plans for the Edict of Nantes, and didn't like it.'

'You don't think they might have had their own candidate for king?'

'I fought at the side of Henry throughout the war. We vanquished the Catholics. What candidate?'

'What about Nicholas de Brûlart?' Anthony asked. Hercule burst into laughter.

'You obviously haven't met him yet. He's as dull as dishwater. He's certainly no evil mastermind.'

'I understand his brother preached and lobbied against the Edict of Nantes.'

'Yes, and Henry had Nicholas slap him down. No, if you're after an evil mastermind, my money would be on Roger de Saint-Lary de Termes, Nicholas de Neufville, or Jean Louis de Nogaret. They all worked for the Catholic League. Actually, not Nicholas; his judgement is excellent, but mastermind is a stretch. Jean Louis's rapacity knows no bounds.'

'And what about you, governor? Where were you in 1593 and 1594?'

'Me! I fought with Henry. Are you serious?'

'I have to ask.'

'I was courting Madeleine. We married in October 1594. Most of the time I was in Brittany, as lieutenant-general.'

'I didn't know you were married.'

'Madeleine died eight years ago.'

'I'm sorry, I didn't know.' Anthony said, as Hercule rose from his chair and tip-toed across the room. He turned the doorknob and jerked the door open.

'If you're so curious, Marie, you'd better come and meet Sir Anthony.' A pretty girl followed Hercule into the room. 'Here is my alibi, Sir Anthony. Do you have young children?'

'Yes I do.'

'And would you risk your life if you would leave a little girl like this practically alone in the world?'

'I'm not a little girl. I'm ten years old. I'll be married soon.'

'Not just yet, my little minx. Who do you intend to marry when I say you're old enough?'

'Charles d'Albert. I like him. I hope he's not one of your suspects, Sir Anthony.'

'No, he is not a suspect at the moment. And, Your Grace, I would not risk my life in such a way. I'll bid you a good day.'

$\Diamond \Diamond \Diamond$

Anthony left the governor's house and crossed the street. He paused by the beggar sitting cross-legged and tossed a few sous into his wooden bowl.

'He's in his early forties, about six inches shorter than me. He has a neatly trimmed, pointed beard and is wearing red silk stockings. I'll be waiting in the tavern. Be careful.'

Anthony made his way to the tavern, a few doors down from the theatre. He paid the innkeeper and went up to the room where he had left his canvas holdall before visiting Hercule. He lay down on the bed and waited. He tried to rest, but kept worrying about Maria. The sun was setting by the time the door opened and Maria came in.

'Thank God you're all right. How did it go?'

'Not bad at all. I made forty-two sous. Most people were far more generous than you. One very kind old lady gave me ten sous.' Maria said, smiling.

'Don't tease me. Did you discover anything?'

'No, Papa. Even by the time you arrived, I thought it was going to be an impossible task. There are people coming and going all the time. I thought that if the man you described left, I'd follow him, obviously. Otherwise, I decided to give him enough time to write a note, then follow the next person who left. I followed a man, but he just turned out to be the owner of a grocery shop. He'd probably just been visiting to pay his rent, or something like that. Can we get this disguise off now? The beard is really itchy.'

'Yes, of course. Sit down on the bed.' Anthony opened the canvas bag and took out a bottle of brandy and a rag. He soaked the rag in brandy and started dabbing it over the beard. He gave it a few minutes to soak in and loosen the spirit gum. Then he started pulling at the edge of the beard. Maria winced, and he dabbed on some more brandy, then pulled again. It came off fairly easily, after the second application of brandy. 'I'm rather pleased with the make up. Mixing the lard with the ground chalk and soot gives it some texture. It makes you look decades older. I think Francis is missing a trick there.'

'Yes, I daresay you're right, but I want it off now.'

'There's a bowl of water and a towel on the dresser.' Anthony said. Maria got up from the bed and washed her face. She looked in the mirror hanging on the wall above the dresser, then washed some more. When she was clean, she stripped off the beggar costume and rummaged in the holdall for her dress.

'What did Hercule have to say, Papa?'

'I don't think it can be him. His wife died a few years ago, and he has a young daughter to look after. Surely he wouldn't put her at risk. He suggested Neufville as a possibility. Neufville worked for the Catholic League, so did Jean Louis and his friend Roger de Saint-Larry. That fellow Nicholas de Brûlart, the one whose brother tried to stop the magistrates agreeing to Henry's treaty, Hercule says he's as dull as dishwater. He laughed at the idea of him being responsible.'

'Perhaps his dullness is his form of disguise.'

'You may have a point, and we won't rule him out. I think we should try Neufville next. Hercule said that although he lacks advanced education, he has excellent judgement. I like the sound of that. If it isn't him, his judgement of his fellow courtiers might be of value to our investigation. I'll see Marcel when we get back to the palace and ask him to arrange an appointment.'

Anthony walked along Rue St. Honore towards the morning sun. He continued into Rue des Halles, which was bustling with shoppers and stall holders, chanting the value of their wares. At the corner of Rue Thibaut, he found Neufville's impressive house, Hôtel de Villeroy. He tugged at the bell pull and a liveried servant soon opened the door. They were expecting him and he was soon sitting opposite Nicolas de Neufville, seigneur de Villeroy.

'I'm not sure why I have the pleasure of meeting you, Sir Anthony. We have hardly spoken, although I remember you recounting your extensive travels to Pierre, who had just returned from his great circumnavigation. That was a cruel trick the queen played on you.'

'Yes, but I owe her a great deal. You spoke with my daughter over dinner.'

'I remember her, a charming young lady. But why has Her Highness arranged this meeting? They led me to believe that you are assisting the dauphin with his speech defect. I don't know how I can help, or, indeed, how you can. The greatest doctors in France have had scant success.'

'We are already making significant progress. It is my interest in language that Her Highness thought might help. We are discovering that an understanding of tongues is more effective than the skill of severing one. However, I also have experience of tracking down murderers. When the queen heard my account of unmasking the serial killer of priests, she thought I might be of use in discovering who is behind the assassination attempts against the king.'

'I haven't heard about any priests being burnt. As Secretary of State, I think it might have come to my attention.'

'It was three years ago, sir, in Italy. To come back to the assassination attempts, do you have any thoughts about who might be behind them?'

'What makes you think anyone is behind them? They are clearly lunatics.'

'Perhaps, but they seem very well informed of where the king will be.'

'Many people know where the king will be. Public events have to be organised. I hadn't given it very much thought, but it seems to me that you would have to be a lunatic to kill a king. It would be certain death. I can only assume that a killer must be in no doubt of the rewards that await him in heaven. They have to be religious fanatics.'

'Yes, I feel sure you're right. But if we assume that someone at court is recruiting and organising them, who do you think that might be? I'm told that you have remarkable judgement.' Anthony asked, staring into Neufville's penetrating brown eyes.

'I don't think anyone at court could be involved, Sir Anthony.'

'But just imagine if there were someone. Who do you think that might be? I assure you, I will keep this conversation entirely between us, unless and until I have some solid evidence.'

'I have your word on that?'

'You do, sir.'

'It would have to be Épernon, and Saint-Lary de Termes, perhaps. They're as thick as thieves, those two. Épernon's ambition knows no bounds. If anyone has an eye on taking the throne, it's Épernon.'

'I believe you have just cause to dislike the duc d'Épernon.'

'Indeed I do, but that was twenty-three years ago. We have had to work closely together since then. I tell you he is ambitious beyond measure. He was in the Catholic League, and the Treaty of Nantes angered him. Yet I still doubt him capable of taking such a risk.'

'You were a member of the Catholic League yourself, were you not?'

'Yes, but if you know of the matter of 1587, then you will know of my cowardice. I'm not your criminal mastermind.' Anthony could tell from his eyes that Neufville spoke the truth.

'I understand that Roger de Saint-Lary uncovered the Biron conspiracy, and that the king made him governor of Burgundy as a reward. What can you tell me about the conspiracy?'

'It was so strange. Charles de Gontaut, duc de Biron, fought with distinction against the Catholic league. He became known as the Thunderbolt of France. The current King Henry made him Admiral of France, then Marshal of France and Governor of Burgundy. Henry sent him to fight the Spaniards in Flanders, where he again distinguished himself. Henry sent him to England in 1601 to announce his marriage to Marie. Whilst he was there, Roger somehow got hold of documents that proved he was engaged in a conspiracy with Spain against King Henry. Biron continued to deny it, but the court found him guilty and they beheaded him in the Bastille in July 1602.'

'And Roger was rewarded?'

'Yes.'

Anthony wondered where he could lead the conversation next. He looked around the room for inspiration. One painting stood out from the landscapes. It was of a beautiful woman reading a book.

'The portrait above the fireplace, she's a very beautiful woman.'

'Yes, she was. Madeleine died fourteen years ago. But I must be grateful for the thirty-five wonderful years we had together. Languages fascinated her, too. The book she's reading is the epistles of Ovid. She translated them from Latin.'

'I'm sincerely sorry for your loss. Did you have children?'

'We had two sons and a daughter, but only Charles survives.'

'I can only imagine what it must be like to lose a child. I really am very sorry. I have troubled you enough, forgive me. I will leave you in peace.' Anthony rose, they shook hands, and he left.

◇ ◇ ◇

When Maria arrived at the tavern, Anthony removed her false beard.

'What happened, Maria?'

'While I waited for you to leave, I thought it was going to be impossible again. There were so many people coming and going. Then, about a quarter of an hour after you left, so did Neufville. I thought you'd flushed him out, and he was going to meet an accomplice.'

'Really? I didn't expect that. Where did he go? Who did he meet?'

'I followed him through the market, and he went to a florist and bought a bunch of roses. Perhaps he has an assignation with his mistress, I thought. He waited outside the florists for a few minutes, then a carriage stopped, and he got in. I had to run to keep it in sight. You should have seen the faces of the people in the streets as I passed. Now I think of it, they probably don't see many beggars running through the streets, let alone with a beard and breasts. Anyway, they stopped just outside the city walls and he got out and went into a cemetery. I sat down by the gate and watched where they went while I got my breath back. I was thinking perhaps there was a message in the bunch of roses that his accomplice would come and pick up. He passed me as he left and put a crown in my begging bowl. There was such sadness in his eyes, Papa. When the carriage had gone,

I waited a while to see if the accomplice would show up. Then, when there was nobody about, I went to find the message, but there wasn't one. The gravestone was inscribed to Madeleine de Neufville, Louis and Marie. I don't think it's him, Papa.'

'Neither do I. He thought that if there were a mastermind, it's probably Jean Louis, duc d'Épernon, or Roger de Saint-Lary, de Termes, duc de Bellegarde, or both.'

'So who do we go after next, Papa?'

'I think Roger. Épernon is the senior of the two, and I want as much on Épernon as I can get, before talking to him.'

'That makes sense, Papa, but what do we know about Roger?'

'He uncovered a plot by Biron against the king, and was rewarded for it. Biron denied the charge, but Roger had documentary evidence. It all reminds me of when I was falsely charged with treason on documentary evidence. If Roger was working for the Spaniards himself, and if they wanted rid of Biron, who had been such a thorn in their side, then false documents could easily have been obtained.'

'We'll have to be careful, Papa. Épernon and Roger both sound dangerous to me.'

Anthony walked to the large town house on Rue St. Honore, which he was told Roger de Saint-Lary de Termes, duc de Bellegarde, occupied when in Paris. A servant let him in and led him to the study. Sunlight flooded the room through large windows overlooking the street. As he approached the desk, Bellegarde continued writing a letter. Without looking up, he indicated for Anthony to sit in the chair facing him across the desk. Before sitting, Anthony glanced out of the nearest window and saw Maria taking up her position across the street. He sat down. Bellegarde finished his letter with a flourish, put down his quill and looked up.

'Sir Anthony, I hope you're not going to ask my advice

on the dauphin's speech impediment.'

'No, Your Grace. The queen has asked me to look into another matter as well, the assassination attempts against the king. She believes them to be coordinated, rather than the acts of random lunatics. Do you have any thoughts on who might be coordinating them?'

'Protestants aggrieved by the king's conversion to Catholicism, I presume.'

'Or Catholics enraged by the Edict of Nantes.'

'Yes, that is also a possibility. Either way, it's a fearful risk to take, to kill a king, Sir Anthony.'

'It is a considerable risk to unseat a duke, is it not?' Anthony watched as Roger looked away, then stood up and walked over to the window. He turned to face Anthony again.

'Damned beggars, they're everywhere in Paris. I assume you are speaking of Biron. It was my duty, Sir Anthony.'

'I would be interested to know how you got the document that incriminated him.' Roger turned away again. After several moments, he returned to his desk and sat down.

'I had had my suspicions for some time. I knew there would be correspondence, so I hired someone to break into Biron's office and search for it. He returned with a great pile of documents. Most were simple letters, reports, and contracts. But one recent one was in cipher. I asked the royal cipher clerk to decipher it, and it was from the Spaniards. It was deeply incriminating.'

'I see. It might have been easy enough to obtain such a document and claim that your agent found it in Biron's study. That is, if one had the right connections with Spain.'

'That's absurd. Why do you suggest such a thing?'

'Well, you gained a lot from Biron's downfall, Burgundy for example.'

'I don't have to listen to this drivel. I think it's time you left, Sir Anthony.'

'Was it your idea, or Épernon's? He introduced you to

court, I believe. You are great friends, are you not?'

'We are friends, and yes, he did introduce me to court. But I alone uncovered the Biron conspiracy, in just the way that I described. Now will you leave, or shall I have you thrown out?'

'Thank you for your time, Your Grace.' Anthony said as he stood up, turned, and left.

Anthony paced the room at the tavern, waiting for Maria to return.

I may have pushed him too far, he thought. I clearly struck a nerve over the Biron conspiracy. He saw Maria from the window. What if he spots her following him? I've put her in danger. I should have taken more time training her in surveillance. Perhaps I should have let her do the interrogation so that I could follow him. How would they take being questioned by a girl? Oh, thank god, I'd recognise the sound of those footsteps anywhere.

The door opened and Maria hobbled in. Anthony took her crutch from her, as she got out of the beggar's costume.

'You certainly spooked him, Papa. You'd hardly turned the corner when he came rushing out. I didn't have far to follow him. He knocked on the door three houses down the road and was promptly let in. He left again about half an hour later. I wondered where he would go next, and whether I should follow him or hang around outside. I needn't have worried, because he scurried straight back to his own house. I was able to keep watch on both houses. Guess who was next to leave the house he'd rushed off to?'

'Épernon?'

'Oh, did you see him too?'

'No, just an educated guess. I hope you didn't follow him.'

'Of course I did, why wouldn't I? Anyway, Épernon went to the Louvre. I couldn't follow him in there, not in this disguise. Shouldn't we be picking their locks and searching their houses now, Papa?'

'Searching for what?'

'You're the spy, Papa. They might have some incriminating documents, an enciphered letter from the king of Spain, perhaps.'

'If I had such a document, I'd hide it inside a book in my library, not in my desk drawer. You've seen the libraries these nobles have. Such a document could be inside one of the books of the fourteen volume set of the history of France, or any number of other innocuous looking tomes. What would you have us do? Enter in the dead of night and pull every book from their shelves? They'd have every excuse to shoot us dead there and then. If I'd thought about it a bit more, before Marie introduced us to all the suspects over dinner, then I'd have tried to go under cover by getting a menial job in a suspect's household.'

'Yes, Papa, but which household?'

'That's the problem, isn't it? But I think we are narrowing it down now. I'd like to have been able to listen in to whatever Bellegarde and Épernon were talking about. If we get the opportunity of forcing them into a private discussion within the Louvre, and if we could identify where they go to converse, then we could listen in from the fireplace in the room above.'

'How could we force them into having such a conversation, Papa?'

'I don't know yet. It would be so much easier for them to have a private conversation while out hunting. They could just separate themselves from the main group, and plot to their heart's content.'

'Your idea about going undercover, Papa. What if we sent a message to bring Antonio to Paris? They don't know him, so he could get a job in one of their households.'

'No, I feel awful enough about the risk I'm exposing you to. Besides, it would be at least a month by the time he got here, and how do we know we have that much time? I think the best thing we can do is put some pressure on Épernon now.'

'When are you going to question him, Papa?'

'Well, not tomorrow. I've got my first induction lesson with Pierre, and we need to keep working on Louis's speech. It won't do any harm to let him stew for a few days.'

Anthony knocked on the front door of number sixteen Rue St. Honore with a tingle of excitement. Madame Dufour answered it. She smiled.

'Welcome, Sir Anthony. I understand you are to induce me into a trance today.'

'I hope you don't mind. It interests me intensely. When I was here last, I drew a portrait of my wife without knowing it. It was quite astonishing.'

'I don't mind at all. I find it rather relaxing, and Pierre has helped me with some troublesome aches and pains. Do come in, we will go up directly.' Anthony closed the door behind him and followed Madame Dufour up the stairs to Pierre's apartment. She knocked on the door, and Pierre opened it. 'Your pupil is here, Pierre.'

'Welcome Sir Anthony, do come in. I think for what I have in mind today, could you lie down on the chaise longue on your back please, Sophia? But first, for the purpose of the lesson, would you mind touching your toes?' Madame Dufour touched her toes, as if the request were perfectly normal. 'There, that's good. Make yourself comfortable on the chaise longue. Now, Sir Anthony, I will induce Sophia into the trance. Since she has been induced many times before, the fact that I shall talk through what I am doing will not affect the process. Do you have any questions?'

'No, but please just call me Anthony. I feel we are friends already.'

'Well then, Anthony, I shall take a chair by Sophia's head. You take the chair opposite me. Good, now I will ask her to focus on the mirror as I move it from side to side.'

You may not know this, but when we are in a dream state, our eyes move rapidly.' Pierre talked softly and steadily to Sophia Dufour. The first thirty seconds or so Anthony remembered from his last visit. He remembered having climbed down to the fifth step, but he did not remember what came next. As Pierre asked Sophia to open the door and enter the happiest place she could be, Anthony recollected standing in the courtyard of his villa in Frascati, with Francesca at his side. 'Now Sophia, your back is like the trunk of an oak tree. You are strong and completely rigid, like a guardsman on parade, only much stronger.' Anthony saw Sophia stiffen. 'Now, Anthony, for the purpose of this demonstration, I have placed the chaise longue at just the right distance from the table.' Pierre stood up and placed a cushion on the table. 'Now, Anthony, would you help me lift Sophia, please? I want to rest her so that her head lies comfortably on the cushion, and her ankles are supported by the back of the chaise longue.'

'Is that wise?' Anthony asked.

'I have done it many times before. I'll lift her at the hips, if you would take her by her shoulders. Right, lift!' They placed her so that her head was on the cushion and her ankles were on the back of the chaise longue. 'You can let go of her now,' Pierre said, and they both moved away. Sophia was spanning the four-foot gap like a plank of wood.

'That's incredible, I would not have thought it possible,' Anthony exclaimed. 'I don't think I could do that.'

'That's not it,' Pierre said, placing a chair by her waist. 'Use this chair to climb and sit on her stomach.'

'Oh no, I really can't. I'll break her back.'

'Trust me, Anthony.'

'Well, if you're sure...' Anthony said, doing as instructed.

'There now, I shall take the chair away for a few seconds. As you can see, you are sitting supported only by the tree trunk that is the trance-induced Madame Dufour. You can get down now,' Pierre said, replacing the chair. Anthony quickly climbed down from Madame Dufour and turned around to check that she was still breathing. 'Shall we put her back on the chaise? You take her shoulders again,' they lifted her, and placed her gently back on the chaise longue. 'I will now bring her back out of the trance. Follow everything I say carefully.' Anthony watched and listened as Pierre had Sophia climb back up the stairs, counting down to one and then telling her to wake up. 'How do you feel, Sophia?'

'Very relaxed, as normal, Pierre,' she replied. 'Shall I make some of your tea now?'

'Yes please, Sophia. We shall continue with Anthony as the inducer afterwards,' Pierre replied as Sophia left the room. 'When I talked last time about somnambulists, they actually walk quite stiffly in their sleep. It is curious, but the larger muscles can be made extremely rigid in the trance state, as you have just seen.'

'It's a very impressive magic trick, but I'm struggling to find a use for it,' Anthony replied. 'Can you make people do things that they don't want to do, using these techniques?'

'In my experience, and that of the Indian masters that taught me, no, you can't. You can help someone overcome inhibitions, so that they can do things that they do want to do. You don't want to feel pain, and I have helped you block out the pain in your leg. Or, I may actually have helped your body physically to repair the problem that you have with your leg; we simply don't know. But as you have seen, the meditative trance has powerful physical and mental effects. I'm sure that one day it will be an important medical technique. It is my opinion that many of the anxieties and problems that we have stem from our childhood. I know that mine do, and I have found meditation to be very therapeutic. I suggest that after tea, you induce Sophia into a trance and ask her about her childhood. I haven't tried that with her yet.'

'What sort of things should I ask her?'

'When she opens the door, tell her that she is three years old and she is at home. Don't say that it is a happy place. Ask her what her mother is doing, and so on. If she becomes distressed, I will take over.'

'Well, if you're sure,' Anthony said.

After tea, Sophia sat in the armchair and Anthony stood over her with the mirror in the palm of his right hand. He began moving the mirror and asking her to keep watching it. He told her she was at the top of a flight of ten steps and started talking her down, a step at a time.

'That's very good, Anthony,' Pierre whispered, 'try to keep your voice in a monotone. This is the only time I can think of when it is an advantage to speak in a monotonous voice.'

Anthony asked her to open the door and told her she was three years old and in her childhood home. He asked her a series of questions, each one leading on from the answer to the previous one. Sometimes Pierre whispered a suggestion in his ear, but in the main, his instinct suggested where to explore next. He discovered that she had three elder sisters. Her father was a lawyer. The family was quite wealthy and owned this house on Rue St. Honore. Her father and mother argued a lot, and sometimes he beat her mother. Her elder sisters had married and moved away, but she had never married, she hadn't wanted to. After Anthony brought her out of the trance, Sophia said she felt refreshed and relaxed. She cleared up the tea things and carried them away to the kitchen.

'That was interesting,' Pierre mused. 'I wonder if the violence started only after Sophia had been born. Perhaps the elder sisters were able to rationalise the violence more, whereas Sophia couldn't, and perhaps that's why she didn't want to marry.'

'I would love to know what my children's childhood was like,' Anthony said.

'Don't you know?'

'No, I'm ashamed to say. Maria and her twin, Antonio,

were conceived just before I had to flee Florence. Then there was one thing after another, and they were almost sixteen before I got back to Florence and discovered that I was a father. I think it would help me if I had a better idea of what their childhood was like. Would you help if I sent Maria round?'

'Yes, of course, but wouldn't you want to be here too?'

'Perhaps, if we can both get away from our duties at the palace, would tomorrow be convenient?'

'I'm busy in the afternoon, but how about the morning?'

'The morning it is then.'

Anthony was almost back at the Louvre Palace when he saw Jean Louis de Nogaret, duc d'Épernon leaving the palace. Anthony followed him. He kept fifty yards behind. Épernon turned left off Rue St. Honore onto Rue de la Ferronnerie. At the next junction, he turned left onto Rue St. Denis. About a hundred yards along, he stopped and let himself into a house on the left with a key. Anthony walked past, glancing at the door. There was a brass plaque which read *Charlotte du Tillet*. He continued down the street before completing a loop back onto Rue St. Honore and returning to the palace.

CHAPTER NINE

Maria was wandering around the great hall amongst the artists and sculptors. She stopped behind an artist who was painting a young woman model, dressed in a simple, blue-cotton dress. The artist had outlined the dress, and was focussing on the model's face. Maria heard a familiar footfall beside her.

'Oh hello, Papa. How did you get on with Pierre?'

'It is astonishing, but let's not speak here. Shall we take a stroll in the gardens as it's such a pleasant afternoon?' Maria nodded, and they left the hall through the French windows that led to the gardens. The gardens were laid out in rows of rectangular flower beds with gravel pathways between them. There were some gardeners at work and a few courtiers strolling. When they were out of earshot of anyone, Anthony spoke.

'This induction into a trance is quite the most exciting thing I have learnt since I picked my first lock. Pierre put Madame Dufour, who is Pierre's landlady, into a trance and told her she was as stiff as a tree trunk. We then balanced her between the chaise longue and the table and I sat on her stomach. It was incredible. Not even you, with your physique, could do that, and she's a middle-aged woman.'

'Are you sure it wasn't some kind of trick, Papa? Perhaps she had a board down the back of her dress.'

'It wasn't a trick. Pierre asked her to touch her toes. This induction is powerful magic.'

'And have you learnt how to do it too?'

'Yes. I have more lessons to complete, but I was able to induce her into a trance.'

'Did you make her as stiff as a board, Papa?'

'No, I got her to… I did some more intellectual experiments with her.'

'I should like to learn this induction myself, Papa. Will you teach me?'

'I think it would be better if you learnt from Pierre. He's free tomorrow morning,' Maria paused for a while, before replying.

'Louis is making such good progress. With the king due back on Monday, I want him to be impressed by the poetic speech we are working on. Would you be able to take over working with him just tomorrow morning? This trance thing sounds so intriguing.'

'Of course. Oh, in the excitement, I almost forgot. As I was walking back to the palace, I saw Épernon, and followed him. He went to a townhouse on the Rue St. Denis, about a hundred yards from the junction with the Rue de la Ferronnerie. The house belongs to a Charlotte du Tillet. Perhaps she is his mistress. I'd like to find out more about her.'

'Perhaps the queen will know something, Papa, or I could speak with Jeanne. We're getting along very well.'

'I'm not sure. The queen seems so close to the duke, I'm not sure she'll be happy with us considering him as a potential suspect. I'm also not sure that we should raise suspicions with Jeanne. You might pass by there after your lesson with Pierre, and observe the house for a while, from the street corner.'

'And have people think I'm a streetwalker? No, why

don't I pick the lock and look around inside at night?'

'No, that's far too dangerous. Just pass by then, look lost for a few minutes. If you see nothing, so be it, but if anyone comes or goes, follow them at a discrete distance. I'll do the same when you take over with Louis again.'

'Very well, Papa. Will you teach me to paint?'

Maria joined Louis in the palace library for their speech class. Louis had suggested the library, since it enjoyed magnificent views of the gardens. He liked to monitor who was strolling with whom. It was also quiet in the library, and they were unlikely to be disturbed. They sat down opposite each other at a long table. Louis took the side which was nearest the window overlooking the gardens. Maria faced Louis and the bookshelves.

'My father taught me about poetry and metre,' Maria began. 'Metre is the rhythm of a poem, like the beat in music. Iambic is one of the most popular metres, because it mimics the heart beat. De dum, de dum, de dum, with the stress falling on the dum. Have you heard of iambic pentameter?'

'Yes, I've heard of it, but I haven't studied it.'

'It's a line of five iambs. De dum de dum de dum de dum de dum. Ten syllables in total. By the time you've got to the tenth syllable, you pause for a second, gather your thoughts, then dive into the next line. A line of poetry is very similar to a line in a song, so we hope that keeping to a rhythm in speech will help you, like singing a song, but without changing pitch.'

'Don't p…poems rhyme?' Louis asked.

'Yes, often they do, but they don't have to. Since you can sing without stammering, we want to use the element of singing that helps you, without making it obvious that you are singing or reciting a poem. We hope that metre, the rhythm, is the key to that, rather than rhyme, pitch or harmony. Why don't you try writing a short speech, using iambic pentameter?'

'I will,' Louis said. After getting up, he went to a desk at the end of the library and opened a drawer. Louis took out a penknife and some quills, and sharpened one. He also took out an ink pot and some paper. 'I think I'll work here, rather than risk spilling the ink.' He sat down and bit on the feather of the quill before writing. Maria got up and walked towards him, examining the books on the shelves as she passed. There were many history books. There was a cabinet of wide, flat drawers. She opened one. It was full of maps. She leafed through the maps, her mind wandering as she sailed Maia from coast to coast. 'I've finished,' Louis said. Maria shut the map drawer and went over to him. She nodded in approval at his work.

'Excellent. Would you like to recite it to me?' Maria asked. Louis nodded and began.

'I am a son of such a great French king
So good, so wise, so strong, in word and deed
When I grow up I want to be like him
And serve my good country like Father has
And bridges build to span each dark abyss
And so unite our fine and pleasant realm
I wish to honour him, our greatest king
But fear my frail and youthful words can't tell
Our people that which I would wish they knew
Too great, too good, too fair, is he our king
For me to paint in speech so cut about
And yet, with Mother's wise and good counsel
I may yet build upon our king's bedrock
I trust you hear me clear, and so farewell.'

Maria was silent for a moment, a tear welling in her eye, which she wiped with her sleeve.

'Your Highness, you should have no fear. You will be a great king too, I'm certain of it now. Your speech flowed beautifully, and it came from your heart, a pure heart. It took you only a few minutes to write. Just think, with practice, how your thoughts will flow.'

'It is so true, for you have shown the way. I owe you much, and hope I can repay. Perhaps one day, when I am king, I may reward you for your fine, inspired aid. Until then, we must work to better build this bridge to finer, fluid, rhetoric.' Louis took a breath, and grinned.

'I think you might be ready to show your new ability to the king, Your Highness. Do you?'

'I do, Maria.'

'Good. I think that's enough for this morning, Your Highness. With your permission, I have an appointment I would like to keep.'

'How intriguing. Who with?'

'Pierre-Olivier Malherbe, Your Highness.'

'Pierre? Whatever for?'

'I, er, my father has bought a boat and taught me to sail. I want to hear all about his voyages.'

'Very well, Maria. We shall continue tomorrow.'

Maria was working on the morning's speech therapy with Louis when there was a knock on the door.

'C...come in!' Louis called out. The door opened and a man Maria judged to be in his late twenties strode in. He was tall and slim, but broad shouldered. He had wavy brown hair that reached down to his shoulders, and a neatly trimmed beard and moustache. He stood and stared at Maria, his eyes beaming and a broad grin spreading across his face.

'I beg your pardon, Your Highness. I didn't know you had a lady friend.'

'C...charles, this is Maria. She's helping me with my stammer. Maria, this is Charles d'Albert, my dearest friend and hunting companion. He's quite the finest falconer in the kingdom.' Charles approached Maria, bowed and held out his his hand, all the time gazing into her eyes. Maria looked quizzically at him. 'He is offering to k…kiss your hand, Maria.'

'Oh, my apologies,' Maria said, holding out her hand, which Charles brushed with his lips.

'Enchanté,' Charles replied, as he stood upright. 'Maria, rather than Marie. Are you Spanish perhaps?'

'No, sir, Italian, although my father is English. I was born in Florence.'

'I see, so I suppose you're a friend of the Concini's then?'

'No, sir. I had not heard of them until my father and I arrived in Paris a few days ago.'

'You should try to hide your distaste for Leonora and Concino, Charles. Mother wouldn't like it.'

'I'm sorry, Your Highness, it sickens me the way they charm riches from the royal purse. I hear Concino is trying to purchase the marquisate of Ancre now. Besides, you know the king was going to have them banished, until the queen intervened. I apologise, Maria, you must find this dull. Your progress with Prince Louis's speech is remarkable. Where did you learn to treat speech defects?'

'From my father, as with many things, sir.'

'Well, I shall have to look in on Prince Louis more often. Would you like some hunting this afternoon, Your Highness?'

'Yes, Charles, now you had better let us get on.' Louis smiled, as Charles bowed, and kissed Maria's hand again, turned, left, and closed the door behind him. 'He's rather handsome, don't you think, Maria?'

'He is certainly that, Your Highness. How does he fit into court?'

'His father, Honoré, is a friend of my father. They fought together. You should be careful. He is quite a rogue with the ladies.'

Maria slept fitfully that night. She was both flattered by the attention that Charles had shown her and scared by it. The skill of the artists she had watched at work dazzled her. The ability to capture a scene, a glance, a feeling, and hold them on canvas, in perpetuity, was a gift. And then she thought about her appointment with Pierre. She hadn't seen Papa so enthusiastic about anything before. She'd seen his love, his annoyance, anger even. He'd been pleased with the boat, but sailing wasn't new to him, not in the way it was for her. This was something that excited him. Would it excite her too? The dawn light shone through the window. She would find out soon enough.

Maria arrived at Madame Dufour's house and was taken upstairs to Pierre's apartment. Pierre welcomed her, and she noticed the way he smoothed his hair and brushed the flecks of dandruff from his shoulder. He found her attractive. If he were ten years younger, and if she didn't already have her own boat, well, her father's boat, but it was much the same thing, then she might be interested in him too. Pierre took a pile of books from the seat of an armchair and placed them on the table.

'Tell me, Pierre, you don't mind if I call you Pierre, do you? Where in the world are the greatest treasures to be found?'

'Not at all, if I may call you Maria?' Maria nodded assent. 'Unquestionably China, closely followed by India and the Malay peninsula. The ancient wisdom will keep me occupied with my writing for years to come. I collected a great many books.'

'Well, I was thinking more of gold. Where did you find the most gold?'

'We did not find any gold. We returned with several tonnes of tea.'

'What's tea?' Maria asked.

'Dried leaves of the camellia sinensis plant. Do sit

down. Shall we start?'

'Yes, who am I going to put in a trance?' Maria asked.

'You should first experience the process yourself before we work on teaching you how to do it. Now relax completely. It is perfectly harmless. Watch this mirror as it moves left, then right, left, then right.'

'Are you going to sit on my stomach?'

'No, not today. Keep watching the mirror.'

'Does it have to be a mirror?'

'No, any object will do, but it works best if there is a reflection. Now relax, and keep watching the mirror.' Eventually, Pierre succeeded in inducting Maria in a trance. 'You are four-years old. What are you doing?'

'I'm playing with Antonio. We're pretending to be soldiers.'

'Where is your mother?'

'She is in the kitchen making lunch. Grandma is with her.'

'Is your grandfather with you too?'

'No, he died when mother was six. She talks about him often. He used to make her wooden dolls with articulated joints. Mother said she made clothes for the dolls and dressed them. She's very sad that he died. He was very kind to her.'

'You're older now. You're ten. What are you doing?'

'Antonio and I are on one of our long walks. When we've finished our chores, we like to go far away from our neighbourhood, where nobody knows us, nobody spits at us or calls us bastards. Mother keeps saying our father will come back one day, but he never does.'

'Does your mother still talk about her father?'

'Yes.'

'Now you're a little older, you're thirteen. What is happening now?'

'I'm working in the wash-house.' Pierre gazed out of the window as Maria described the wash-house and those who worked there. 'I make a little money, which helps mother.

She wants Antonio and I to attend school once a week, if we can afford it. I want to learn, but, no, get off me, no. I don't want...' Maria writhed in the chair and lashed out with her arms, forcing Pierre to move away. He paused before continuing.

'Maria, you're older now, you're fifteen. What is happening now?'

'Father came back, but then he had to leave again. He said he will return and bring a great treasure. Mother says we will have a brother or sister soon, poor bastard.'

'Now you're older, and your father has returned. What is happening?'

'He's teaching us many things. We're learning to wrestle. I wish we'd been able to do this before. Nobody would have assaulted me or spat at me then. He's teaching us languages too. They're less useful than wrestling, but he says they're important.'

'Does your mother still talk about her father?'

'No, she doesn't, not now.'

'I'm going to count now, from one back to ten.' Pierre brought Maria out of her trance state. 'How do you feel?'

'Relaxed. What happened?'

'Nothing much. We just talked about your childhood. Don't you remember?'

'No, not a thing. What happens next? When do I learn how to do it?'

'Next time. I'll work out a schedule and as you have duties, I'll alternate between you and your father's lessons. I look forward to seeing you next time,' he said as Maria left. She looked at the sundial on the building opposite and was astonished to see that she'd been there for over an hour. She set off to find the house on Rue St. Denis. It didn't take her long to find it, and she strolled past it. There was a patisserie near the corner, so she lingered there admiring the pastries, and glancing at the Tillet house. After a few minutes, a man in his early thirties, wearing good but shabby clothing, brushed past her. He turned and apologised to her. He had long greasy hair, which looked like it hadn't seen a comb in months. He carried on walking down the street, talking to himself as he went. To Maria's surprise, he stopped at the Tillet house and knocked at the door. An attractive woman, also probably about thirty, opened the door and invited him inside.

'Can I interest you in any pastries, mademoiselle?' the patissier enquired.

'Er, no, I was only looking,' Maria said, and set off back to the palace.

CHAPTER TEN

Anthony and Maria were both working with Louis on Monday morning when Marcel arrived.

'Your father would like to see you, Your Highness.'

'I'm sure he will be impressed, Louis. If you're not sure, start a sentence with "I am" and let it flow from there,' Maria said.

'You should both wait here. I'm sure we won't be very long. His Majesty has a lot to attend to,' Marcel said, as Louis got up, and they left the room. Maria paced back and forth, and Anthony gazed out of the window.

'This is ridiculous. I feel nauseous on Louis's behalf. If he's half as nervous as I am, he'll forget his poem, and the king will think we've been a complete waste of time.'

'Calm down, Maria. I'm sure he'll be fine. You've been fantastic with him. He's been over that poem dozens of times, and hasn't stammered at all.'

'Yes, but we're not the king.'

'True, but he's his father first and foremost.'

'That's what worries me.'

After what seemed like an hour, but was only twenty minutes by the clock on the wall, Marcel returned.

'His Majesty would like to see you both now. Please follow me.'

'How did Louis get on?' Maria asked.

'I cannot say as I was not present.'

The king's study was about the size of the small dining room. Behind his desk was a window looking out over Notre Dame. There were paintings of battle scenes adorning the walls. Marcel closed the door as he left, leaving them standing just inside the doorway. In the centre of the room, two men were standing at a table, examining a drawing of a bridge. There were several other drawings and documents strewn across the table. Both men were dressed in black, but the man on the right wore a white ruff whilst the man on the left had a simple white linen collar.

'Yes, I approve it. Have the masons make a start at once,' the man with the ruff said. 'Ah, you must be Sir Anthony, and you are Maria, I assume. Please come and take a seat. This is Sully, my right-hand man. Maximilien de Béthune, duc de Sully to give him his full title. He's been at my side since he was eleven, and a more capable organiser you will not find.' Sully pulled two chairs out from the table and indicated that they should sit. The king paced back and forth. 'Please sit, don't mind me. I've had my arse in the saddle most of the morning, so would rather stand. Sit down, Sully, it might make them feel more comfortable. There, that's better,' he said, as Anthony and Maria sat down, and Sully did, too. 'You knew Marie when she was a child, I understand. She thinks very highly of you. Well, so do I. I think we can give that surgeon his marching orders now. Cut half the boy's tongue out, indeed. I never thought that would work, but you have both worked wonders.'

'Thank you, Your Majesty,' Maria said.

'Yes, thank you, Your Majesty,' Anthony added.

'I also understand from my ambassador to Tunisia that you are both formidable fighters. The pair of you saw off a couple of pirate galleys, did you not?'

'We could not have done it without François and Anne,

Your Majesty. They loaded our rifles so that we could keep up a rapid rate of fire. François crawled across the deck, bringing them to us under heavy fire. As they finally caught us and boarded, Anne shot the pirate leader, who would certainly have slain me, since my sword was stuck in one of his men.'

'Really?' King Henry exclaimed, raising his right eyebrow. 'I had him down as a pen pusher. Damn smart one, of course. They can't have been very good shots though, these pirates, if you managed to pick most of them off before they could board you.'

'We had the advantage of rifles, whereas they had only muskets, Your Majesty.'

'Rifles eh, very accurate but too expensive for all but a few sharpshooters.'

'And half as accurate again with the projectiles we were using. I bought my rifles from a gunsmith named Fanzoj, from Ferlach in Austria. He told me he had been experimenting with cylindrical projectiles pointed at one end, and had found them much more accurate than balls. He sold me some moulds, along with the rifles,' Anthony explained.

'I should like to see your rifles, and these projectiles,' King Henry said, then noticing that Maria seemed far away, and gazing at a letter on the table, he walked around the table and picked up the letter. 'Do you have them with you here?' he asked, walking over to his desk, opening a drawer, and putting the letter inside, then locking the drawer.

'Yes, Your Majesty.'

'Do I have any free time soon, Sully?'

'I can make you some time, Your Majesty.'

'Excellent! Let Sir Anthony and Maria know when, and we shall try out these rifles and the fancy projectiles in the garden. I'm a man of action, Sir Anthony, a sword in my hand and my arse in the saddle. That's my motto.'

'His Majesty belies his greatest virtues,' Sully added. 'He is the greatest of warriors, but he is the greatest of peacetime kings, too. A chicken in every pot, is his other motto.'

'Well, what good is winning a war if you lose the peace? Build bridges and roads, keep the people fed, and educate them. Now thank you both for what you have achieved so far with Louis. I shall look forward to seeing you and your rifles tomorrow, but in the meantime, I have some business to be getting on with.' Anthony and Maria rose, bowed, and left. Once they were out of earshot, Anthony turned to Maria.

'What was that letter you were staring at?'

'I don't know, it was in cipher. I'd love to have a go at deciphering it. Perhaps it's something to do with the attempts on his life.'

'How could it be? Nobody would write to him in cipher, about a plot to kill him, would they?'

'Perhaps not, but I'd still like to crack it. I'll wait until midnight, then pick the lock to his study, do the same with his desk drawer and take it.'

'Are you mad, Maria? He saw you looking at it, so if it goes missing, you're the first one he'll suspect.'

'I'll make a copy of it then.'

'No. You'd need a candle, and if the sentry sees a light, they'll investigate.'

'All right, I'll bring it back here to make the copy, and then replace the original.'

'It's still far too dangerous for something that probably doesn't have any relevance. You're in the king's good books, and you've befriended the future king. Don't blow it. Promise me you won't pick your way into the king's study.'

'I suppose you're right, I promise, Papa.'

Anthony arrived for his second lesson in the art of inducing the meditative trance. Sophia Dufour took him straight up to Pierre's apartment. Pierre invited him to sit down at the table. When Sophia went to make the tea,

Pierre sat down opposite Anthony. Anthony seized his opportunity to find out what Pierre had learnt of his twins' childhood.

'What did you learn from inducing Maria, Pierre?'

'She had a tough childhood, I'm afraid. She and her brother, Antonio, isn't it?' Anthony nodded. 'They were called bastards, and spat at. They went for endless walks to get away from their neighbourhood. That must have been hard for them. However, they had a very loving mother, and grandmother, but they sorely missed having a father, and the normality and respectability that brings,' Anthony's head dropped. 'Maria seems to have a powerful desire to amass a fortune. I suspect she wants to buy respectability, or at least have it as security. In our society, it's hard not to associate respectability with wealth.'

'Yes, I see that.'

'She was much happier when you returned. She was particularly happy to have learnt to wrestle from you, and languages, although wrestling seems to be the thing you taught her that she values the most. I assume, as with wealth, that they are defences against the bigotry she endured as a child.' Pierre paused for a few seconds.

'What is it, Pierre? Is there something else?'

'I think there was something much worse than bigotry. She was twelve, and working in a wash-house. She writhed and hit out, shouting no, and get off me. I think, I can't think of a gentle way to put this. I think someone raped her, Anthony.'

'God! No! Can you be sure?'

'Not completely, no. She was so distraught, I thought it best to move her on in time. I didn't know what else to do. I haven't come across this situation before, you see.' Anthony clenched and unclenched his fists. Then, with his right arm, he swept the books from the table in front of him. He stood up from his chair and walked to the window, peering down at the street below.

'I must go to Florence now. I'll find this wash-house and

whoever was responsible, and I'll kill him.'

'No, Anthony, that's not the answer. The impression I got was that it was the son of the wash-house owner, a child himself. Let him bear the burden of his guilt for the rest of his days. That is my advice.'

'Guilt! You talk to me of guilt. If only I'd stayed with Francesca in Florence, I would have been there when she was born, when they were born. I would have taught them to wrestle as soon as they could walk, and this would never have happened.' Pierre watched Anthony's back convulse as his sobbing began. When Anthony took a deep breath and pulled a handkerchief from his pocket, and wiped his eyes, Pierre spoke again.

'If I had a sou for every "if only" I have heard, or uttered myself, I would build a fleet of ships. Anthony, we cannot change the past. There are plans for the future that we can make. We can build sound ships and equip them well. We can train our crews, but you know as well as I what respect fate has for our plans. All we really have is the present.'

'All right, the present. What do we do now, Pierre? How can we help her?'

'I have learnt to unlock the deepest dungeons of the mind; but how to slay the demons that lurk there? No, that is beyond any knowledge I know of. She has built a strong dungeon with sturdy locks. I think it's best that we leave that demon in chains there.'

'It would explain a lot. She hasn't shown any interest in marriage. Are you certain there isn't anything we can do to help her?'

'I don't know. Just keep loving her, as you do. Is your wife much younger than you, Anthony?'

'Yes, twenty years younger. How is that relevant?'

'Oh, it's just that your wife clearly idolised her father, who died when she was six. She spoke about him very often, apparently. She stopped talking about him when you reappeared. I think she was looking for a father figure. Ah, here is Sophia with the tea.' Pierre picked the books up from the floor and replaced them on the table. Anthony sat down. He took the cup of tea that Sophia handed to him, but spilt some as he raised the cup to his lips. He brought his left hand up to steady his right. Pierre cleared space for Sophia to sit. When they had all finished their tea, Pierre continued. 'Anthony, do you feel able to continue with your lesson?'

'Yes, yes, I must.'

'Very well, I have an idea that I think you will find interesting. I have seen it done, but haven't tried it myself yet, so I too am curious. Please select a book from the shelves, any book' Anthony stood up and surveyed the shelves. Then he picked up the chair and placed it near the far end of the shelves, climbed on the chair, and took down a large, leather-bound volume.

'Will this do?' he asked, handing it to Pierre.

'Oh yes, classical Malay. It's old Malay, heavily influenced by Arabic. Now I want you to handle the induction, with no interference from me. Open the book wherever you like and ask Sophia to study it for a minute or two. Put a bookmark on the page, close it, and then begin the induction, as I showed you before. Once Sophia is in the trance, ask her to go to the table. Ask her to sit down and take the quill. Then ask her to draw what she remembers of the page on a blank sheet of paper. Have you got all that?'

'Yes, I think so.'

'Are you ready, Sophia?' Sophia nodded. 'Then the floor is yours, Anthony.'

Anthony selected a page from the book, taking care to not use one of the pages to which the book seemed to fall open from frequent use. He asked Sophia to study it for a while, then he marked the page, and asked Sophia to settle comfortably into the armchair. He took the mirror in his right hand and began the induction.

'Look into the mirror, Maria, I mean Sophia. Let your eyes follow it as it moves. You are standing at the tenth step, no at the top step of a flight of ten steps…'

'I'm sorry, Sir Anthony, the mirror is shaking and your voice is rather anxious. I don't think this is going to work today.' Sophia said.

'Yes, Anthony, you have had rather a shock. I think we should leave this for another day.' Pierre added.

'Yes, you're right, of course. All I can think about is Maria, and what she must have suffered. I must go.'

'Let me know when you feel able to continue, and we'll carry on where we left off.' Pierre said as Anthony left, forgetting to close the door behind him.

It took a lot of brandy before Anthony fell asleep that night. The shattering of the jug of water awoke him. It had been on his bedside table. He looked around in the dim morning twilight, but there was nobody else in the room. His bedsheets were soaked with sweat. His nightmare drifted back to him. Maria had been following Épernon, but Épernon had spotted her. He'd turned into a dark alley and waited for her, his dagger drawn. He'd held the knife to her throat as he'd forced himself upon her. Then, when he was done, he'd slit her throat. She lay there, dead, with rats crawling over her.

'Are you alright, Papa? I heard a crashing sound.' Maria asked from the open connecting door. 'You look like you've seen a ghost.' She walked over and sat on the bed beside him, putting her arms around his shoulders. 'Have you wet yourself, Papa? The sheets are damp.'

'No, it was a nightmare. I've been thinking. Perhaps you should do the questioning of Épernon when we have time.'

'You think I'm not up to following him, don't you?'

'No, it's not that. You said you wanted to be involved in the interrogation, and I persuaded you to do the surveillance. Now I'm offering to let you do the interrogation. That's all.'

'You're lying, Papa. I can tell. You don't think I'm up to

the surveillance, that's what it is. You're worried that he'll spot me and try something. Well, heaven help him if he does. You don't trust me, do you?'

'I admit I am worried about you.' Anthony stood up and walked to the window. He wiped his eyes before turning back to face her again. 'When I was hunting down the priest killer with Hugh, I did most of the interrogation, but it was Hugh who knew when someone was lying. Cardinal Aldobrandini had the same sense of when I was lying. He said it was all the confessions he'd heard. You have that talent too, and I think we'll need it with Épernon. We'll discuss beforehand what questions to ask, and what direction to take it. You'll be better at homing in on his lies.'

'Well, I'm glad you agree about that, Papa. It's female intuition, you know. But aren't you worried about what he might try to do to me, if he sees I suspect something?'

'Of course I'm worried, intensely worried. But I'm more concerned about what he could do to you in a dark alleyway than in a house or palace. Besides, I'll be right outside, ready to take action if you don't reappear.'

'What about the disguise, though?'

'I'll ask Gaston to make me a suitable costume, and I already have a beard. The makeup will work just as well on my skin as yours.'

CHAPTER ELEVEN

There was a knock from her father's side of the connecting door, and Maria opened it. She recoiled as a hunched, dirty beggar in a stained brown coat with a hood concealing much of his face stood before her.

'What do you think, Maria? Hasn't Gaston done a good job with the costume?'

'He has, Papa. I didn't recognise you at all.' Maria sat in the chair by the window, and Anthony sat facing her. 'I've been trying to think how to approach the interrogation of Épernon. He's clearly a close friend of Bellegarde, and you certainly spooked him because he dashed straight round to see Épernon. Then there was the discussion that they had about the king's ambitions regarding Julie. I don't see a connection, though. How do I go about it, Papa?'

'First, identify an object you can throw, a paperweight for example. If he makes any kind of a physical threat against you, throw it through the window. I'll be through his front door in no time and join you. Promise me that.'

'I promise, Papa, but I'm more interested in the sort of questions I should ask.'

'I don't think you'll need to ask too many questions. He will attempt to take control. He'll be curious about why you're interviewing him rather than me. You could say that I'm busy, or you could say that you persuaded me to let you interview him. That would gain his interest. He may feel flattered. You could play on that. It's important to keep him talking, whatever it's about. You do as much listening as you can, and use that female intuition of yours to tell when he's lying. Then you can compose some more questions to probe that a little deeper.'

'My friend Cecile calls it body language, rather than female intuition. Women are better at it. It's all about recognising the physical expression of emotions, rather than the verbal ones. Babies can't speak, you see.'

'I see. That makes sense. Well, use that. I think the other thing is to use open questions.'

'What do you mean by open questions, Papa?'

'Well, a closed question would be one to which the answer is short, like yes, no, Thursday, or never, for example. There's a place for those to clarify something. But I've found that it's much better to ask questions that invite an explanation. Why and what are my favourite questioning words. You might start with, what do you think is behind the attempts on the king's life?'

'Yes, I get the idea.'

'Have a good look around the room as well. I think a man's possessions say a lot about him, his interests, what he values. I'm sure something will come to you, you're an intelligent girl. Then there's the question of his relationship with Charlotte du Tillet. See what you can find out about that, although it's best if he doesn't know that I followed him to her house, or that you saw that scruffy fellow enter.'

'Shall I tell him that Bellegarde let it slip?'

'That's an interesting idea. If he had let it slip, would he have warned Épernon of having done so? But since he didn't, because I forgot to ask, he won't have done. I don't know. Inserting some perceived deceit between Bellegarde and Épernon might be an interesting tactic. What are the alternatives? You could say that someone else told me about her, the queen perhaps. But since she hasn't, and as they're so close, I think not. Yes, why not? Insert some doubt in his mind about his pal Roger, and how far he can trust him. Tell him Bellegarde let it slip to me.'

'I have a feeling I'm going to enjoy this, papa.'

'Just be careful and throw something through the

window if he threatens you. We'll try to make an appointment for tomorrow afternoon. I believe the dauphin will be out hunting in the afternoon.'

Without glancing behind her, Maria knocked on the duc d'Épernon's front door. A liveried servant opened the door and led her up the grand staircase to a door on the first floor. He knocked, and when he heard the acknowledgement, he opened the door.

'Would you take off your shoes, mademoiselle, and leave them by the door? His Grace is most particular about his carpets.' Maria slipped off her shoes, as instructed, and cast her gaze around the room. Épernon sat writing at a large desk at the end of the room to her right. There were two empty chairs on this side of the desk. Light flooded the room from five large windows set in the wall opposite the door. The wall behind Épernon's desk was fitted with bookshelves. They were full of books, which appeared to be arranged by size. At the other end of the room, a tapestry depicting a grand chateau covered the wall. Portraits lined the wall behind her. She recognised King Henry and Marie, and assumed the others were family members. She heard the door close behind her and saw Épernon beckon her towards the desk. As she crossed the room, the exquisite carpets drew her eyes downward. There were three large carpets stretching the length of the room, with only two feet or so of floorboards at the margins of the room. The carpets were of the most vivid colours. One of them depicted a room, not unlike the palace she had seen in Tunis, in which seven men in turbans were sitting on cushions around a feast laid out on a carpet. The next carpet was decorated with animals the like of which she had only heard about. She thought the large one must be an elephant, and the stripped one a tiger. The carpet furthest from her was of a floral pattern, perfectly geometrically arranged. She approached Épernon's desk.

'Your Grace, I can see why you are particular about your carpets. They must be immensely valuable. I have never seen their like, not even in the Louvre.'

'Thank you, mademoiselle. They are valuable, but particularly valuable to me.'

'The large animal, is that an elephant? Like the ones that Hannibal used to cross the alps?'

'Similar, but Hannibal used African elephants. Do sit down.' Maria sat. 'I am surprised to see you. I had heard that your father has been interviewing people about the atrocious assassination attempts on His Majesty. Is he not well?'

'No, he is perfectly fit. Thank you, Your Grace. I persuaded him to let me interview you.'

'Why is that?'

'We had such a charming discussion at dinner a few days ago that I thought it would be amusing to continue it. Of course, I must ask the necessary questions first. What do you think is behind the attempts on the king's life?'

'Don't you mean who is behind it?'

'Of course, if Your Grace knows who is behind it, please tell. I imagined you would already have done so, if you did, which is why I thought we should discuss the motive before speculating on culprits.' She watched his face colour slightly.

'I assume that the culprits are deranged religious fanatics. That fellow Barrière, then a little later, Châtel. The others since haven't been caught, unfortunately, but I don't doubt that they are the same sort.'

'Why then, Your Grace, did you say, who is behind it?' She watched his eyes bore into hers.

'I simply meant whether they were Protestant extremists or Catholics. What their motivation was.' He paused, and when he saw her lips start to move, he jumped in. 'My guess is Protestant fanatics. His Majesty's conversion must seem like a brutal rejection to them, however good and just his reasons.'

'Perhaps, Your Grace, but I have heard that the Treaty of Nantes has not gone down well with the Catholics. Is that not so?'

'It disappointed some hardliners, that is true. But if it is in the interests of securing peace, then it is to be welcomed. His Majesty always acts in the best interests of the common people. Have you interrogated me enough yet? Shall I call for some wine, so that we can continue our discussion more convivially?'

'I'm sure that would be most pleasant, Your Grace.'

'Excellent! Please call me Jean Louis, Maria.' Épernon rang a bell on his desk and when the liveried servant opened the door, he instructed him to bring a decanter of wine and glasses. Moments later, the servant placed a silver tray with the decanter of red wine and cut crystal glasses on the desk. Épernon dismissed the servant, poured the wine and handed a glass to Maria. They both took a sip at the same time.

'This is an excellent wine, Jean Louis. We have a vineyard, ourselves, in Frascati. Is this from your chateau?'

'Thank you, Maria, but no. The Chateau du duc d'Épernon was somewhat run down when I became duc. I am having it completely rebuilt. In any case, the area is rather better known for its brie than its wine. This is a wine from near the town I was born in Caumont. The tapestry at the far end of the room is of my chateau. It looks rather less grand at the moment.'

'Is your wife overseeing the rebuilding?'

'My wife died seventeen years ago.'

'I'm sorry, I didn't know. Do you have children?'

'I have a son, Henri. He's nineteen. He's overseeing the works. I get down there as often as I can. It's an easy day's ride.'

'You said that the carpets are of particular value to you, Your Grace. Why is that?'

'My grandfather left them to me. We were very close. He enthralled me with the tales of his travels.'

'Where did he travel, Your Grace?'

'I am interested that you asked if I am married. Do have some more wine,' he said, while refilling both glasses. 'Shall we adjourn to the drawing room? It is more comfortable, and we can get better acquainted.'

'Might we be in any danger of being interrupted by Charlotte du Tillet, Your Grace?'

'Charlotte who?'

'Why, she is your mistress, is she not?'

'Whatever makes you think that?'

'The duc de Bellegarde suggested it to my father, Your Grace.'

'I am afraid that I have other appointments awaiting me. If you're looking for someone who wants the king out of the way, I suggest you investigate Concino Concini. His Majesty threatened to have him banished for the drain he has become on the royal purse. Marie fought tooth and nail to keep her companions with her. I cannot see the king's patience lasting much longer. Now, you must go. Good day, Maria.' Maria got up, bowed and left the room.

Maria paced the floor of the room in the tavern near the theatre. Eventually she heard footsteps coming up the stairs, but they were slow, deliberate steps. She grabbed a candlestick from the table and hid behind the door. She raised the candlestick as the door creaked open and was about to strike when she recognised Anthony.

'It's you, Papa.'

'Who did you think it was?'

'I don't know. It didn't sound like you. What happened?' Maria asked, putting down the candlestick. Anthony slumped into a chair.

'You talk, while I get my breath back.'

'Are you hurt, Papa?' Anthony shook his head and waved his hand in front of his mouth. 'Alright then, I think it went well. It came to an abrupt end when I told him that

Bellegarde had told us about Charlotte du Tillet. Until then, he'd been quite calm and interested in me. His wife died, and he has a son aged nineteen called Henri. He thinks Concino Concini could want the king dead. Apparently, the king has threatened to have him banished for the drain he's become on the royal purse. It reminded me of something Charles d'Albert said. He's a good friend of the dauphin. Concino is trying to buy a title. I can't say I took to him or his wife when we met Marie the first time.'

'Neither did I. Was there anything else?'

'Well, he was born in Caumont, and still gets his wine from there. Oh, and he has the most amazing carpets, better than anything I've seen in the Louvre. I was told to take my shoes off before walking on them. His grandfather gave them to him. I think he was very fond of him. Are you feeling better, Papa? What happened?'

'Yes, I'm getting my breath back now. I'm not as young as I was. After I saw you leave, and knowing that you would have implicated Bellegarde, I expected him to come out and walk the short distance to Bellegarde's house. Instead, his stable doors opened, and I was almost run over by the coach and horses that came flying out. I glimpsed him in the coach, and as it headed towards St. Honore, I assumed he was heading to Charlotte's house. I ran there as fast as I could, but my old injuries hampered me. When I got to the end of Rue St. Denis, I saw Charlotte and the scruffy fellow climb into the coach. Épernon climbed in after them and the coach drove off. I couldn't keep up with them, so I don't know where they went.'

'What do we do next then, Papa?'

'Well, two ideas come to mind. I think I'll let myself into Charlotte's house and see what I can find. They obviously cleared out in a hurry, and might have left something behind.'

'Good idea, Papa. I'll come with you.'

'No, it's too dangerous. I'll do it alone.'

'Nonsense. With two of us, one can keep watch, while

the other does the searching.'

'I don't like it, but you have a point.'

'Good. We'll go in tonight, Papa. What was the other idea?'

'Well, we should follow up on the Concinis. I don't like either of them one little bit. And if the king has threatened to expel them, then they have an obvious motive. The problem is that Marie is so protective of them that she certainly won't agree to let us interrogate them.'

'We could still follow them though, Papa.'

'Yes, we don't need an appointment to do that. You can follow her, and I'll follow him. But first the du Tillet house. I suggest we return to the palace and try to get a bit of sleep. We'll go to the house around midnight and observe. When it looks as if all is quiet in the house, and on the street, I'll pick the lock while you keep watch.'

'Can't I pick the lock, Papa?'

'I know you're good at it now, but not as good as I am. Your eyes and ears are younger than mine, and our safety depends on each of us doing what we're best at. I'm going to change out of this beggar costume, then let's get back to the palace. What did you say the name was, that fellow who told you about Concino buying a title?'

'Charles d'Albert. Why do you ask?'

'I've heard the name somewhere. Now, where was it? Oh yes, Marie told me about him. She said he was far too young to have been involved in most of the attempts. Now I think back, she told me about him teaching hunting and falconry to Louis. But there's something else I just can't remember…'

'It'll come to you when you're not trying to think of it, Papa.'

'Papa, that's it. When I interviewed Hercule, his ten-year-old daughter was listening at the door. She's a precocious one, and her name is Marie. She wants to marry this Charles d'Albert fellow. That's what it was. Anyway, let's try to get a little sleep before we search the du Tillet house.'

All was quiet on Rue St. Denis when they arrived at the du Tillet house. There was a half moon providing some light, and there appeared to be an oil lamp glowing in an attic room.

'You wait in the shadows here. I'll go around the back of the house and see if there's another way in, with more cover,' Anthony whispered.

'Yes, Papa,' Maria whispered back, as Anthony walked towards the end of the street and turned the corner. She pressed close against the wall, and held her breath as a wagon rattled past. By the time it was out of earshot, she saw her father walking towards her.

'Off the next street, there's an alley which leads to the back of the house. Let's go,' Anthony whispered.

'Alright, Papa. The oil lamp has just gone out.' He nodded, and they both made their way around to the back of the house. The garden gate wasn't locked. Anthony took a small bottle from his pocket and uncorked it. 'What's that?' She whispered.

'Oil,' he replied, and poured a little on the hinges of the gate. He waited a few minutes, then slowly opened the gate. They tiptoed to the back door. Maria kept watch as Anthony knelt at the back door and took out his lock picks. Maria heard the faint sound of the gates falling into place as Anthony worked the lock. He turned the handle, and the door opened. They tiptoed inside and closed the door behind them. Anthony stood still, listening. Maria did the same. They were in the kitchen. There was a glow from the range, but it was otherwise dark. Anthony felt his way around a table, over to the range. He ran his hands around the range, then poured a little oil on the hinges of the firebox. After a brief wait, he opened the firebox door. He took a candle from his pocket, blew softly on the glowing embers, and lit his candle. He took another candle from his pocket and lit that too, before handing it to Maria. Anthony felt in his pocket and took out two pieces of cloth. He wrapped one around the base of the candle he was holding and passed the other cloth to Maria. She followed his example. Anthony made his way to the door opposite the door they had entered from. He poured a little more oil on the hinges before opening it. Maria followed him into the hallway. There was the sound of snoring coming from upstairs. They tiptoed along the hallway. There were rooms on either side of the corridor, both doors were open. Anthony went into the room on their left, and Maria followed. There was a dining table in the centre, with eight chairs. Anthony opened the doors of a cabinet and looked inside. He carefully pulled open the drawers, then closed them again. Maria looked out of the front window. All still seemed quiet outside. Anthony pointed to the room across the corridor, and they both left the dining room. The second room was a sitting room with armchairs and a chaise longue. There was a writing desk with the drawers open. There were a few papers scattered on the floor. Anthony picked up some of the papers and examined them in the candlelight. Maria remained by the door, listening to the snoring. 'They obviously left in a hurry,' he whispered. Maria nodded. Anthony put the papers in his pocket.

'Shall we go up?' Maria whispered. Anthony nodded. Anthony led the way up the staircase. They both froze as a stair creaked. They listened as the snoring continued. There was no sound of movement from above. Anthony continued to the first floor landing, and Maria followed. The snoring sounded like it was coming from the third floor. There were three doors on the second floor. Anthony opened the first, and Maria followed him in, closing the door behind him. 'This must be the main bedroom,' she whispered. Anthony examined the dressing table, while Maria felt underneath the pillows and the mattress.

'Find anything?' Anthony asked.

'No.'

'Nor me. Let's try the next room.' The next bedroom was of a similar size to the main bedroom, but with three single beds and a cot. Anthony worked his way around the room, opening drawers and feeling under the pillows and mattresses. Maria stood guard at the door, listening and looking along the corridor. Anthony joined her and pointed to the third room. They made their way to it. Anthony opened the door and went in. Maria again stood guard at the door as Anthony worked his way around the room. It was a smaller room with a basic single bed and a chair. Anthony let out a slight gasp.

'What is it, Papa?' Maria whispered.

'Just the reflection of my candle. There's a small mirror in a stand on the chest of drawers. It startled me. I'll look in the drawers. You keep watch.' There was nothing in the drawers apart from some old clothes. Anthony looked under the mattress, under the pillow, and under the bed. 'Nothing here. Let's see what's on the third floor.' They made their way up the next flight of stairs, the snoring getting louder with each step. There appeared to be three bedrooms again. The snoring was coming from the first. They tiptoed past it. Anthony put his ear to the door of the second room before opening it. He peered inside, then shut the door again. 'I could hear breathing. Someone's asleep in there.' He led the way to the third door. He opened it and peered inside before entering. Maria stayed by the door, listening for any sound. 'Just an attic storage room. I've taken a few papers we can examine later. Let's go while our luck holds,' He whispered, leading the way back to the staircase.

They made their way back down both staircases to the kitchen. Anthony closed the firebox door of the range, then blew out his candle before leaving by the backdoor. Maria followed suit, and Anthony locked the door. They closed the garden gate behind them and made their way back to the Louvre.

'We can look through the papers I took in the morning. You did well, Maria.'

'Thank you, Papa. It was rather exciting. I almost screamed when you startled yourself with your own candle.'

'I'm glad you didn't. Now let's try to get some sleep. You have more work to do with Louis in the morning, and I've got my next lesson with Pierre.'

CHAPTER TWELVE

When Anthony arrived at Pierre's lodgings, Sophia let him in and took him up to Pierre's room.

'Do you feel able to proceed, Anthony?'

'Yes, Pierre. It was such a shock, hearing about Maria being raped, but I think I can control myself now.'

'Then, please choose another page from the book, and we shall continue.' Anthony selected a new page from the Malay book, and Sophia studied it for a few seconds. Then she settled down in the armchair. Anthony took up the mirror and began the induction. Every few minutes, he glanced at Pierre, who nodded approvingly. Once Sophia had stepped through the door into her happy, comfortable place, he asked her to stand up and walk to the table. He asked her to sit down, and he placed a sheet of paper, the quills, and the inkpot in front of her. He asked her to draw what she remembered from the page of the book. She took a quill and dipped it in the ink, then began to draw. When she reached the bottom of the page, she put the quill back in the jar and placed her hands flat on the table. Anthony asked her to return to the armchair and began the count, back up the stairs. When Sophia awoke from the trance, she looked around.

'Would anyone like more tea?' she asked. Pierre nodded, and Sophia went downstairs to the kitchen.

'Let's have a look,' Pierre said.

'I couldn't tell how accurately she was reproducing it. I recognise the Arabic influence, but to be honest, it could all have been simple doodling to me,' Anthony commented.

'Right, this is the page. Let's compare.' They both scanned Sophia's drawing and referred back to the book. It took them ten minutes to be satisfied, whereas Sophia had taken perhaps two minutes to study the page, and only a little longer to reproduce it, from memory. 'There are places where the hand is different, but the symbols are the same. How can that be?'

'I don't know. I surmise that everything we see, hear, smell, and taste is locked away inside our brain. Our conscious mind is preoccupied with the present and the future, but when we allow it, our subconscious can tap into old memories, or recent ones, in considerable detail. That, I think, is the great thrill of meditation, unlocking the unknown power of the subconscious mind. Anyway, you did well, Anthony. I don't think there is much more that I can teach you about meditation and induction.'

'Thank you, I am most grateful, Pierre. If there is anything I can do for you, you must ask.'

'You seem far away, Anthony. Are you all right?'

'Oh yes. I am quite all right. It's just that I think I can see an immediate use for this. I must get back to the palace at once.' He put on his coat and shook Pierre's hand.

'But what about your tea?'

'Oh, yes, would you give Sophia my sincere apologies? I really have to get back.' Anthony rushed out and flew down the stairs, two at a time. When he reached the ground floor, Sophia was emerging from the kitchen, carrying a tray. 'My apologies, Sophia, I have to leave. Something important has cropped up.'

◇ ◇ ◇

'It's me,' Anthony said, as he knocked on Maria's door. Maria opened the door, and Anthony stepped inside.

'You're looking pleased with yourself, Papa. What is it?' Anthony stood for a few moments, staring into Maria's eyes, searching for her pain. But he couldn't find it. He would have to think about how to deal with her trauma later. 'Papa, what is it?'

'Pierre showed something to me that can be done with induction into a trance. I selected a book at random from his shelves, and we got Sophia to examine it for a few minutes. It was in classical Malay. After that, we closed the book. I put her in a trance, and then asked her to draw out the page she had examined. She drew it perfectly, even though she couldn't read Malay. Don't you see? I could put you in a trance and ask you to sketch out what you saw in the king's letter. You studied it for at least as long as Sophia did.'

'Well I could give it a try,' Maria said, 'but I really don't think I memorised any of it.'

'Right, make yourself comfortable in the armchair. Is there a small mirror anywhere?' Anthony said, looking around. 'I know,' he said, opening his purse and taking out a gold ducat coin. 'Your eyes will follow this, that's for sure,' he smiled. Anthony put Maria into a trance and then got her to sit by the table. He gave her a sheet of paper, a quill, and an inkpot. Then he asked her to reproduce the king's letter. Her quill skimmed across the paper. Occasionally she dipped the pen in the ink, then carried on. When she had finished, she put the quill down. Anthony asked her to return to the armchair, then he brought her out of the trance. As she opened her eyes, he smiled at her. 'I think it's worked. You have written what looks like a cipher. Come and see.' Maria followed him to the table, and they both sat down. Maria started running her eyes back and forth across the text.

```
O Y S V    A M D I U T O    E    M A    X B I M U I J
T Y    V I X Y V T    T F M T    Q I    F M R T
U I K S V I J    T F I    U S X X Y V T    Y H
M B B    I B I K T Y V U    T F M T    O Y S V
A M D I U T O V I X B M K I    V S J Y B H
M U    F Y B O    V Y A M Z    I A X I V Y V
```

'Shall we assume the base language is French, Papa?'

'It's written to a French king, so that would be a reasonable starting point,' Anthony replied, as he too ran his eyes over the cipher. 'Of course it could be Latin, Italian, German, Spanish, English or even Greek. But we have to start somewhere.'

'I have counted sixteen Is, eleven Ms and eleven As, Papa,' she said, taking a piece of paper and dipping the quill in the ink, 'so let's assume that the cipher I is really E, that works for most languages. I'll base the key on that.' She began writing.

```
A B C D E F G H I J K L M N O P Q R S T U V W X Y Z
E F G H I J K L M N O P Q R S T U V W X Y Z A B C D
```

'Right, so let's see what the message is,' Maria murmured, as she used the key to decipher the message.

KUOR WIZEQPK 'No, that's obviously not right, but I is so far ahead, it should be E. In Latin the most common letter is I, Let's try that. Oh, no that's stupid of me if I is I then that's no cipher at all. What if I is A? Let's try that.' She wrote out a new key

```
A B C D E F G H I J K L M N O P Q R S T U V W X Y Z
S T U V W X Y Z A B C D E F G H I J K L M N O P Q R
```

'I must have it this time, surely.' WGAD IULQCBW 'No, nothing again. Have you got any ideas, Papa?' Maria asked, throwing the quill down on the table.

'No, I would have done exactly the same as you. It has me stumped too,' Anthony said, running his fingers through his beard.

'It must be that I didn't remember the letter at all. Aargh! This is so annoying, stupid trance induction, it's all mumbo-jumbo. I should pick the lock and check. It'll only take me a minute to see if I have got it correct.'

'No, absolutely not. We've discussed this, and anyway, I

saw you write this out, and you did it without hesitation, just as Sophia did with the Malay. I'm sure you have transcribed the message correctly. We're just missing something. Why don't you work on Louis's next lesson, and let me work on this. After all, I've had more practice.'

'All right, Papa. Oh, I've just remembered something from when I went to see Pierre. The meeting with the king and this confounded cipher put it out of my mind. After I left Pierre's, I went to see the Tillet house. While I was there, a very shabby-looking man of about thirty went by, talking to himself as he went. He went up to the Tillet house, knocked on the door, and a very attractive woman, also about thirty, opened the door and let him in. What do you think of that?'

'I don't know. If she's the duke's mistress, I'm surprised she'd let another young man into the house, particularly a shabby, insane one. We need to find out more about both the duke and her.'

Anthony was wandering around amongst the artists and sculptors in the great hall, running the cipher through his mind, when he heard footsteps behind him. He turned and saw Marcel.

'Sir Anthony, I have been looking for you everywhere. The king has an hour free this afternoon, and would like you to show him your rifles. Does that make sense?'

'Yes it does, Marcel. Where and when would he like to meet?'

'At two o'clock, in the garden. The gardeners are stacking some straw bales and erecting targets.'

'Thank you, Marcel. I will be there.'

Marcel turned and left, and Anthony made his way to his room. When he got there, he found Maria sitting at the table with the cipher.

'Papa, I've tried almost every letter in the alphabet, and this just doesn't work for any language. It's driving me insane.'

'We will crack it in the end. It's only a matter of time. Meanwhile, I have an appointment with the king this afternoon to show him our rifles. Why don't you come too? You can show him your sharpshooting skills.'

'Excellent idea, Papa, although my eyes are hurting from staring at this damned cipher. I don't think I could hit a barn door at fifty yards at the moment.'

'Then rest your eyes. I'll wake you when it's time.'

At a quarter to two, Anthony and Maria went into the garden, carrying a rifle each, in the leather holsters slung over their shoulders. Anthony also had his saddle bag, in which he was carrying a stock of the cylindrical projectiles, a gunpowder pouch, and half a dozen musket balls of the same calibre. They walked down a path with red rose bushes to the left and white rose bushes to the right. Behind the rose bushes were neatly trimmed hedges. At intervals of twenty paces, on either side of the path, there were openings in the hedges, which revealed the most exquisite knot gardens. When they reached the end of the path, Anthony saw the straw bails and targets at the far end of the garden, about three hundred yards away. The targets had a gold circle in the centre, a red ring around that, a blue ring around the red, and a black outer ring. Anthony heard voices and turned to see the king and Sully approaching, followed by Marcel. Marcel was carrying a musket.

'Sir Anthony, I am keen to try out these rifles of yours. Let's get a bit nearer. I want to get my eye in with my trusty musket first.'

'In that case, Your Majesty, I agree we should get a little closer.' They walked forward until they were about a hundred yards from the target. Marcel loaded the musket and handed it to the king.

'Right, you go forward and report back, Marcel. Stay well clear until I've fired. Leave the powder and balls here,' the king ordered, and Marcel obeyed. When Marcel was in position, the king cocked the musket, took aim, and fired. Marcel inspected the target, cupped his hands to his mouth, and shouted back.

'Blue, Your Majesty.'

'What do you say to that? Not bad, eh? Let's see if I can do any better,' The king licked his finger and raised it to assess wind direction. Then he reloaded the musket, cocked it, and took aim. He fired.

'Blue, Your Majesty.'

Anthony loaded his rifle with one of the spherical musket balls. 'Try the rifle with a ball, Your Majesty,' he said, offering the rifle to the king. The king took it and aimed. He fired.

'Red, Your Majesty.'

'Good lord,' the king exclaimed. 'Now, can we try one of your special projectiles?'

'Too easy from this distance, Your Majesty, let's walk back a couple of hundred yards to the hedge line,' Anthony replied, smiling.

'Are you mad, Sir Anthony? Marcel's a damned fine servant. I wouldn't want to hit him.'

'You won't, Your Majesty, trust me.'

'Very well, on your head be it,' the king replied, and they walked back to where Anthony had first observed the targets. 'STAND WELL CLEAR!' the king called to Marcel, as he waved his arm. Anthony loaded the rifle with one of the cylindrical-pointed projectiles and passed the rifle to the king. He tested the wind again, and took careful aim, then fired. They watched Marcel examine the target and cup his hands as he shouted back.

'Gold, Your Majesty.'

'A lucky shot, but impressive,' the king said.

'Not lucky at all, Your Majesty,' Maria smiled. 'May I try?'

'A girl? Although, I suppose you took your share of those pirates. It's most extraordinary, but why not?' the king nodded, and waved at Marcel to stand well clear. Maria loaded her rifle with a projectile, and Anthony reloaded his. Maria took aim and fired, then Anthony passed Maria his rifle, and took and reloaded hers. Maria fired again, and they continued until they had completed six rounds of rapid fire. 'Is that it? You won't have got anywhere near at that rate. I'm just glad, for your sakes, that Marcel seems to be still standing.' He signalled to Marcel, and Marcel took the target from the bail and came running towards them. He was panting as he arrived, and handed the target to the king. There were two holes in the blue ring about four inches apart, and one in the red. The gold had one hole about an inch-and-a-half off centre, and six holes, partially overlapping, around the dead centre. 'I have never seen anything like this. What was the name of the gunsmith again?'

'Fanzoj, from Ferlach in Austria, Your Majesty.'

'Get in touch with the fellow, Sully, and order me a couple of dozen of these rifles, and moulds for the projectiles,' the king ordered. 'Equipped with these, our sharpshooters would be unbeatable.'

'Your Majesty, congratulations on your excellent marksmanship,' a familiar voice called out from behind them. They all turned to see Queen Marie accompanied by Leonora and Concino Concini.

'Where the devil did you spring from, my darling?' The king asked.

'We were enjoying a stroll around the knot gardens, my dearest,' Marie replied. 'You carry on playing with your rifles. We shall take tea, I think. Come Leonora, Concino, we shall take the route back through the knot gardens to my apartments.' The queen's party disappeared from view.

'Come, Sir Anthony, Maria, we shall take some wine,' the king said, slapping them both on the back, and leading them back to the palace. The king was walking with Sully on his right-hand side. They were talking in low voices, so Anthony quickened his pace to get a little nearer. He still couldn't quite make out what they were saying. He thought he heard the word electors, when the king brushed past a rose branch, which whipped back and struck Anthony across his left cheek. He stifled a gasp and dropped back.

The king led them back to his study, and invited them to sit around the table, while he took out a decanter of red wine and four glasses. He poured them and sat down himself.

'Sir Anthony, you have scratched yourself,' he said as he handed him a glass of wine.

'It is nothing, Your Majesty. I walked into a rose bush. I wasn't looking where I was going,' Anthony said, rubbing his cheek and smearing blood across his face. Maria took a handkerchief from her pocket and passed it to him. He wiped his cheek.

'Your Majesty, with one of these rifles a man could pick you off from a rooftop two hundred yards away. Would you consider wearing an armour breastplate in public? It would glisten and make you appear even more magnificent,' Sully suggested.

'And young Maria here could shoot me through the eye socket from the same rooftop. Would you have me wear my jousting helmet too, Sully? Don't worry, if God wanted me dead, I've already given him every opportunity; and it appears he doesn't.'

'Your Majesty, if I may say something,' Anthony interjected, 'the queen is very concerned. I understand there have been several attempts on your life. Do you have any idea who might be behind them?'

'None at all, but there really is no reason to concern yourself. How do you like the wine?' the king asked. Anthony swirled the red wine around his mouth, then swallowed.

'Very much, Your Majesty, it is bursting with fruit, notes of blackberry, hints of cherry, rich in tannin, yet shades of mineral, too. It is a very round wine. Where is it from?'

'Saint Jean de Luz, in Navarre, near where I was born. You have good taste, Sir Anthony.'

'Thank you, Your Majesty. If I could ask one more thing, what would happen, in the hopefully very unlikely event, of your being taken from us, before your time?'

'That depends on when it might occur. In five-and-a-half years' time, Louis will be fourteen, and he would become king. Thanks to you and Maria, I have much more confidence that he will become a successful king. If I were to be taken before that, then there would be a regency, until he became of age.'

'So I assume that the queen would be regent until he became fourteen.'

'The queen will be guardian of Louis, but the administrative matters of kingship are forbidden to women in France. It is Salic law. Normally the administrative role would fall to my eldest brother, but as I have only a sister, that will not apply either. There will be a council formed to administer the realm, composed of Sully here, the dukes, Épernon, Vendôme, Lorraine, Montbazon and Bellegarde. The queen will sit on the council, but only have one vote. Sully, I think Sillery and Neufville should be on the council too, and Pierre Jeannin. Draw up a paper, would you? I want my wishes to be clearly known, should this come to pass, which, of course, I'm sure it won't.'

'Pardon me, Your Majesty, but I am curious to know why this Salic law pertains to France, whereas we English have had Elizabeth, Mary and Matilda as queens, in their own right. There may have been more. History was never my strongest subject. I thought that France and England shared a lot of common history, particularly since the normans invaded,' Anthony asked.

'Law emerges from events, and they establish precedents to suit the law makers. Men are indisputably the stronger sex,' the king began, as Anthony saw Maria clenching and unclenching her fists under the table, 'so it falls naturally to man to rule and defend the realm. The female English rulers, you cite, ruled in the absence of a male heir, though I grant you that Elizabeth made a fine and formidable monarch. Where was I? Events, that's right. When Louis the tenth died in 1316, he left a daughter, Joan, and his wife Clementia, who was pregnant with his son, John. Louis's younger brother Philip pronounced himself regent, and when John died after only five days, Philip had himself crowned king. There was a challenge on behalf of Joan, but Philip saw that off, on the grounds of her youth, and cast doubts on her parentage. That set the precedent for what we know as Salic law.'

'I see,' Anthony mused, 'but Catherine de Medici was regent in her own right, wasn't she?'

'She was a quite remarkable woman, one might say unprecedented,' the king laughed. 'She and Marie share a common ancestor, but the Medici family are large and powerful. You have to go a long way back, to Giovanni di Bicci de Medici, who was Marie's grandfather with five greats in front. Catherine married Henry, Duke of Orleans. Unfortunately, Henry didn't find Catherine attractive, and he had fallen deeply in love as a fifteen-year-old boy with the widow, Diane de Poitiers, twenty years his senior. Catherine played the model of what it was thought a woman should be. She went to the king, her father-in-law, Francis, and said that she would retire to a convent, or whatever was necessary to allow Henry to remarry, if that was what the king wished. Francis was very touched and decided that he would insist that his son produce heirs by Catherine. They rumoured that he may have been present in the bedchamber, to encourage his son along. Anyway, it worked, and Catherine produced nine royal children, including five sons. When his brother died, Henry became king. That was in 1547, I think. Henry died in a jousting tournament in 1559, and his eldest son Francis was fifteen and had been married to Mary Queen of Scots since he was fourteen.'

'Good heavens, what a small world it is. I saved Mary's life when her then husband, Lord Darnley and his uncle, murdered David Rizzio, her secretary. She knighted me for it. Oh, I am sorry, Your Majesty, I interrupt,' Anthony said, catching the king's glare.'

'Where was I?'

'Francis the second, Your Majesty. I think you were going to explain Catherine's continuing performance,' Sully prompted.

'Thank you, loyal friend, you are right. Although Francis was fifteen, and therefore could have been king in his own right, he was a sickly child. He also had a stammer, by the way. I apologise if I was tetchy, Sir Anthony, I should not forget the great service you and Maria are doing us. Anyway, Catherine once again portrayed herself as the very model of a grieving widow. There was quite a lot of skirmishing in court over who should advise the king. The bishop, Jean du Tillet, a fervent Catholic and supporter of the Guise family, began the debate. Although Francis wanted his mother to rule for him, she passed the role to his wife's uncles, the Guise family. Du Tillet argued that the king had the right to appoint his own advisors. Du Tillet's anti-Guise adversaries claimed that only princes of the royal blood could advise a young king. Francis died within a year, and her second son Charles, who was ten, became king. Since the Guise family had no ties to Charles, Catherine cashed in her carefully accumulated credit as a grieving widow and devoted mother, and piece by piece cemented her control of the regency. My father, Antoine was the first prince of the blood, and my uncle, also a Charles, was in prison. Catherine made a deal with my father to intercede on his behalf with Spain, over parts of Navarre that they had taken, and in return my father supported Catherine, during the regency. Catherine was a devoted mother, and her son, King Charles the ninth, relied on her and defended her right to rule on his behalf, assisted by my father.'

'So what happened to Charles, Your Majesty? When did you become king?' Maria asked.

'Religious conflict re-ignited after the Saint Bartholomew's Day massacre of the Huguenots. Catherine timed that to kill as many Protestants as possible. They had gathered for my wedding to my first wife, Margaret, the then king's sister. Two years later, the king died childless, and his brother Henry became King Henry the third. When it became apparent that the king preferred men in the bedchamber, and that there would be no heir, the War of the Three Henrys began. My principal opponent was Henry duc de Guise, founder of the Catholic League. I won, and here I am. I converted to Catholicism to achieve it, but as I said, Paris is well worth a mass.'

'So, since Catherine rules as regent, with your father's help, does that establish the precedent, that your queen, Marie, could control the regency, if you died prematurely?' Maria asked.

'Much as I admire her, I don't think that Marie has quite the same cunning as her distant cousin, Catherine. Anyway, I find all this talk of my death rather depressing. Let's finish our wine.'

Maria was sitting in an armchair in Anthony's room, while Anthony gazed into the mirror, examining the scars on his cheek inflicted by the rose bush.

'Well, I think this Salic law is outrageous. Why shouldn't a woman be monarch? As he said, your Elizabeth was a very good queen, wasn't she, Papa?'

'Yes, although she was a bit tight with her purse strings, and she didn't recognise me as I deserved, not at first anyway.'

'I don't see why it should automatically be the elder son, either. It should be the best person to do the job, never mind what sex they are, or how old they are, or who their parents are. Catherine was clearly the cleverest person at court to pull off what she did. She would have made a good queen.'

'Well, I don't think the Saint Bartholomew's Day massacre was her finest hour. The streets were running in blood, all over France.'

'That rubbish about men being the best fighters is nonsense, too. I think I've proved that. I can best Antonio at least half the time; and I can shoot straighter than the king of France. Greta's training to be a doctor. Women can do anything men can do. Are you listening, Papa?'

'Yes dear,' Anthony said, running the tip of his finger over his scars, as he studied his face in the mirror, 'that's it, I think I've got it?'

'What, a solution to misogyny?'

'Mis, what? No, I think I can crack the cipher. I've been so stupid. The trouble is that all the ciphers I've cracked have been Spanish, and the pope himself said how notoriously simple the Spanish ciphers are. I've been touching the scar on my left cheek, but it's on my right cheek in the mirror,' Anthony turned away from the mirror, went to the writing desk, and sat down. He took a piece of paper and began to write. Maria got up from her chair and went to look over his shoulder. 'look, we think E is I in the cipher alphabet. And we started our cipher key on that premise. But who is to say that they have to run in the same direction? If I run the cipher alphabet backwards, we get this as the key.

```
A B C D E F G H I J K L M N O P Q R S T U V W X Y Z
M L K J I H G F E D C B A Z Y X W V U T S R Q P O N
```

Now let's see if that helps.' Anthony took out the paper that Maria had written from memory in her trance.

```
O Y S V   A M D I U T O   E   M A   X B I M U I J
T Y   V I X Y V T   T F M T   Q I   F M R T
U I K S V I J   T F I   U S X X Y V T   Y H
M B B   I B I K T Y V U   T F M T   O Y S V
A M D I U T O   V I X B M K I   V S J Y B H
M U   F Y B O   V Y A M Z   I A X I V Y V
```

He then began working from his new key.

YOUR MAJESTY - 'look, that's it, we've cracked it!' I AM PLEASED TO REPORT THAT WE HAVE SECURED THE SUPPORT OF ALL ELECTORS THAT YOUR MAJESTY REPLACE RUDOLF AS HOLY ROMAN EMPEROR

'That's it. Actually, it's a damned foolish cipher to use really, because with the alphabets going in different directions, T is still T and G is G. It should be easier to crack.'

'Well, it had us both beaten until the rose bush intervened, Papa. But who is Rudolph, and what does it mean for us finding the assassin?'

'Rudolph is the Holy Roman Emperor. The empire is now, effectively, Germany, Austria, Savoy, Hungary and Bohemia. I have heard that the pope is trying to take back control of Austria and Hungary, and that Rudolph is a weak man. If Henry were to take over, then that would be to fight back against the Catholics.'

'If Henry is veering towards his original Protestant religion, as this would suggest, and if the Catholics have uncovered it, then are we looking for Catholic extremists?' Maria asked.

'I think we might be. It's certainly an avenue to be explored.'

'This Salic law had got me so riled up, but now I've calmed down a bit. What about that bishop, Jean du Tillet? He's got to be related to Charlotte du Tillet, don't you think?'

'Yes, yes I do. But we don't know where Épernon has moved her to. We also need to follow up on Concino.'

Anthony was deep in thought, wandering the corridors of the Louvre, when he saw Concino Concini emerge from Marie's apartment. Anthony stopped. Concino walked away from Anthony, and Anthony followed him, staying around

fifty paces behind him. Concino turned a corner, and when Anthony got to the corner, he was just in time to see Concino enter an office. It was Nicholas Brûlart de Sillery's office. Anthony approached the door, but couldn't hear anything through the thick wooden door. Anthony thought about what rooms were above and below, and whether he might be able to listen in via the chimney. He had walked twenty paces towards the nearest staircase when he heard the door open. He glanced around and saw Concino walking towards him. Anthony had taken three steps up the staircase when he heard Concino pass by. Anthony retraced his steps and knocked on Brûlart's door.

'Sir Anthony, do come in. How are your investigations going? Please take a seat.'

'They are going quite well, I think. I couldn't help noticing that you have just received a visit from Concino Concini. Would you be able to tell me about it?'

'Is he one of your suspects?'

'I have heard that the king has threatened to banish him, yet I have also heard that he is purchasing a title. I am puzzled.'

'You are well informed, Sir Anthony, but it is not a secret. He has just made payment, and, as chancellor, I shall draft the necessary paperwork for His Majesty to sign. Concino Concini will become the Marquis of Ancre.'

'Why will His Majesty sign? I understand that he considers Concino a drain on the royal purse?'

'He is, but at least this way the royal purse recovers much of the money the queen gives him. A king needs his queen, and the queen, it seems, needs Leonora and Concino.'

'Can you buy a marquisate? I assumed you had to inherit it?'

'The title had become extinct, so was available to sell. In France, there are several routes to nobility. First there is immemorial nobility, which comprises families that have always lived nobly. Then there is ennobled nobility, which is granted by the king via letters patent. You can become ennobled in a number of ways. Certain official positions carry nobility with them. Sometimes the king has clear views concerning who should hold the office, but when he has no clear view, the office will go to the highest bidding candidate. That is known as the nobility of the robe. The nobility of the chancery is a special case of that type. Then there is the nobility of the bell, which is for people made mayor or alderman of certain towns. There is military nobility, for someone holding high military office, and finally there is nobility by letters patent. It's a useful way for the crown to raise revenue, or in this case, recover some.'

'Why didn't the king simply banish him, as I understand he had threatened to do?'

'As I said, Sir Anthony, the king needs his queen. I don't know the details, but she prevails. Perhaps His Majesty has more important things on his mind.'

'Yes, perhaps he does. But I can't understand why Concino would part with so much money. Is it vanity?'

'It may be. Many of us care very much about our titles and place in the pecking order,' Nicholas replied as Anthony nodded, 'but maybe he has ambition. The queen relies on his counsel. If something were to happen to His Majesty, God forbid, and the queen became regent, then I can imagine Concino becoming her closest advisor.'

'Closer even than the duc d'Épernon?'

'I know that the queen and Jean Louis are close, Sir Anthony. There are people that are useful, and there are people you feel you can trust. I should say no more.'

'I see. Well, I should be going. Thank you for your time, Your Grace.'

'You're welcome, Sir Anthony, but I'm not a duke. Sir would suffice.'

CHAPTER THIRTEEN

Anthony was writing at the desk in his room when he heard the door open. He glanced up.

'How was he today?' Anthony asked.

'He still stammers now and then, but he's getting better all the time. What are you writing, Papa?'

'I'm making a list of suspects, what we know about them, and their possible motives. I'll just be another ten minutes, then I'll hand it over to you to check, and add what you know.'

'All right, Papa. I'll take a lie down until then. It's a tiring business teaching a future king how to speak normally.'

When Anthony had finished, he took the list to Maria. She was fast asleep on the bed, so he checked that her door was locked, then put the list on her desk. He slipped back into his own room and locked the connecting door. Then he lay down and had a nap himself. The rattle of the door handle woke him. Then he saw the key to the connecting door fall to the floor. He heard the familiar sounds of a lock being picked, and thirty seconds later, Maria grinned at him.

'What did you lock the door for?'

'I saw you fast asleep, so I left the list on your desk. I felt tired myself, and didn't want anyone getting past me and finding our list. You're getting much faster at picking locks now.'

'Good thinking, Papa. I've added my thoughts to the list,' she said, handing him the paper. Anthony got up from the bed and went to his desk to study the list.

1. Nicolas de Neufville, seigneur de Villeroy - Secretary of State for three kings. Hates Épernon. Accused of embezzling funds. Not much backbone. Well liked by Catherine de Medici.

2. Roger de Saint-Lary de Termes — Introduced to court by Épernon. Uncovered a plot in which the duc de Biron, who had fought against the Catholic League was later conspiring with Spain and Savoy.

3. Jean Louis de Nogaret de la Valette, duc d'Eperon — a favourite of the queen.

4. Maximilien de Béthune, duc de Sully — King's right-hand man.

5. Sillery ?

6. Duc de Vendôme?

7. Duc de Lorraine?

8. Duc de Montbazon?

9. Pierre Jeannin?

10. Françoise de Montglat - governess.

11. Jeanne de Harlay—Françoise's daughter and assistant governess.

12. Concino Concini—Came to court with Marie. Married Leonora. Trusted confidant and advisor of Marie. Buying nobility using Marie's money, probably has ambitions. The king has threatened to banish him, but Marie insists on keeping him by her side.

13. Leonora Concini—Has fits, may be possessed. Came to court with Marie. Confidant of Marie, and longest, closest friend.

14. Charlotte du Tillet—possibly mistress of Épernon. May be related to radical Catholic Jean du Tillet

'We've discovered quite a lot, but still have many unknowns,' Anthony said, running his left hand through his beard. 'I suggest we each ask questions about our unknowns; the thing is who do we ask? I might as well see what Marie knows; she's queen, after all; a clever woman and we're working for her.'

'Shall I ask Pierre, the sailor that is?'

'What can he know? He's been at sea for twenty-seven years. Why don't you ask Louis? Children are invisible, but they hear things; and they're smarter than we think.'

'Good idea, Papa.'

'Well, we might as well start straight away. Do you think Louis will be free?' Maria nodded. 'Excellent, I'll see if I can catch Marie on her own. Then we'll compare notes again.'

By the end of the day, Anthony and Maria had fleshed out their knowledge of the suspects. They sat at Anthony's desk and examined the list again.

1. *Nicolas de Neufville, seigneur de Villeroy—Secretary of State for three kings. Hates Épernon. Accused of embezzling funds. Not much backbone. Was well liked by Catherine de Medici.*

2. *Roger de Saint-Lary de Termes, duc de Bellegarde— Introduced to court by Épernon. Uncovered a plot in which the duc de Biron, who had fought against the Catholic league, was later conspiring with Spain and Savoy.*

3. *Jean Louis de Nogaret de la Valette, duc d'Éperon—a favourite of the queen. Fought on the Catholic side in the French wars of religion. Favourite of Henry III, but after his assassination in 1589, Épernon opposed the accession of the current king and attempted to install an independent government in Provence. His attempt failed, and they forced him to submit to the king. Overheard whispering with Roger, after dinner, about Julie, Rudolph, and the king's ambition.*

4. *Maximilien de Béthune, duc de Sully—King's right-hand man. Protestant who had fought with William of Orange. Then*

joined current king when he was Henry of Navarre; fought loyally with him. Excellent soldier and military engineer. Injured badly at battle of Ivry. Widowed. Advised Henry to convert to Catholicism, but remained a Protestant himself. Richly rewarded by Henry.

5. *Nicolas Brûlart de Sillery*—Chancellor and keeper of the seals. Clever but dull. Age sixty-four.

6. *César, duc de Vendôme*–age 16—illegitimate child of Henry, by his favourite mistress, Gabrielle d'Estrées (deceased). Married to wealthy heiress Françoise de Lorraine when he was 14, and she was 16. Her father had been head of the Catholic league in Brittany.

7. *Henry duc de Lorraine.* Age 47. Widower of Catherine de Bourbon, the king's niece. It was a political alliance. He then married Margherita, daughter of the duc of Mantua.

8. *Hercule, duc de Montbazon*—Fought with Henry against Catholic league. Governor of Paris and Ile-de-France. Master of Hounds. Age 41.

9. *Pierre Jeannin,* Age 68—Superintendent of Finances. Lawyer by training. Negotiated the Treaty of Lyons bringing peace with Savoy.

10. *Françoise de Montglat*—governess.

11. *Jeanne de Harlay*—Françoise's daughter and assistant governess.

12. *Concino Concini*—Came to court with Marie. Married Leonora. Trusted confidant and advisor of Marie. Buying nobility using Marie's money, probably has ambitions. The king has threatened to banish him, but Marie insists on keeping him by her side.

13. *Leonora Concini*—Has fits, may be possessed. Came to court with Marie. Confidant of Marie, and longest, closest friend.

14. *Charlotte du Tillet*—may be mistress of Épernon. May be related to radical Catholic, Jean du Tillet.

'Well, I don't know what you think, Maria, but a few stand out for me. I don't like Épernon at all, or Roger. You heard them whispering about Julie, Rudolph and the king's ambition. Now that we know what that ambition was, and which Rudolph they meant, that makes me very suspicious.'

'Yes, but who do you think Julie is, Papa?'

'I don't know. I think we can rule out Neufville and Sully. Neufville doesn't have the courage that a conspiracy requires, and we have seen ourselves how concerned Sully is for the king's welfare. Vendôme is the king's son; it's possible, but I doubt it. Sillery seems a bit old, so does Jeannin. I can't imagine Françoise or her daughter being involved. Charlotte may be pumping Épernon for the king's movements, and feeding them to Jean du Tillet. I have a bad feeling about Concino. He's clearly ambitious, or why would he buy the Marquisate of Ancre? He must feel threatened by the king, and if the king died, and Marie became regent, as her advisor, his ambition would have free rein.'

'So what do we do next, Papa?'

'I think we should start with Épernon, and Bellegarde. Let's find out as much as we can about them; see what Louis knows about them. I'll try asking Marie.'

'Do you think you'll get anywhere with her, Papa? She seems to be on very close terms with Épernon.'

'You may have a point. I'll try asking Sully. Since he is so concerned about Henry, I feel I may reveal our hidden purpose. He seems as concerned about the assassination attempts as Marie is. We need to find out who this Julie is too, and how she's involved.'

'I can't be sure it was Julie. As I said, they were whispering. It could have been Juliet, Julian, Julius, July even? Perhaps they plan to act in July.'

'You have a point there. I hope it is July. That gives us a bit of time.'

Anthony asked Marcel where he could find Sully. He

was told that he was at work in his study, which was next to the king's study. He went there and knocked on the door. He heard a muffled acknowledgement and went in. Sully was sitting behind a desk, almost as large as the king's, reading a letter.

'Sir Anthony, come in, sit down. I have just sent an enquiry to that gunsmith of yours, in Austria. How can I help you?'

'Do you mind if I speak with you confidentially, Your Grace? It is a sensitive matter?'

'Of course not,' Sully replied, putting down the letter. 'What is it?'

'The queen did send for me to help the dauphin with his speech impediment, but there was another reason, too. She is most concerned about the attempts on the king's life; and she wanted me to find out who is behind them. I know you share her concern, so I hoped you might advise me, in confidence. I wouldn't want the king to know that the queen had engaged me in the matter.'

'I see. She thinks, there is some mastermind behind the attempts then; that they are connected? They seem to have been entirely random so far, a boatman from Orleans and a tailor's son. We got nothing from them through torture. We didn't catch any of the others, and there seems to be no connection, besides their faith.'

'The queen wonders how they know where the king will be.'

'A visitation from the king involves a great deal of preparation. Hundreds of people are involved in the planning. For instance, I am busy making preparations for the queen's coronation. I was reading a quotation from a cake maker, as you came in. So many people are involved: confectioners, bishops, guards, caterers, carriage-builders, cabinet-makers. The list is endless. They all have to know dates and locations.'

'The queen's coronation, Your Grace? You mean she isn't queen yet? They have been married for almost ten years, haven't they?'

'She hasn't mentioned it to you then. That is interesting. The king and queen have had their difficulties. There have been the most unseemly quarrels between the queen and Catherine de Balzac, the king's favourite mistress. He has also taken issue with some expenses she incurs. To give her her due, she has provided heirs, and that is her crucial role. The court has also been unhappy with her apparent unwillingness to become fully French. She speaks Italian much of the time and insists on having those frightful Concinis around her. His majesty has deferred her coronation for, shall we say, political purposes?'

'I see, so why are you busy organising it now?'

'I can't give you any details, you understand, but His Majesty may need to be absent for a period. During his absence, the queen may need to serve as regent, for a while. The coronation makes that more legitimate.'

'How many people know about the king's possible absence?' Anthony asked.

'Only myself, it is a secret.'

'After dinner last week, I overheard the ducs of Épernon and Bellegarde talking about the king's ambition concerning a certain Rudolf, and Julie. Might that be relevant?'

'My god!' Sully exclaimed, rubbing his chest, 'damn indigestion, it's getting worse. They can't possibly know anything about it. Would you excuse me? I have a lot to do.'

'Of course, I'm sorry to have taken up your time,' Anthony stood and went to the door.

'Sir Anthony. If you hear any more such asides, let me know.'

'Of course, Your Grace.'

Maria knocked on the door of the library and entered when she heard Louis's call. Louis was sitting at the long table with a map in front of him. Maria went and stood behind him.

'Good morning, Your Highness. No poetry this morning?'

'No, I wanted to find out where something was.'

'Where what was?'

'Jülich. My father is going to lead an army there. I overheard him talking to Sully about it. He's made a pact with the Protestant union. It's here look, in Germany, half-way between Cologne and Maastricht,' Louis pointed at the map. Maria bit her lip. 'Sully doesn't want him to go; but he says he must. He's very brave, my father, not afraid of anything. Shall I write another verse?'

'Yes, Your Highness, although your last verse is going to be hard to improve on. You spoke of your mother's good counsel; would you like to develop that further? I understand she is to be crowned soon. Are you looking forward to that?'

'Yes, I want to make a good impression with my verse. Mother and Father have tried to shield me from the public. I've been something to look at, rather than be listened to. I want to show the bishops and ducs, and the people, that I can speak now. One day, I will be king. I know I can be now.'

Maria finished the lesson with Louis as soon as she could, and rushed back to find Anthony.

'It's not Julie, or Julian, or July, Papa. It's Jülich in Germany. Henry is sending an army there to support the Protestant union.'

'Of course; it's the price for becoming Holy Roman Emperor. The Catholic league will not like it. What timing! He sets himself up as a target and then arranges the queen's coronation; where he'll be on display to all and sundry. The man has a death wish.'

'No, Papa, he just thinks he's invincible. How do you think Épernon and Bellegarde found out about Jülich? It took us ages to crack the cipher, and only then because you scratched your cheek.'

'You can't send an army off on campaign and keep it secret. How did you find out about Jülich?'

'Louis was looking it up on a map in the library. He'd overheard the king talking with Sully about it,' Maria replied. Anthony paced up and down between his bed and the window, running his fingers through his hair.

'How do Épernon and Bellegarde think they can get away with it? If they launch an attack on the king, that is? Will they have a hired sniper on a rooftop? Is it just revenge, on behalf of the Catholic league, or do they intend a coup to seize power themselves? Are they strong enough to do that? Where would the other nobles stand? Henry is clearly a much-loved king.'

'Épernon is very close to the queen. Perhaps he doesn't want outright power, just to influence her regency, should the king be killed.'

'Yes, but as we heard, Marie will have governorship of Louis, not administrative power. She will have one vote on a council. What can we do now? What should we do now?'

'I don't know, Papa,' Maria said, watching Anthony pace back and forth.

'I must think. Marie worried that there was someone behind the attempts on the king's life; a good king loved by his people. The king is planning to become Holy Roman Emperor, perhaps siding with the Protestant union. So the Catholic league, if they know about Henry's intentions, will want him out of the way. If Henry were to succeed, he would become ruler of virtually all of Europe, except Spain, Russia, the Papal States and the British Isles. We know that Épernon and Bellegarde are aware of Henry's intentions, and that Sully is worried. What would they hope to gain?'

'Catholic league gold, perhaps?'

'They're dukes, for heaven's sake. Don't you think they have enough gold already?'

'Isn't France enough of a realm? How much gold did you need, Papa, before it was enough to return to Mother and us?'

'It wasn't like that. It's just that it took so long to get and keep enough that I thought Francesca would have married someone else. I didn't know about you.'

'Which brings me back to my point. How much is enough?'

'Mea culpa, I'm so sorry. This is not helping us work out what to do next.'

'I'm sorry too, Papa. I didn't mean to hurt you; I love you. What about the regency? There will be a council. Épernon and Bellegarde will have votes. The other votes are held by Marie, Sully, Sillery, Vendôme, Lorraine, Montbazon, Neufville and Jeannin. Sully is Protestant, and, with Henry and Montbazon, fought against the Catholic league. Sillery is clever, but dull and sixty-four. Vendôme is young, and married to Françoise de Lorraine. Her father had been head of the Catholic league in Brittany. The duc de Lorraine might therefore also have radical Catholic leanings. Neufville is weak, and Jeannin is sixty-eight, and a peacemaker. It looks to me as if Sully and Montbazon will be the chief opponents of the Catholic league on that council, with several possible league supporters, and some sitting on the fence.'

'You have a good brain, Maria. I think it skipped a generation. But what are we going to do?'

'I hate to even consider it, but what would happen if both Henry and Louis were assassinated on the same day?'

'My god! Surely that's not possible during the ceremony, but they have to get through the streets to the cathedral. No, they will be well guarded. Anyway, little Nicholas would be next in line, so what would be achieved by that? But if Marie were to be killed, then who would be appointed regent? I think we have to find out when the coronation is going to take place. On that day, one of us should stay close to the king, and the other to Marie.'

'I'll take the king, Papa. Marie contacted you. It's you that has the special attachment to her. But won't they be in the same coach?'

'I suppose they probably will. I hadn't thought of that.'

Anthony made his way back to Sully's study. As he turned the last corner, he saw several people clustered around Sully's door. As he got closer, they were making way for someone coming out of the study. It was a liveried man; there was something behind him. The cluster of people parted, and Anthony saw he was carrying a stretcher. It was Sully on the stretcher. He was muttering something and clutching at his chest with his left hand. His face was ashen. Another liveried stretcher bearer emerged, and as he cleared the door, Henry passed him to walk beside his friend, taking Sully's right hand in his left.

'You'll be all right, dear Sully. They will take you to the hospital at the Arsenal; where you will be in expert hands,' Henry wept as he spoke. Everyone followed the stretcher down the corridor and out through a side door, where a cart was waiting, hitched to a team of four horses. They loaded Sully onto the cart, and two men climbed up to be with him. The king nodded, and the driver cracked his whip. Gravel flew up, hitting Anthony in the face, as the horses galloped across the courtyard, out through the gate, and headed south east towards the Arsenal. Anthony, stunned, looked around him. There was a body of figures on the far side of the courtyard, barely visible through a dust cloud, that the cart and horses had kicked up. Standing beside him was a man he recognised. He was standing next to Marcel.

'What happened, Marcel?'

'Oh, Sir Anthony, they think it's his heart.'

'Who does?'

'Those men who have gone with him. They are the king's physicians. They say he has been working too hard, what with the coronation on top of everything else.'

'When is the coronation?'

'The day after tomorrow, Monday the fourteenth,' Marcel replied. As the dust cloud settled, the body of men became clear. There were three ranks of ten men each, a captain of the guard in front of, and facing them. They were all in red and yellow tunics with a coat of arms emblazoned on their chests. The arms comprised a white cross-potent on a red background, at the top; with, on the left, a green tree against a white background beneath; then a white bell against a blue background, in the centre and, at the right, a sort of red cross potoncé, with a yellow edge, and yellow balls at each tip of the cross; all against a red background.

'Who are they?' Anthony asked.

'Part of the guard of honour for the king on coronation day,' Marcel replied. 'They are the duc de Épernon's men.'

Anthony went to find Maria and tell her about Sully. She wasn't in her room, so he went to see if she was in the library. She was there with Louis. They both looked up as he came in.

'Oh, Your Highness, there is bad news. I'm afraid that the duc de Sully is ill. They have taken him to the Arsenal.'

'I am sorry to hear that. Was it p…poison?'

'The doctors think it is his heart, Your Highness,' Anthony replied. Louis paused.

'I have no faith in doctors. Why should I? My tongue would from my head be ripped, if it had been left up to them. Poison may be deadly as a dagger, the heart to still, and send man to his grave.'

'Your mother's coronation takes place the day after tomorrow. We fear for all your lives, but particularly your father's, given his impending campaign to Jülich. However, I am also concerned for your mother. We would like to stay close to them, on the day. Do you think that would be possible, Your Highness?' Anthony asked. Louis paused for thought before speaking.

'For my small part, I would like you to be there too. But Mother is the one to ask for that.'

'Thank you, Your Highness. I will seek an audience,' Anthony said, bowed, nodded to Maria, and left.

Anthony found the queen in her salon, with Leonora Concini. He bowed. Leonora looked a little breathless.

'I'm afraid there is bad news, Your Highness.'

'If it's about Sully, Leonora has just rushed to give me the news. I hope he will make a swift recovery. I wouldn't want him to miss my coronation.'

'I hope so too, Your Highness. I would like to speak with you about my purpose here.'

'Of course, Sir Anthony. What is it?'

'I would rather speak alone, Your Highness.'

'Oh, I see. Leonora, dear, would you leave us, just for a while.' Leonora rose, bowed and left, throwing Anthony a dirty stare, as she closed the door behind her.

'I fear for your safety as well as the king's, Your Highness. I would be happier if Maria and I travel close to you and the king on the way to and from your coronation.'

'I see your role as uncovering the conspirator before an assassination attempt, Sir Anthony. We will have no shortage of guards. Dear Jean Louis leads the guard of honour. Then all the other dukes will have their men with us too,' Marie said. Then, seeing the downcast look in his eyes, her tone softened. 'We will be well protected, but yes, you must come too. Our carriage is full, but I will try to find out if anyone else has space in their carriage. Leave it with me.'

'In that case, Your Highness, I think it would be better if we ride as part of the guard.'

'We can't have un-liveried riders in our guard; it would look out of place. Besides, Maria is a girl.'

'Do you think Gaston could make us some uniforms in time? He has our measurements already? With a tight-fitting doublet, and a hat pulled down low, Maria might pass muster, Your Highness.'

'Very well, if you think it best. Is that everything?'

'Forgive me, Your Highness, French ceremonial is not my specialist subject. Where does the coronation take place?'

'Neither was it mine. They crown French kings in the cathedral of Reims, queens in the Basilica of Saint Denis, on the northern outskirts of Paris. Saint Denis is where all the regalia of a king's coronation are stored, the sword of Charlemagne, the sceptre of Dagobert, the throne itself. They take it all to Reims in a grand procession for a king's coronation. It's less bother to do it in Saint Denis, for a queen.'

'How far is it from here to Saint Denis, Your Highness?'

'Just under six miles, I'm told. Is that all, Sir Anthony?' Anthony nodded. 'In that case, would you mind asking Leonora to re-join me on your way out?' Anthony bowed and left. He passed Marie's request to Leonora and walked thoughtfully back to his room. A lot can happen in six miles, he thought. Perhaps the best thing we can do for now is for Maria and I to ride the route. Time spent in reconnaissance is never wasted.

On Sunday, Anthony and Maria saddled their horses, rode out of the stables, through the courtyard to the north gate, and chatted to the sentries before turning east onto Rue St. Honore. Anthony glanced behind him at the tower of the west gate of the city wall, and the windmills slowly turning beyond that. As he turned back, people were spilling out of the church to his left. Through the general buzz of conversation, he heard several mentions of the coronation. They trotted on along the wide, cobbled road, studying the white-washed buildings with their red-tiled roofs to either side. About three hundred yards short of the junction with Rue St. Denis, the wide avenue of Rue St.

Honore ended. The shortest route to join Rue St. Denis was the road off to the left, arcing through the Les Halles market, before joining Rue St. Denis a quarter of a mile further north. Straight ahead, Rue St. Honore became Rue de la Ferronnerie, pinched between churches to left and right.

'A marksman would get an excellent shot from either bell tower, as the carriages turn here,' he said to Maria, who had stopped beside him.

'Yes, but it would be a bit of a suicide mission. Guards would surround the church within seconds. I'd go for a shot from an upper storey window. Any of these terraced houses would be perfect. By the time you look up, the window could be closed, and you wouldn't know which house to search,' Anthony nodded and flicked the reins to continue left through the empty market, its market-stalls shuttered, wasps feeding on rotting fruit and vegetables in the open sewer. They left the market and turned left onto Rue St. Denis, heading north. 'There's the du Tillet house,' Maria called out. 'Pity it's a Sunday. That patisserie has a marvellous display. I wouldn't mind a pastry.' They continued trotting along the wide avenue of Rue St. Denis. It was quiet, as most churchgoers had returned home. A few children played in the street. The aromas of chicken roasting made Maria salivate. Then they passed through the city's northern gate and open fields replaced the serried rows of buildings, with scattered village churches, and settlements to either side.

'I see little to worry about along here, open countryside, not much cover, and there will be few crowds outside the city.'

'So can we turn back and find somewhere for lunch?' Maria asked.

'You can turn back, if you like. I'm going to look around the basilica.'

'Do you think we can find somewhere to eat in St. Denis? I'm starving.'

It took them about an hour and a half in total to reach St. Denis. The basilica dominated the town at its centre. Workmen were busy putting the finishing touches to timber barriers, to keep the area in front of the basilica free for the carriages to arrive, and disgorge their nobility. They dismounted and tied their horses to a rail. A monk came scurrying over to them.

'I'm sorry, sir, this area is out of bounds. We are making preparations for the coronation.' Anthony reached inside his doublet and pulled out his warrant with the king's seal. He passed it to the monk, who examined it and handed it back. 'I beg your pardon. Have you come to check arrangements? I'm Abbot Francis. I can show you around, if you wish. The bishop is busy rehearsing, and we have set up the thrones, and arranged the seating.'

'Yes please, Abbot Francis.' The Abbot led them towards the central portal of three. Anthony and Maria paused to admire the intricate carving on the stone tympanum and lintel over the massive doors. Abbot Francis saw them gazing up.

'It is the last judgement. It dates from 1135.' They passed through the doors into the atrium. They caught their breath as they took in the beauty of the massive stained-glass windows all around them. 'All the kings of France, from Clovis the first, are buried here,' the abbot said.

'And the queens?' Maria enquired.

'Yes, the queens too. See, here are the tombs of Henry the second and his queen, Catherine de Medici,' he said, pointing to their marble effigies. Anthony cast his eyes over the deathly cold model of the woman who had stolen a year of his life. He dragged himself back to the present, as Abbot Francis continued the tour, first to the crypt, and then up the bell tower. When they had finished the tour, they thanked the abbot and asked if there was anywhere they could get some lunch. He took them to the monastery refectory. After a plain, but filling meal, they mounted and rode back to Paris.

'What do you think, Papa? If I were going to try something, I think it would be in the city. There's very little cover outside the city walls, and the basilica will be crawling with guards.'

'I agree. My favourite spot would be where Rue St. Honore ends and you turn into Les Halles. The carriages will slow at the turn.'

'What can we do about it?'

'I have no idea. Keep our eyes open, and react as necessary.'

◇ ◇ ◇

Anthony and Maria rode side by side through the gate back into Paris, Anthony showing his royal warrant to the sentry. When they reached Les Halles, Anthony reined his horse in. Maria did likewise.

'What is it, Papa?'

'We're assuming it's Épernon and Bellegarde, and it might well be. But how? We mustn't forget Concino. He has every reason to want the king, who threatens to expel him, dead. If Marie becomes regent, he'll be her chief advisor. He's bought a title for that reason.'

'Yes, but how?'

'He overheard our rifle demonstration to the king. What if he buys a rifle, and has some moulds made for the pointed-cylindrical projectiles? He could feign illness on coronation day, then slip out and work his way to one of these rooftops. With a rifle he could kill the king from quite a distance, then make his escape back to the palace and his sickbed.'

'I thought rifles are quite rare.'

'They are still very expensive, but I first fired a rifle right here in Paris, forty-three years ago. With the money he has, he could have bought one and had the moulds made. I fear that my demonstration of the rifles may have sealed the king's fate.'

'Don't blame yourself, Papa. The king insisted on seeing them. I have an idea. If Concino doesn't appear as part of

186

the queen's retinue, one of us can drop out of our place in the guard and go back to the palace in order to follow him. We can catch him red-handed.'

'On the face of it, that sounds like a good plan. However, I don't see how he could sneak out of the palace, carrying a rifle, and make his way to a rooftop to be in position by the time the procession sets off. He would also have to get back to his sickbed unnoticed.'

'He'd obviously need Leonora to be in on it. If she told Marie that Concino was sick, shortly before they board their carriages, then it would be too late for Marie to go and see how he was. He could have left the palace hours before, and already be in position, up there, on one of those rooftops. He could have rented an apartment, just as you rented the room in the tavern near the theatre, for us to change in. In the pandemonium that the assassination would cause, he could get back to his sickbed.'

'That sounds plausible, but how does it help us? By the time we notice that he's failed to show up to take his place in the procession, it's too late for one of us to follow him.'

'You're right, of course, Papa. One of us will just have to seek him out on the coronation morning. If he's nowhere to be found, we know it's him, and that he's taken up position. Then we insist that the procession route be changed.'

'I fear the king may insist on the route that the people will expect him to follow. But I can't think of a better option.'

CHAPTER FOURTEEN

I n the morning twilight, Anthony left his room and made his way to the rooms that the Concinis occupied, next to Marie's apartments. He bent double and listened at the keyhole, and could hear nothing but snoring. Anthony tried the handle, but the door was locked. After taking out his lock picks, he opened the lock, turned the door handle, opened the door, and entered. He tiptoed through the sitting room and tried the handle on the bedroom door. It was unlocked. He opened the door inch by inch, the snoring growing louder as he did so, and approached the bed until he could discern the head of Concino Concini on the pillow nearest to him, and his wife on the far side. He backed away and made his way out of their apartments, locking the door behind him. Then he went to find Marcel in the servant's quarters. Marcel was already organising the other servants, assigning their duties for the day.

'Marcel, may I have a word?'

'Of course, Sir Anthony. How can I help?'

'I know how busy you must be, but if there is anyone you can spare, can you have someone check on Concino Concini, once or twice an hour? If he has disappeared, please inform me immediately.'

'That seems very irregular.'

'It is a matter of utmost importance. The servant needn't do much, just ask if there is anything he requires. But if he is nowhere to be found, I must hear of it.'

'Well, we would ensure that the queen's entourage has everything they require anyway, so yes, Sir Anthony. I will ensure that you hear if he disappears.'

'Thank you, Marcel.' Anthony made his way back to his room.

About an hour later, Gaston delivered their red and yellow uniforms, emblazoned with the Épernon coat of arms. He made some last-minute adjustments to Maria's uniform, to conceal her bust as best he could. Around five minutes after he left, there was another knock at Anthony's door. He opened it to find the sergeant-at-arms of the duc d'Épernon.

'Sir Anthony, I am Sergeant Bernard. I understand that you and your,' he hesitated, 'daughter, are to join our troop for the day. Her highness sent word that you were to be invited to breakfast with my men, and that I am to give you instruction, so that you don't look too out of place.'

'Did someone mention breakfast?' Maria said, striding through the connecting door.

'We won't be a minute,' Anthony said, unlocking the wardrobe, and taking out the flintlock pistols and his rifles with their holsters. 'You don't mind if we bring these, do you?'

'Not at all, sir. All the guards will be well armed. We shall need to stop at the stores on the way to breakfast and get you some regulation riding boots.' The barrack block was behind the guardroom, and after trying several pairs, they found boots that fitted tolerably well. As he led them into the canteen, the hubbub died away as all eyes fell upon Maria. 'Get on with your breakfast and put your eyes back in their sockets,' he barked. 'I'm sorry, mademoiselle. Are you able to ride a horse, like a man, I mean?'

'No, not as badly as most. I'm sorry, sergeant, I've never ridden sidesaddle. I think you'll find I won't embarrass you.' They got through their breakfast without further incident. Then they collected their horses from the stable. Anthony fitted the rifle holsters to the saddles, and they joined the rest of the guard in the courtyard. The sergeant introduced them to the captain of the guard, and then to the troopers who would ride closest to them.

'Will the duc d'Épernon be at the head of the guard?' Anthony asked.

'Yes, he'll be riding alongside the captain, behind the royal carriage,' Sergeant Bernard explained.

They had about an hour of drill, riding in a column of two around the courtyard, wheeling left and right as commanded. Neither Anthony nor Maria had any trouble staying in formation, and Sergeant Bernard seemed relieved. All the while they trotted in formation around the courtyard, carriages had been arriving and disgorging dignitaries in elaborate apparel, who entered the palace. After another hour, the king and queen came out, followed by the elder children with their governesses, and then the dukes and other nobles. They queued, making small talk, and shuffling forwards as the coachmen opened the coach doors and they boarded. Anthony saw Jean Louis striding across to join the captain of the guard. A trooper was holding his horse ready for him. As the royal coach set off, the guard split in two, with half the guard leading the royal coach and the other, including Anthony and Maria, following it. Anthony glanced back at the remaining coaches, that the lower ranking guests were boarding. He turned to Maria.

'I heard nothing from Marcel, and I think I just glimpsed Concino boarding a coach. It seems I may have been wrong about him.'

They turned right, as expected, onto Rue St. Honore. Anthony and Maria scanned the cheering, waving crowds who lined the road. Their gaze flicked from the crowds on the street to the rooftops, the windows and back to the crowds again.

'At this pace, you'd have to be incredibly lucky to get a kill,' Maria called across, above the clattering hooves.' Anthony nodded. As they approached the turning into Les Halles, Anthony saw the king tap his coach driver on the shoulder. The procession came to a halt. 'What the hell is he doing, Papa? He's a sitting duck now.' Anthony clenched his teeth and kept scanning the crowd and the buildings. Jean Louis rode up to the royal carriage and spoke with the king. Then the king got out of his coach and climbed into the second coach in the line. Jean Louis spoke with the captain, and the captain spoke to Sergeant Bernard, who then rode back to Anthony and Maria.

'The king wants to visit the duc de Sully in hospital, at the Arsenal. He's joining the duc de Montbazon in his coach. Half the guard will accompany him, and the other will stay with the royal coach. He says he only wants ten minutes with him, to put his mind at rest. We're just transferring the royal crest to the Montbazon coach.'

'You stay with the queen, Papa. I'll go with the king.' After a few minutes of intense anxiety, Anthony was riding after the royal coach through Les Halles market. He turned his head to see Maria following Montbazon's coach into Rue de la Ferronnerie.

Maria turned in the saddle to see Anthony riding off after the queen into Les Halles. As she turned back, she caught sight of a face that was familiar from somewhere, standing in the crowd on the corner. She looked again, but it was gone. The coach carrying the king and the duc de Montbazon was pushing forwards, through the crowds on the street. The guardsmen she was with in the rear rode after it. She glanced left and right at the people cheering and waving from every window. She scanned them again for any sign of a gun, or anyone not smiling and waving. The carriage came to a stop, and so did the guard. Maria broke away from the guard, urging her horse to push through the crowds so that she could see what was causing the hold up. In front of the coach was a wagon carrying an enormous wine barrel. One of its rear wheels was at an acute angle. It appeared as though the axle had broken. The king was leaning out of the coach shouting at the duc d'Épernon, to get the wagon moved out of the way. The guards in front

191

went to the wagon and dismounted. They were all heaving at the wagon, and members of the public were helping too, but the weight of the barrel was too much. The king issued more orders, which Maria couldn't make out against the general noise of the cheering crowd, but the guardsman, with her in the rear, dismounted and pressed forwards to help with moving the wagon.

Maria stayed where she was, in the saddle. She scanned the windows again, sensing danger. Her eyes flashed back to the king, and she saw again the face she had glimpsed at the corner. It was the shabby man she had seen entering the du Tillet house. He was close to the king now, who was still leaning out of the coach, shouting to Épernon. She saw the sun glint off a blade, and then the king slump over the side of the coach. Montbazon tried to pull him back into the coach, and Maria saw the shabby man strike again. Montbazon recoiled back inside the coach. She urged her horse forwards through the crowd. The assassin was making off towards Rue St. Denis, the crowds parting as his blade flashed left and right. She gave chase. As she passed the stricken wagon, she gained a little speed. She didn't take her gaze from the assassin, who was running now. He jinked left into a narrow alley, too narrow to proceed on horseback. Maria lept from the saddle and ran after him. When she thought she was close enough, she dived and caught his right ankle. He fell. They both struggled to their feet, and he turned, the bloody knife in his right hand. He lunged at her. She caught his wrist in her right hand, dropped into a crouch, pulling him into her, as he fell across her twisting torso, and threw him hard onto his back. The impact, as he hit the ground, smashed the breath from him, like an inflated pig's bladder hitting the pavement. The knife clattered onto the cobblestones.

'Why?' she asked, as he starred up at her, trembling.

'The voices. I didn't want to, not really, but the voices.' Épernon's men pushed past her and dragged him to his feet.

'Well done, mademoiselle. We've got him now,' she heard Sergeant Bernard say as they dragged him away.

'Where are you taking him?' She shouted after them.

'To the Bastille, of course.'

'The king, is he alive?'

'I don't know, mademoiselle. They're taking him, and the duc de Montbazon, to the Arsenal.'

Maria watched them drag the assassin back onto the street. Charlotte du Tillet, she must have something to do with this, she thought. Maria ran back to the street, but couldn't find her horse. She ran to the corner and turned onto Rue St. Denis. From the corner she could see the du Tillet house, and she could also see the woman who had opened the door mounting a horse, held for her by one of Épernon's men. Maria ran towards them, but they galloped away before she could reach them.

The queen was with the bishops in the Basilica of St. Denis, as they rehearsed the ceremony, over and over again. Jeanne and Françoise de Harlay were looking after the younger children. Anthony was with Louis. They heard the great door creak, and a beam of pure sunlight mixed with the red, green, and blue light from the stained-glass windows. A guard rushed to the queen. He bowed, then whispered to her. Anthony saw the bishop's jaw drop. Queen Marie wailed and dropped to her knees. Anthony was rooted to the spot. Louis reached up and put his hand in Anthony's.

'I must go to him,' Marie said. She approached Anthony. 'Someone has attacked Henry. They have taken him to the Arsenal. I must be with him.'

'I'll come with you.'

'No, Anthony. I shall have my guards. Please stay and look after Louis and the children.' She turned and walked through the sunbeam towards the main door, followed by the rest of the guard. The door shut behind them. Anthony

193

was trying to think, but fear for Maria forced everything else from his head. They had failed. He had no notion of time, and as word spread around the guests, voices echoed around the hallowed walls. Then there were familiar footsteps, and he looked up.

'Papa, have you heard?'

'Thank god, you're all right,' he said, and pulled her close to him, wrapping his arms around her, squeezing her. 'What happened? Was it a marksman?'

'No, a knife. It was that shabby man I told you about, the one who went into the du Tillet house.'

'I wonder what happened to Charlotte.'

'That's the funny thing. In the mayhem, I thought of her straight away. I forgot Épernon had evacuated her and the assassin from her house after I'd interviewed him. I rushed round to the du Tillet house, after Épernon's men took the assassin from me, and another group of his men were galloping away with her. I can only assume that Épernon discovered that we had searched the house, and thought it was safe to move her and the assassin back in there. It was conveniently located near the route of the procession. Maybe it was safer for him to have them there, rather than wherever he took them.'

'They took the assassin from you?'

'Yes, Papa. There was total confusion. The axle of a wagon carrying a massive wine barrel had broken, blocking the road. The guard were trying to get the wagon shifted, when the assassin rushed at the king and stabbed him. Montbazon tried to help, and he was stabbed too. The assassin fled, and I went after him. I caught him in a narrow alleyway, and had just disarmed him when Sergeant Bernard and a few men arrived. They took him from me. They've taken him to the Bastille. Just before they arrived, I asked him why. He said the strangest thing.'

'What did he say?'

'He said, "The voices. I didn't want to, not really, but the voices." He was crying. I felt sorry for him somehow, even after what he'd done.'

'I don't feel s...sorry for him.'

Maria writhed free of Anthony's arms and knelt down to hug Louis.

It seemed as if nobody knew what was happening, in the time between the shocking news arriving, and the queen returning from the Arsenal. Priests had been circulating amongst the dignitaries handing out mint tea laced with sugar and brandy. When the queen returned, she went directly to the bishops. Anthony and Maria got as close as they could, and Louis stayed with them.

'The king's dying wish was that the coronation go ahead. Let us begin,' she said. The Bishop of Paris signalled to the choirmaster, and the choir sang. The well-rehearsed ceremony staggered into action, and everyone took their allotted places. Anthony didn't take very much in. He mumbled the words of the hymns and psalms that he knew. The words were going through his mind, "the voices". Anthony shook himself when he saw Louis bow to the queen, turn and address the audience, with a line from the speech that Maria had worked on with him. The one that went, "and yet, with mother's wise and good counsel, I may yet build upon our king's bedrock." He heard a gasp from the audience. Perhaps the emotion of their young king's sentiments impressed them, or perhaps they were just impressed that he had spoken them at all. A fanfare startled Anthony, and the congregation turned to watch the newly crowned queen lead the procession from the church, followed by Louis, then the other children with their governesses, and the rest in strict order of nobility.

'What shall we do now, Papa? We've failed, haven't we?'

'We have lost a king, but I sense you have been the making of one, too. I need to speak with Pierre.'

CHAPTER FIFTEEN

A nthony bounded up the steps to Madame Dufour's front door and knocked loudly. He heard her approaching, then she opened the door.

'Is Pierre in?'

'Yes, Sir Anthony, but he's just about to go out.'

'I won't keep him long,' Anthony said, squeezing past her and running up the stairs, two at a time. He tried the doorknob and opened Pierre's door.

'Good heavens, Anthony,' Pierre exclaimed, 'what's the hurry?'

'I'm sorry to be so rude,' Anthony gasped. 'I have to check something. You said that in an induced trance, it is not possible to make someone do something against their will. Is that right?'

'Yes, as I told you.'

'Could someone be persuaded to commit a crime?'

'I don't know. If the person in question feels inclined to commit the crime, then it may be possible to remove, or at least reduce, the inhibitions that otherwise would stop them. Perhaps they might want to steal, because they need the money. Then it might be possible to help them do it. But theft is a serious crime. The penalties are severe. As well as removing the inhibition, there is a natural sense of self preservation. That is a powerful force.'

'Yet men steal.'

'They do, if they think they can get away with it. They have to weigh the rewards against the consequences, as well as their inhibitions, their social conditioning. If someone could persuade them that it is the right thing for them to do, and that they will escape the consequences, then I suppose that it might be possible.'

'What about a greater crime, murder, let's say?'

'Murder? My god, is this about the king? We just heard.'

'It may be. Is it possible?' Pierre slumped into an armchair. Anthony walked around to face him. 'Well Pierre, is it?'

'This is on another level altogether. I don't know. If the fellow already sees evil in the king, perhaps. Say he is a Catholic extremist, and believes the king to favour Protestants, then someone could work on that. Or vice versa, a Protestant extremist could see the king as a Catholic enemy. If someone could lead him to believe that it were for the good of society, that he kill the king, then… But it would be certain death. The sense of self preservation is so strong.'

'Men can be persuaded to walk into battle, Pierre. How is that possible?'

'They have to believe, I think, that they will be one of those happy few who survive. Despite the odds, they want to believe that.'

'Yes, you are right. Hope is a powerful force, too. So let us assume that there is a candidate, a Catholic extremist. You build upon the good to come from removing the evil, Protestant sympathising king. You promise him he will be a national hero. Perhaps you promise him other rewards, too. You persuade him he will escape. Perhaps you promise him you will help him escape. Can it be done?'

'The competing forces are so strong. The mental turmoil would be enough to drive a man insane, but, yes, perhaps. Anthony, you aren't suggesting that I did this? I love the king. He sponsored my voyage. He is sponsoring my history of the voyage.'

'No, Pierre, I don't for a second think you did this. But how many others here know how to induce a trance?'

'I don't know of anyone else in France who has brought back the knowledge. I made a very intensive study of the Indian yogis and priest caste. I've only been back a few weeks.'

'Has anyone else taken an interest? You told me that Sophia was an excellent subject to practise on. Have you taught anyone else?'

'No, only you and Maria.'

'I can't be sure. I may be putting two and two together and making five. Forget that we spoke.'

It was growing dark by the time Anthony got back to the palace. His inclination was to find the queen and tell her of his suspicions, but he couldn't think how to put it. He wanted to be with Maria. She had had a narrow escape. He went to their rooms.

'What is it, Papa? What did you learn from Pierre?'

'It was what you said about the voices. I imagined being in an induced trance and being told to kill the king. I wondered if it was possible.'

'What did Pierre say?' she asked. Anthony related as accurately as he could the discussion he had had with Pierre. 'Papa, I have no doubt that man had been driven insane. I could see it in his eyes.' Maria paced the room for a few minutes in silence. 'What would an elephant be if it weren't African?'

'I don't know. An elephant is an elephant, isn't it? Where are you going?'

'To the library.'

There was nobody in the library when Maria arrived. A fire was still burning, and she lit an oil lamp from an ember, using the brass tongs hanging at the fireplace. She passed the map drawer and examined the shelves. She stopped in front of a five volume set. It was Historiae Animalium by Conrad Gesner. Maria took down the fifth volume and found the index, then returned it, and took down the first volume. She leafed through the pages and smiled, then replaced the book on the shelf, blew out the lamp, and returned to find her father.

'Papa, there are two types of elephant, African and Indian.'

'What have elephants got to do with it? The king was stabbed. You saw it. A stampeding elephant did not crush him. You'd better get some sleep. You've had a terrible shock. We all have.'

'Pierre learn't the induction into a trance from Indian yogi, didn't he?'

'Yes. Where are you going with this?'

'So if he didn't teach anyone other than us how to do it, someone else might have. Someone who had also learnt it from an Indian yogi. When I interviewed Épernon, he was very precious about his carpets. He had inherited them from his grandfather, to whom he was very close. One carpet depicted enormous creatures, and I asked him if they were elephants like Hannibal used to cross the alps. Guess what he said.'

'Yes?'

'No. He said Hannibal used African elephants. I found a set of books about animals that I'd seen Louis refer to. I looked up elephants, and that's where I found out that there are Indian elephants too. They're smaller than African elephants and have smaller tusks and ears.'

'So he has a carpet with Indian elephants on it. Where does that get us?'

'He changed the subject. I think he thought he'd said more than he should. So what if his grandfather learnt induction from an Indian who sold him the carpet? What if his grandfather taught him how to do it? If there is an induction angle to this, then it has to be Épernon.'

'Yes, that makes sense. You saw the assassin enter the du Tillet house. After you spoke with Épernon's guards, they informed him and he rushed round there and took Charlotte away somewhere. But we need evidence. We found nothing in the house.'

'But we did, Papa. We just didn't realise. The mirror that spooked you when your candle was reflected in it. It reminds me of the mirror that Pierre uses.'

'You may have something,' Anthony said, stroking his beard. 'We need to know more about Épernon's grandfather, and if possible, from whom he got his carpets. I think in the morning I'll have a talk with Nicholas de Neufville again. He's no fan of Épernon, but he's known him most of his life. He may know something about his family history.'

◇ ◇ ◇

'Sir Anthony, I didn't expect to see you this morning. It's shocking, isn't it. I heard your daughter apprehended the assassin. She's an extraordinary young lady.'

'She is, sir. Please call me Anthony. May I call you Nicholas?'

'Yes, of course. Please sit down. How can I help you?'

'I know you have known Jean Louis, duc d'Épernon for many years. I also feel confident that you are not in league with him.' Anthony studied Nicholas's face and saw him nod. 'I wondered if you knew anything about his grandfather.'

'His grandfather?'

'Yes. What do you know about him?'

'He was a military man. He served Louis the twelfth with great distinction.'

'Do you know if he served in the Far East?'

'Not that I know of. He got as far as Naples, I believe.'

'So he didn't travel to India then?'

'India, you say. I assumed you meant his paternal grandfather. His mother's father was a trader on the Silk Road. He made his fortune from trading in silks, spices, carpets, that sort of thing. I believe he spent a lot of time in India. Why do you ask?'

'I must go.' Anthony said, standing up and shaking Nicholas's hand. 'You have been a great help, Nicholas.'

Anthony left the Hôtel de Villeroy and rushed to the

Rue St. Honore to see Pierre again. When Sophia opened the door, Anthony smiled at her and bounded up the stairs.

'Pierre, have you ever spoken with the duc d'Épernon about induction?'

'No, I haven't.'

'Oh.'

'You seem disappointed.'

'I had hoped that you might have been able to tell if he knew about induction.' There was a pause. Pierre paced over to the window and looked out onto the street below.

'Well, that's the funny thing. He wouldn't speak about induction. I sat next to him at a dinner, shortly after I returned from my voyage. Induction fascinates most people, as it did you. I tried to talk to him about it, but although he humoured me, he wasn't interested. I thought it was most odd, rude almost.'

'Do you think he might also have known about it?'

'If he did, wouldn't he have enjoyed speaking about it?'

'Not if he wanted to keep his knowledge a secret.'

'Do you mean… do you think it's him?'

'I do, but please keep this to yourself. Thank you, Pierre, you have been a great help. Now I must go.'

Marcel showed Anthony into the queen's salon, and then left. It disappointed Anthony to see that she had Leonora Concini with her again.

'Sir Anthony, do come in and join us. Please sit down. Marcel said that you wish to speak with me.' Anthony sat at the table opposite the queen and Leonora.

'Yes, Your Highness, although I am afraid it is a most confidential matter. Please accept my most sincere condolences for your tragic loss.'

'Dear Leonora has been a great comfort to me. You would not have me send her away, at the hour of my greatest need.'

'Unfortunately, Your Highness, it is a matter most

pressing and dangerous.'

'The king is dead. I can hardly see what is more dangerous. I had hoped you might prevent it.'

'Your Highness, I can tell my story to you alone. Once you have heard it, you may do with it as you deem fit. I will have done what I can.'

'Very well. Leonora, would you send Marcel in to light the fire? I feel cold. Have him bring some more brandy to me. Would you like a glass, Sir Anthony?'

'It is early, but in the circumstances, yes please, Your Highness.' Leonora left the room and Marcel set down two goblets of brandy on the table. He went to the fireplace and took some tinder from a brass container. He arranged it in the fireplace, then took out a flint and steel. The steel sent a shower of sparks over the tinder as he struck the flint. After blowing on the glowing tinder, he set some twigs over it. After blowing some more, he arranged a few logs on top.

'I think the fire will be satisfactory now, Your Highness.'

'Yes thank you, Marcel. You may leave us.'

When the door had closed, Anthony told his story. He began with the lessons he had had in trance induction from Pierre, how he had seen Épernon visit the house of Charlotte du Tillet, and how Maria had seen a shabby man also visit the du Tillet house. Anthony explained how he had overheard Épernon and Bellegarde whispering about the king's ambition in Jülich, and how shocked Sully had been to hear that. Then he recounted Maria's experience from the day before, how she had recognised the assassin as the shabby man who had visited the du Tillet house, how she had apprehended him and what he had had to say about the voices. He explained everything that Pierre had told him about what could and could not be achieved under a trance, and how Épernon may have learnt the technique from his maternal grandfather who had spent much time in India. Anthony recounted how the duc d'Épernon had rushed to the du Tillet house after Maria had questioned him, and how he had taken Charlotte and the assassin into hiding somewhere for a day or two. He closed with how Épernon had avoided speaking with Pierre about induction, suggesting he might wish to conceal his knowledge of the art of induction.

'So you see, your highness, the way it looks to me, is that the duc d'Épernon may be behind the assassination. I can't prove it, but that's how it looks to me. I understand he fought with the Catholic league in the War of the Three Henrys, so the king deciding to side with the Protestant league, in the Jülich campaign, may have triggered the recent tragic events. Also, Épernon's men removed Charlotte du Tillet from the house, just as Maria got there.' The queen took a large swig of her brandy, and Anthony followed suit.

'This is a most serious accusation. I can now see why you wanted to tell me alone. I'm sorry if I was curt. This is very awkward, although it is not yet a crime to be a good Catholic. I shall ask how the interrogation of the assassin is progressing, and what has been done with the du Tillet woman.'

'What will you do with Jean Louis, Your Highness?'

'Nothing, for now.'

'I see. May I ask how the duc de Montbazon is, and Sully also?'

'They are both recovering. Sully is being treated with digitalis, for his heart. It comes from the foxglove, I am told. Oh, what shall I do? We shan't assemble the council until after the execution, so we must get that over with quickly. That will be quite a spectacle. Oh, I have forgotten to thank you, Sir Anthony, and your daughter. Maria is quite a woman. You must be very proud of her.'

'I am, Your Highness.'

'Despite this terrible shock, you have both worked miracles with Louis's speech. That is something to celebrate, at least. Will you stay with us until we settle things?'

'Of course, if you wish it, Your Highness.'

'Good, then that is all for now. Please send Leonora back in as you leave. Ask her to bring Concino.' Anthony bowed and left.

Anthony took the long way back to his room, meandering and thinking hard. He couldn't understand why Marie would not move against Épernon? Did she fear him or love him? Could she be implicated too? He couldn't believe that. Yet she resented the number of mistresses the king had, and why shouldn't she? Could she and Épernon be lovers and have planned this themselves? If that were the case, then she wouldn't be thrilled to hear about the du Tillet woman. Perhaps it was just that she doesn't know who she can trust at the moment. He thought how unfortunate it was that both Sully and Montbazon were out of action at the moment. He felt sure she could trust them, and that they could move for her against Épernon and Bellegarde, if required. As he reached his room, Marcel was just knocking on Maria's door. She opened it.

'Prince Louis, I mean King Louis, would like to see you, mademoiselle,' Marcel said.

'Papa, how did you get on? Do you want to come and see Louis too?'

'He just asked for you, mademoiselle,' Marcel said. Maria shrugged.

'I'll see you later, Papa.'

Marcel led Maria past the queen's salon, and the dauphin's dayroom. He then led her up a flight of stairs to the right, and then back along a corridor. He stopped and knocked at a door. Maria heard Louis call out, and Marcel opened the door.

'Thank you, Marcel, that will be all,' Louis said as Marcel bowed, left, and closed the door behind him. Maria looked around the room. It was dominated by a full size, four-poster bed with a blue tapestry canopy, and velvet hanging curtains, which were tied open. Tapestries depicting hunting scenes hung on the walls. On the opposite side of the room to the bed, there was an unmade fireplace. Louis was sitting in a small armchair by the window, next to a small table, with another child's armchair on the other side of the table. The chairs faced the bed. On the table, some of the wooden carved soldiers that had been in his dayroom were arranged.

'You will be more comfortable sitting on the bed, Maria,' Louis suggested. She sat on the bed, facing him. 'Now I want you to tell me everything you know about yesterday, and the events leading up to them. I heard some of your father's story through the chimney, but then mother had a fire lit, and it became difficult to hear.'

'Goodness, father said that he learnt a lot by listening at fireplaces. Is this room directly above your mother's salon?'

'Yes, it is. I learn a lot from listening. Now please proceed.' Maria told him everything from her father's overheard snippet of conversation, through the sessions with Pierre, how she had remembered his father's ciphered message in a trance, and their deciphering of it. She recounted the events of yesterday, and their reasons for suspecting the duc de Épernon.

'What do you think will happen next, Your Highness? I haven't talked with my father since he spoke with your mother.'

'She will do very little until after the council meeting. I know what she wants, she wants to be regent for administration as well as governorship. Épernon will support her in that, because he thinks he can control her. The council is finely balanced.'

'I thought that wasn't possible because of satanic law.'

'You mean Salic law, although, as a woman, you can be forgiven for calling it that. Mother shares some blood with Catherine de Medici, and she has studied her, and her methods. She will play a cautious hand. Épernon is strong, and she will need to build a coalition against him, if she is not to be controlled by him.'

'But surely Épernon should be arrested at once, Your Highness.'

'Do you think your evidence would convict a duke in a court of law? No. It is sufficient for me, but he is a powerful man, with many friends. Mother will think this through very carefully, and so shall I,' Louis said, before turning to the table, reaching out his hand and flicking his finger to knock over one of the red and yellow soldiers. It took all the other red and yellow soldiers down with it. 'Thank you, Maria. I know I can count on your loyalty and silence. Will you teach me how you overcame the assassin?'

'I could try, Your Highness, but it is difficult to practise wrestling with an opponent of a very different size. But we could try.'

'I would like that. I have been learning to fence, hunting, and shooting. I take great joy from them. But the wrestling sounds interesting too. I sense that in fencing, for example, my opponents lose to me deliberately, just to please me. I don't think you would.'

'You have a wise head on young shoulders, Your Highness.'

Maria, dressed in her riding clothes and prepared a vacant stall in the stable block to serve as a wrestling area. She placed bails of straw around the sides and spread a thick layer of straw on the ground. Louis recruited Charles, the youngest of the cook's three sons, to act as his opponent. It was a good match, as they were the same age and height. Maria began by explaining that learning how to fall, without getting hurt, was the first step. She demonstrated the slight body twist, keeping one arm tucked in and curving her body, as she rolled over each shoulder in turn, slapping the ground with her free arm as she landed on her back. After a hesitant start, both boys were soon running and rolling around the stable, to her satisfaction. At ten o'clock, Anthony arrived.

'Perfect timing, Papa. We shall now demonstrate throwing techniques. My father will pretend to be my assailant. I will talk you through how I defend my…'

'I'm sorry, Maria, would you mind doing the falling? I'm feeling my age. I suppose my injuries are catching up with me.'

'Of course, Papa.'

Maria demonstrated frontal and rear attacks on Anthony, which he deflected and harnessed her momentum to throw her onto her back. After three repetitions of each throw, Louis tried throwing Charles.

'You must resist, Charles,' Louis said. 'I won't learn anything if you just drop to the ground as soon as I grab your wrist.'

'I'm sorry, Your Majesty, I fear hurting you.'

'Well don't.'

Charles resisted, and Louis became frustrated at not being able to throw him, as Anthony had Maria. Maria offered a great deal of encouragement, kneeling down beside Louis and Charles as they were in mid-throw, showing Louis how to get his centre of gravity beneath Charles's, getting him to feel the point at which Charles was just on the tipping point, and then making one more heave. The smile on Louis's face as Charles left the ground and balanced across Louis's back before being flung onto the ground lit up everyone's humour. Maria insisted the boys take it in turns to be assailant and defender. Although Louis was reluctant at first, wanting to learn the techniques, rather than have them practised on him, Maria persuaded him that true learning came from experiencing the techniques from both angles. Anthony added that practice bouts against a skilled opponent were necessary, so Charles had to learn too.

The daily wrestling instruction and practice seemed to help everyone forget the tragic events, if only a little, and just for an hour or two. Louis could vent his rage with physical activity, and it passed the time until the execution.

Cook occasionally dropped by, concerned that her beloved son should not cause the king injury or displeasure. As the days passed, she beamed at the bond that was developing between the boys, and left them to get on with it. They progressed from throws to hold downs, and escaping from hold downs. As they writhed around the stable floor, Louis trying to keep Charles pinned down, and Charles trying to escape, Charles let out a yelp. Louis released him and Charles felt his back. Maria rushed over to examine him.

'It's only a scratch. There must be a nail or something on the floor. I'm afraid your smock is torn though,' she felt around on the floor and held up a bent nail.

'Don't worry, Charles, I shall have Gaston make you some new clothes. I shall ask him to make us both some wrestling garments, thick and strong,' Louis said.

The following day, as promised, Charles and Louis fought in made-to-measure wrestling outfits, tailored from tough canvas. They moved on from simple hold downs to both arm and leg locks, and finally strangleholds. Both Anthony and Maria went to great lengths to emphasise the importance of counting to your own heartbeat, and releasing the hold after twenty beats, or immediately, if the opponent slumped into unconsciousness. Both boys were learning well. Charles appeared to have slightly the upper hand in the throws, but Louis was better at holds, locks, and strangle holds.

Eleven days after the assassination, Marcel found them practising and called to Louis. The boys paused their fight while he took Louis aside and spoke with him. Louis thanked Marcel, who then left.

'The interrogation and trial are complete and the execution is set for the day after tomorrow, in the Place de Grève,' Louis announced. 'We shall watch from the mayor's banqueting room. There will be a fine view from there. Maria, you and Anthony must come, given your role in catching him. I'm sorry Charles, space is limited. A place at an overlooking window is worth a year's wages for a master-baker, I am reliably informed.'

'What did the interrogation discover, Your Majesty?' Maria asked.

'Not a great deal. The fellow's name is François Ravaillac. He's thirty-two years of age and comes from Angoulême. His father was a merchant and mother was always rather unpopular, very bigoted, the locals said. His parents and his brother have been exiled, never to return, on pain of death. The chief inquisitor says that he has never seen a clearer case of demonic possession.'

'How will he be executed, Your Majesty?' Anthony asked, fearing another burning.

'Oh, I wouldn't want to spoil the surprise. I can reassure you it will be a magnificent spectacle. I think we shall end wrestling for the day. We can begin again after the execution.' Charles bowed and ran off towards the kitchen. 'Wait a moment, Maria, Anthony, I should prepare you. I find it just as distasteful as you undoubtably will, but the duc d'Épernon will watch with us. I know, I know,' he said, raising a hand, 'but for the time being, it is necessary that he doesn't suspect that we know about his role in the affair. You will both have to behave cordially towards him. Do you think you can do that?'

'Have you anyone who can give us acting lessons, Your Majesty?' Maria replied.

'Well, let me see, there is very little time. There is the Hôtel de Bourgogne on Rue Mauconseil. They mostly perform farces. I have been watching performances there since I was five, and know the manager well. I shall send word—'

'Forgive me, Your Majesty, I was only joking,' Maria said, smiling. 'If you wish it, then I'm sure Papa and I can contain ourselves, can't we, Papa?'

'Just make sure I don't drink too much wine, Maria.'

Sunday, the twenty-seventh of May, 1610, dawned bright and fair. There was a knock on the door and Anthony opened it to find Gaston and an assistant, with black garments draped across his forearms.

'May we come in, Sir Anthony? I knew you would not have brought anything suitable with you, so I have taken the liberty of making some mourning clothes for you and your daughter. I understand you will attend the execution, and it will be expected.'

'Yes, of course, please come in.' Hearing voices, Maria opened the connecting door. 'Come through Maria, Gaston has kindly run up some mourning clothes for us to wear to the execution.'

'Oh I see, Papa. Yes, I hadn't thought about what to wear. I am rather puzzled, though. Why should we dress in mourning clothes for the execution of the king's assassin?'

'Yes, it may seem odd,' Gaston replied, 'but the mourning is for the king, not, of course, his assassin. The execution is a very public affair, and everyone must show their respect and grief for the king. The king lies in state for quite some time, while the whole of France grieves. Servants pretend to feed him, to suggest that his spirit is still with us. The burial is planned for the first of July. The dispatch of his assassin is to be a swift spectacle, so that we may all continue to mourn our loss.' Gaston took a voluminous black dress from his assistant's arms and handed it to Maria. 'I wonder if you would mind trying this on, mademoiselle. It may look as if it would be rather hot, but some wicker hoops, which will keep the silk away from your legs, create the volume in the skirt. The bodice is also silk with lace decoration, so that should be quite cool.' Maria took the dress from his arms and went back to her room, closing the connecting door behind her. 'And if you would try this on, Sir Anthony. Would you like us to step outside for a moment?'

'No, that won't be necessary,' Anthony undressed and put on his mourning clothes, also made from silk with lace trim. 'It feels very comfortable,' Anthony said as Gaston walked slowly around him, his experienced eyes running over every slight wrinkle and crease. He stopped occasionally to pull at a seam, here and there.

'Could you take it off again please, Sir Anthony? It may seem like nothing, but I have a reputation to maintain. You may be comfortable, but I will not be comfortable until the jacket hangs perfectly. I should take in the left leg of the breeches a little too, just at the knee. It will be a matter of minutes only, if I take in this seam just a bit, it will make such a difference.' Anthony undressed again, and handed the costume back to Gaston. He was standing in just his silk drawers when the connecting door opened and Maria reappeared, wearing her mourning dress.

'Oh, I've never seen your scars, Papa. I'm not surprised you didn't want to be thrown the other day.'

'I've lived with them for a very long time. It's only recently that they have started to pain me again. You look wonderful.'

'Indeed you do, mademoiselle,' Gaston said, examining her as she twirled one way, then the other. 'I think my reputation will be safe with you. I'll just finish this slight alteration for Sir Anthony, and then we will be on our way.' Gaston completed his stitching and then passed the garments back to Anthony. He put them on again. 'Yes, the jacket hangs so much better, and the breeches are also perfect. We will be on our way. I hope you enjoy the execution,' Gaston said as he and his assistant left.

'Well, I suppose now that we are suitably dressed, we should find out what happens next. Do you fancy a stroll?' Anthony asked. They closed Anthony's door behind them and set off towards the queen's apartments. As they turned the corner of the corridor leading there, they almost bumped into Marcel.

'Sir Anthony, mademoiselle Maria. I was just coming to see you and let you know the arrangements. Gaston has done an excellent job, I see. I shall come to your room and collect you in around half an hour, if that is all right. You will be amongst the first to be taken to the banqueting-house. The queen and King Louis will be the last to arrive. I will take you to your carriage, and the coachman will see you to your destination. You will have a brief wait, I'm afraid, as the dignitaries will arrive in a set order. There will be refreshments, so you will not go hungry or thirsty.'

'Thank you, Marcel. I wasn't worrying about going hungry,' Anthony replied.

◇ ◇ ◇

Anthony and Maria were amongst the first to arrive. It had only been a short carriage journey, since the mayor's house and banqueting hall were just off the north bank of the Seine, with the towers of Notre Dame casting their shadows towards them. The Place de Grève was heaving with people, laughing and jostling to get to the front. From their elevated position in the carriage, they could see across the swaying heads to a wooden platform in the centre of the square. Soldiers formed a ring around the platform, and there were wooden trestles to keep the crowds clear of the execution site. Stalls and trestle tables were set up around the square, for vendors to keep the spectators fed with bread and stew, and refreshed with wine and beer. There was a corridor kept clear, leading to the mayor's house, with barriers and more soldiers. It was clear that there would be a one-way system for carriages, as there was not enough room to turn. As the coach pulled up, the footman jumped down and opened the carriage door. They stepped down, Maria first, hitching her dress up with one hand, and taking the footman's hand with the other. Anthony climbed down after her. The footman climbed nimbly back to sit beside the driver, the whip cracked, and the carriage rattled forwards, leaving the square to the north.

'Welcome, monsieur, mademoiselle, please follow me,' said a liveried man, leading them inside the mayor's house. By most standards, it was very grand indeed, but compared to the Louvre, the paintings were from an inferior hand,

and the carpets not as sumptuous. The servant led them up three flights of stairs and showed them into the banqueting hall. They were immediately greeted by two other servants, in the same livery, one bearing a tray of meat and pastry, the other goblets of wine. Anthony and Maria took refreshment and thanked the servants. A plump man, dressed in mourning, but wearing a gold chain of office around his neck, came across and introduced himself as the mayor. They introduced themselves, and Anthony could see the mayor mentally rehearsing their unfamiliar names. He took them to the long side of the room, where chairs were arranged by the large, open windows. He had to raise his voice above the noise rising from the square, to introduce them to some of the civic dignitaries already present. They made polite conversation, not feeling able to mirror the joyous, excited chanting of the crowd outside. One by one, guests of progressively higher rank arrived. Anthony and Maria were delighted to be joined by Pierre.

'Anthony, Maria, it is good to see friendly faces on such an occasion. I have hardly been able to sleep since we spoke. To think of what might be done by induction, in the wrong hands…'

'Dear Pierre, you should not feel that way. It is what a man does with knowledge that matters. In any case, I may be wrong, it may all be a set of surreal coincidences,' Anthony said, putting his hand reassuringly on Pierre's shoulder. 'Please, tell us more of your voyages, to take our minds off all this. How is the book coming along?'

'I have just rounded the Cabo das Tormentas, as the Portuguese explorer Bartolomeu Dias named it. That is towards the southern extremity of Africa,' Pierre said The room was filling up. There was no sign of Sully or Montbazon. Anthony assumed they were still recovering. Nicholas de Neufville was speaking with Nicholas de Sillery, and the young César, duc de Vendôme, and his wife joined them. More people that he did not recognise arrived, then from the corner of his eye he saw Épernon enter, with

Bellegarde. Queen Marie and King Louis followed them, holding hands. Anthony stopped a passing waiter and asked if he could have a little water in his wine. The waiter returned after a couple of minutes with a jug of water, from which he topped up Anthony's goblet. Maria requested the same. Shortly after that, the mayor clapped his hands for silence, made a brief speech about how honoured he was, and asked people to take their seats at the windows. The queen and Louis sat at the centre window. Anthony, Maria and Pierre took a window at the far end of the hall, as far away as they could get from Épernon.

A drum roll began and they could see Ravaillac being led in chains towards the platform. They dragged him roughly up a short set of stairs onto the platform, flanked by soldiers on both sides. They could see his eyes darting around the crowd. A captain of the guard, also standing on the platform, unrolled a scroll and began reading the judge's sentence. At the end, they forced Ravaillac to lie on his back. A man appeared carrying a bucket. Four of the guards put on leather gauntlets, two of them took an ankle each, and the other two took a wrist. They pulled at each limb, as the man with the bucket spilled some yellow liquid onto the prisoner's shoulders and hips. They saw smoke rising, and Ravaillac writhe, a split second before the screams reached their ears, followed by cheers from the crowd.

'What are they doing, Pierre?' Anthony asked.

'It is an acid of sulphur. I understand it loosens the joints, and reduces the strain on the horses,' he replied. Four more guards appeared on stage carrying coils of rope. Another four guards pushed through the crowds to the platform on horseback. They threaded the ropes through a loop on each of Ravaillac's shackles, whilst the guards, with their leather gauntlets, held Ravaillac as still as they could. Another guard undid the padlocks securing the chains to the shackles. They threw the loose ends of the ropes to each horseman, who tied a bowline in the rope and looped it over the pommel of their saddle. The crowd moved willingly, expectantly, as the horsemen spread out, pulling the ropes taut. The captain raised his hand, checking the alignment of the horsemen. When he judged the moment just right, he dropped his arm. The horsemen dug their spurs in, the horses strained, and the sea of people parted to give the horses room. The horses' eyes bulged, as their front hooves lifted, and their rear legs strained, then it was done. They reined the horses in after a few yards, the ropes dropped off the edges of the platform, taking the four limbs with them. They saw the spark of life leave the limbless Ravaillac. There was the glint of steel as members of the crowd hacked at the limbs for a souvenir of the great day, something to show their grandchildren, that they were there when Good King Henry's assassin got his just desserts. Anthony excused himself, he felt a desperate need to find a privy.

◇ ◇ ◇

Maria looked around for her father, as she saw Jean Louis de Nogaret de La Valette, duc d'Épernon, making his way towards her through the other dignitaries. She looked around to Pierre, but he got up and walked away. She stood up just as Épernon reached her.

'Mademoiselle Standen, I did not know when we dined together a few weeks ago, exchanging small talk, that I was addressing a future celebrity. My men told me it was you who apprehended Ravaillac. I can hardly believe it is possible, did he slip?'

'No, he made a lunge at me and I threw him. What do you find impossible about that, Your Grace?'

'I should have thought it was obvious, you are a woman, the weaker sex.'

'I assure you, Your Grace, that there is nothing weak in my sex. I was with my mother when she gave birth to my younger siblings. A woman can bear pain, that a man can only imagine, even on a day such as today.'

'Yes, but it is unnatural. Women were born to bear

children, suckle them and make a home. Men were born to roam and hunt, to bring back food for the pot. That is the natural order of things. Women were born to gather food and herbs, not to hunt and fight. You are unusual, a little interesting.'

'Thank you, Your Grace,' Maria replied, trying to force her rising rage back down. 'I believe it is not uncommon, in the animal world, for the females to hunt and kill.'

'Is that right? Well, however it happened, you have done France a great service. I hope you have enjoyed the fruits of your handiwork. It was quite a spectacle, wasn't it? Thankfully regicide doesn't happen very often. I hope we will meet again. Good day, Mademoiselle Standen,' Épernon bowed slightly and Maria forced herself to curtsey.

'Thank you, Your Grace.'

CHAPTER SIXTEEN

The days following the execution were an anti-climax for Anthony and Maria. Louis spent almost every hour with his mother in her apartments. Marcel brought Maria a message advising her that Louis would not require any speech or wrestling tuition until further notice. They even had their meals taken in to them. Thankfully, both Sully and Montbazon appeared to have recovered well, but they, too, spent most of their time in Sully's office. Épernon and Bellegarde could be seen walking the palace gardens. Maria and Anthony took their meals in the dining room by themselves. When others came to eat, they sat as far from Anthony and Maria as possible, and spoke in whispers, if at all.

'Why is everyone avoiding us, Papa? Do you think they blame us for not catching the assassin in time?'

'No, I don't think it's that.'

'What then? The execution seems to have set everyone against us. Nobody wants to speak to us, apart from Marcel.'

'I think it's rather that they're preoccupied with each other. Haven't you seen the way they're talking in cliques? Then someone joins one clique, before shifting to the other, bouncing between the two? I've been watching, and it seems as if Épernon is the head of one, and Sully the other. It must be this council meeting that Marie mentioned. You remember, they're going to assemble the council that will administer the regency, and govern France. I bet they're all jostling for position, trying to get the best jobs.'

'Well, that makes sense, but I'd just like to get our money and go home now. This hanging around doing nothing is boring me senseless.'

'Me too, Maria.'

That afternoon, they strolled around the great hall, admiring the artists at work. On the way back to their rooms, they met Marcel in the corridor.

'Good afternoon, Marcel. Would you mind asking the queen what we are to do? We wish to be of service, of course, but it would seem that our services are no longer required. I'm sure you'll be tactful, and choose the right moment, but we would just like to go home now,' Anthony said.

'I quite understand, Sir Anthony. I shall do my best.'

At dinner time the same day, they were once again dining alone, when Marcel came in.

'Sir Anthony, I put your request to the queen. She quite understands your predicament, but asks that you be patient just until the day after tomorrow. She is very preoccupied at the moment, but may yet have further need of your services.'

'Preoccupied, you say. Is it the council meeting that is pre-occupying everyone?'

'Yes, Sir Anthony. They will hold it on Thursday, the day after tomorrow. Once that is out of the way, I'm sure the king and queen will want to see you both.'

Thursday came and went, with no call from Marie. On Friday morning, Marcel found Anthony and Maria admiring the art in the great hall again. There was no news from Marie, but Louis would like to see Maria. Maria dashed off to see him, and Anthony continued pacing around the great hall.

'Thank you for coming, Maria. Mother and I are sorry to have kept you and Sir Anthony waiting. The lead up to the council meeting has been a very testing time for everyone, but it is now settled, mainly.'

'What do you mean by mainly, Your Majesty?'

'I was coming to that. Épernon proposed that mother should be regent with full authority until I become of age. Bellegarde seconded that motion. Sully opposed it, arguing that the council should govern France on my behalf. My half-brother, César, duc de Vendôme, was with Sully, as was Nicolas de Neufville. He probably would have voted for the council anyway, but he detests Épernon. Jeannin also voted for the council, and mother put on a magnificent display of reassuring the council that if appointed regent in full, she would make a government of minsters, and listen carefully to their wise counsel. Lorraine voted in favour of mother's regency, so it was all in the balance. Mother would vote for herself, so everything depended on Sillery. The poor old fellow didn't seem to know what to do. So that's when I stepped in. I'd been rehearsing my piece for days. It was a longer version of the poem I wrote for mother's coronation. I gave them a heart-rending account of my love for father, and how I hoped one day to rule as he would have wished. Then I heaped praise on mother, how good and kind she is, and how wise her counsel would be. I watched the tears roll down Sillery's cheeks, and he voted for mother. Then mother hugged me, and accepted the decision gracefully, adding to her earlier speech about forming a government, and giving due heed to their wise counsel. I didn't stammer once during the whole thing.'

'Congratulations, Your Majesty. I hope you don't mind me asking, but why did you do it?'

'She is my mother. I know how to influence her, which levers to pull on. She is also much wiser than you might imagine. Others dismiss her as a weak and fickle woman, but she is not. I should know. In the final balance, I trust her more than I do the councillors. One day, I will need my own Sully. I shall begin the search immediately. That now leaves only one remaining problem, what to do with Épernon. In the lead up to the council meeting, mother and I had such rows about it. In the end, I struck a deal with her. I would speak for her, but Épernon had to go. His charm still takes her in, despite what we believe he did, but she agreed that he would try to use her. Unfortunately, even Sully doesn't think we could convict him on the evidence, and nor could we banish him. So that's where you come in.'

'Me, Your Majesty? What can I do?'

'He suspects you. He thinks that somehow you know what he did. I think he's angry that you caught Ravaillac. He will want to dispose of you if he can find the opportunity. Why don't you kill him first? I would pay you handsomely. Will you do it?' Maria opened and closed her mouth, unable to find the words. The words, how much, almost emerged, but something stopped them.

'I am sorry, Your Majesty. I don't think I can kill a man. I almost did once, in a rage, but I broke his knee instead.'

'But you have killed many men. It was in the ambassador's report.'

'Oh, that, yes. But that was quite different; it was self defence.'

'That is a pity. The day will come when I can order an army of innocent men to kill another army of innocent men, or die trying. But you, I cannot. Are you sure? I'm certain that you could provoke him. He lunges at you with a dagger. You throw him, and somehow he lands on his own dagger. I could arrange witnesses.'

'I am so sorry, Your Majesty. You have my complete loyalty in all things, and yes, I can kill a man. I have killed men. But I cannot plan on killing a man. Perhaps it is a womanly weakness.'

'You are a woman, but not a weak one. I hope you don't think badly of me for asking.'

'Not at all, Your Majesty, he probably did plan to kill your father. It is such a pity we cannot prove it. I could break into his house perhaps, and search for evidence.'

'I am certain that you would find none. He isn't that stupid, not stupid at all. I shall have to be content with ensuring that we exclude him from government. I'm sure I can convince Mother to do that, at least.'

Anthony was feeling a little put out. Maria had gone to see Louis over an hour ago, but he hadn't heard a thing from Marie. He chatted for a while with an artist called Rubens. He was eager to get back to Antwerp, where he was setting up his own studio. Anthony could see he was rushing. The fellow was painting furiously. He'd get nowhere until he calmed down. Attention to detail, that's what was missing. Anthony considered giving him some artistic advice when Marcel returned.

'I'm sorry, Sir Anthony, I didn't think you'd still be here. I looked for you in your room, and then the gardens. The queen would like to see you.' Anthony walked briskly to the queen's apartments. He knocked and heard her call, then entered. He was relieved to see that she was alone this time.

'Dear Sir Anthony, I understand that you are keen to return home. I'm sorry to have kept you waiting, but with all this business of the regency, I have been somewhat preoccupied. Still, I have good news, the regency is mine in full. I shall rule France until Louis is of age. In part, I owe it to you. Before you and Maria came, Louis could not possibly have been able to speak as eloquently and movingly as he did. Isn't that great news?'

'Yes, congratulations, Your Majesty.'

'Not Your Majesty, although it has a certain ring to it. Louis is the king, he warrants Your Majesty. I simply wield his power on his behalf.'

'So you overcame the problem of Salic law, Your Highness?'

'Yes. I shall appoint a government, and I shall listen to their counsel, but I shall wield the power. Oh, how I've dreamt of this moment. We shall amply reward you. Have no fear of that. Maria caught the assassin, even though you may not have been able to prevent Henry's murder. You seem a little distant, ah, Jean Louis perhaps. Well, there is little we can do without more evidence, and we are unlikely to find any. It will have to be enough, for now, to bar him from government office. I should like to do more, of course, and my son certainly would. But a ruler must be pragmatic, don't you think?'

'Yes, Your Highness.'

'Come and see me again after breakfast tomorrow, with Maria. Louis and I will give you your rewards, and our thanks, then you may return home.'

'Thank you, Your Highness.'

The following morning, after breakfast, Anthony and Maria went to the queen's apartments, as instructed. Louis sat beside his mother. Anthony bowed, and Maria curtsied. The queen stood and handed them each a leather purse. They were quite heavy.

'There are two thousand ducats for each of you. I see you are shocked, Sir Anthony. Don't be. You have both earned it. Without you, Louis would be missing half his tongue, and I would be under the council's thumb.'

'Thank you, Your Highness, Your Majesty,' Anthony and Maria said in unison. Maria continued. 'If there is anything I can do for you in the future, that is within my power, Your Majesty, please don't hesitate to ask.'

'Thank you, Maria, I'm sure I will. I also respect your limitations. I trust we will say nothing more of it. Is there anything more we can do for you?'

'Well, there is one thing, Your Majesty. I realise I am a tomboy, but I think the dresses that Gaston made for me will delight my mother. I don't think they will fit in our saddlebags. Is there someone who could enlarge our saddlebags, perhaps?' Maria asked.

'I will send the royal saddle-maker to your assistance. I'm sure he will do something,' Louis replied, beaming.

Anthony and Maria rode side by side, through the southern city gate, on the first leg of the journey back to

Marseille.

'What did Louis mean about your limitations?'

'He asked me to kill Épernon, Papa. I couldn't do it.'

'My god! Nine years of age, and he tries to hire you to kill a man. I suppose it must be in the blood. What did you make of Marie? I can't help wondering if she engineered the whole thing. She seemed overjoyed to effectively be France's monarch.'

'Why shouldn't she be? Why should France not have a female ruler?'

'I don't know, but it seems such a burden, let alone dangerous. Why would she want to be?'

'Papa, you said when we were drinking with François and Anne, after the battle with the pirates, that Marie, the queen, was only seven when her brother died. Her mother was already dead, then I presume. A short while afterwards, her uncle murdered her father and stepmother. What would that do to you, at that age? Just think about it. All that loss, and then presumably, she grew up with the man who murdered her father, until she could be married off to the highest bidder. Don't you think that after all that you would want some power over your life? Don't you think you would want to pull the levers that affect your world, rather than just have bad things happen to you all the time, orchestrated by others?'

'I don't remember saying all that?'

'You were a little the worse for wine, Papa.'

'I'm sure you're right. That was an awful thing to happen to a young child. It affects you, doesn't it, your childhood? I know mine did, and I had much better-than-average childhood. I'm so sorry that I wasn't there when you were young. I can't explain how much.'

'You've made up for it, Papa. We did quite well, didn't we? Four thousand ducats is a tidy sum, for one failure and one resounding success.'

'Two failures, Maria?'

'Two? Failing to stop the king's assassination, and what

else?'

'I haven't been able to marry you off to a duke. Your mother will be furious.'

'Which duke would you have me marry, Papa?' Maria laughed, 'the spineless one, the one with a weak heart, or the one with a black heart?'

CHAPTER SEVENTEEN

It was a beautiful evening in late June when Anthony and Maria arrived home. Antonio was clearing weeds from amongst the vines. He put down his fork and came straight over to greet them. Maria jumped down from the cart and hugged him.

'It's good to see you, Maria, Papa. What happened?'

'It's a long story,' Anthony replied, climbing down from the cart. 'How is everyone?'

'We're all well, Papa. William, Anna and Catherine have gone to bed…'

'Darling, I've been so worried,' Francesca called, as she rushed over from the kitchen door. She and Anthony hugged and kissed, while Antonio and Maria took their luggage from the cart and carried it into the villa. A few minutes later, Anthony and Francesca joined them. 'I think the chicken will be enough, but I'll put a few more carrots and turnips on. Lay another two place settings, could you, Antonio? I expect Maria's tired after such a journey.'

'I have something to show you, Mama,' Maria said, opening one of their trunks and taking out her dresses. Francesca glanced over her shoulder and put down her kitchen knife and the carrots.

'Mamma Mia, I've never seen such dresses. I told you to get her a nice dress, Anthony. But these must have cost a fortune.'

'They didn't cost us anything, Mama. The queen's dressmaker made them for me. Papa has some quite fancy outfits too.'

'You must both put them on for us, but after dinner. You wouldn't want to get food down such fine garments.'

225

'So, did you help the dauphin with his speech defect?' Francesca asked, as she sliced another piece of bread and took a bit more cheese.

'Yes, Mama. He barely stammers at all now. Papa asked him if he could sing, which he could, so we got him to talk with a rhythm, and minimise his use of the sounds which trouble him most. It takes him a little longer to compose what he wants to say, but then he can say it very well. And you'd be a fool to interrupt a king as he's about to speak.'

'Dauphin, dear, isn't it?'

'No, he's king now…'

'Yes, you'll find out soon enough, darling,' Anthony butted in. 'Although our help with the speech defect was required, Marie, the queen, that is, wanted us to investigate assassination attempts that have been made against King Henry. Unfortunately, we were less successful at that than with Louis's speech. Henry was murdered.'

'I knew it! I knew you weren't telling me the complete story.'

'We didn't want you to worry, my darling. But you should know that Maria is now one of King Louis's closest confidants and friends. Isn't that right, Maria?'

'Yes, I am, Mama.'

'You should be very proud of her. I am.'

'Of course, I'm proud of Maria. How did you become one of Louis's greatest confident's, my dear?'

'Papa let me do most of the speech work with Louis, whilst he started the investigation. But then I got involved in that too.'

'So what went wrong with the investigation, and how have you escaped being blamed for the murderer's success?' Francesca enquired.

'It's a long story, but Maria deserves most of the credit. We worked our way through interviewing suspects. I became convinced that one of Marie's closest confidants, Concino Concini, from Florence, was probably the assassin. But Maria picked up on two vital clues. One was the role that induction into a trance played, and the other was that the duc d'Épernon's grandfather might have gained the knowledge of induction from his time as a merchant in India.'

'So why weren't you able to stop him?' Francesca asked.

'I didn't realise the role that induction played until the assassin told me it was the voices that made him do it. Then I remembered when we searched the du Tillet house, that there was a small mirror, like you use to help induce a trance…'

'The assassin told you, Maria?' Francesca said.

'Yes, when I caught him. Are you alright, Mama? You look a little pale.'

'Have some more wine, darling,' Anthony said, filling Francesca's goblet. 'Yes, Maria caught the assassin and disarmed him. She also put the case together against the duc d'Épernon, who we are sure was the mastermind behind it.'

'You were supposed to marry her to a duke, not arrest one.'

'I know, darling, but you should be very proud of her. He's far too old for her, anyway.'

'Too old! She's twenty-one. How can anyone be too old for her? I should be a grandmother by now. What with Antonio falling in love with a doctor, and Maria following in your footsteps, I don't know what will become of them.'

'It's late, my darling. Why don't we go to bed?'

Anthony couldn't sleep, and he could tell from Francesca's breathing that she couldn't either.

'Are you awake, my love?' He asked.

'Yes, of course.'

'This induction into a trance. It's an amazing thing. An explorer called Pierre taught it to us. It's like he puts you to sleep, but he can delve deep into your memory. You can even accurately draw an intricate pattern that you've only seen once. When he delved into Maria's memory, he found something. It might explain, but it's hard to bear. It's that he thinks someone raped her when she was young.'

'Raped? My god, she never said anything. When?'

'She was working in a wash-house in Florence. It seem's the wash-house owner's son did it. I wanted to kill him, but Pierre said he thought he was only a child himself.'

'There was a day. She was very quiet. I just thought it was one of her moods. Why didn't she tell me?'

'I don't know. Perhaps she felt ashamed. Who knows? It's just that I think it might be why she's so difficult to get interested in men.'

'Is there anything we can do about it? This induction? Can that help?'

'Pierre doesn't think so. He said she's locked the memories away in a dungeon in her mind, with thick walls and sturdy locks. He thinks it's best to leave it that way. But like you, I think we must try to find some medicine, something to help her.'

'Yes, you're right. We must wait for the medicine, the strongest medicine of all.'

'What medicine, darling?'

'Love. Maybe twenty-one isn't too old. We just have to wait for the right man to come along.'

ABOUT THE AUTHOR

David V.S. West was educated at St. Edmund Hall, Oxford, where he took a B.A. in Engineering Science. During a career in engineering and project management he was commissioned by Gower Publishing to write a book on Project Sponsorship. This led him to study creative writing with the Open University, and a new career as a writer. The Spy who Sank the Armada is the first novel in the series The Sir Anthony Standen Adventures. The second is Fire and Earth. He lives in Wiltshire.

AFTERWORD

I hope you have enjoyed *The Suggested Assassin*. Please leave a review on Amazon, they are extremely helpful. In the short period between finishing Fire and Earth and starting this book, I did some work on my family tree. Imagine my delight to discover that my 10th great-grandfather was Edmund Standen, Sir Anthony's younger brother. For those readers who have dipped into my work at this, the third book in the series, Sir Anthony Standen was Francis Walsingham's spy who fed him detailed information on the preparation of the Spanish Armada. The first book in the series, The Spy who Sank the Armada, is my attempt to tell his story by weaving my imagined why and how into the known fabric of Sir Anthony's life.

I intend to take a few weeks break before starting work on the fourth book. Where it will take us, I do not yet know. I am intrigued to discover whether Maria will find love, and if so with whom. Louis is Louis XIII, the king that Alexandre Dumas's three musketeers served, so there is fertile ground ahead. Cardinal Richelieu doesn't become chief minister until 1624, but in the meantime there is much adventure ahead for some of the more minor characters in this book.

Printed in Great Britain
by Amazon

16396496R00139